Alex CROSS
Must Die

In 1993, James Patterson wrote *Along Came a Spider*, which introduced the world to Alex Cross, a young detective working out of Washington, DC. Since then, every Alex Cross thriller has been an international bestseller. *Alex Cross Must Die* is the thirty-first novel in this extraordinary series.

James Patterson is the author of other bestselling series, including the Women's Murder Club, Michael Bennett and Private novels. James has donated millions in grants to independent bookshops and has been the most borrowed adult author in UK libraries for the past fourteen years in a row. He lives in Florida with his family.

Why everyone loves
James Patterson and Alex Cross

'It's no mystery why James Patterson is the world's most popular thriller writer. Simply put: **nobody does it better**.'
Jeffery Deaver

'No one gets this big without **amazing natural storytelling** talent – which is what Jim has, in spades. The Alex Cross series proves it.'
Lee Child

'James Patterson is the **gold standard** by which all others are judged.'
Steve Berry

'Alex Cross is one of the **best-written heroes** in American fiction.'
Lisa Scottoline

'Twenty years after the first Alex Cross story, he has become one of the **greatest fictional detectives** of all time, a character for the ages.'
Douglas Preston & Lincoln Child

'Alex Cross is a **legend**.'
Harlan Coben

'Patterson boils a scene down to the single, telling detail, the element that **defines a character** or moves a plot along. It's what fires off the movie projector in the reader's mind.'
Michael Connelly

'James Patterson is **The Boss**. End of.'
Ian Rankin

WHO IS ALEX CROSS?

PHYSICAL DESCRIPTION:

Alex Cross is 6 foot 3 inches (190cm), and weighs 196 lbs (89 kg).
He is African American, with an athletic build.

FAMILY HISTORY:

Cross was raised by his grandmother, Regina Cross Hope - known as Nana
Mama - following the death of his mother and his father's subsequent
descent into alcoholism. He moved to D.C. from Winston-Salem, North
Carolina, to live with Nana Mama when he was ten.

RELATIONSHIP HISTORY:

Cross was previously married to Maria, mother to his children Damon and
Janelle, however she was tragically killed in a drive-by shooting. Cross
has another son, Alex Jr., with Christine Johnson.

EDUCATION:

Cross has a PhD in psychology from Johns Hopkins University in Baltimore,
Maryland, with a special concentration in the field of abnormal
psychology and forensic psychology.

EMPLOYMENT:

Cross works as a psychologist in a private practice, based in his home. He
also consults for the Major Case Squad of the Metro Police Department,
where he previously worked as a psychologist for the Homicide and Major
Crimes team.

PROFILE

A loving father, Cross is never happier than when spending time with
his family. He is also a dedicated member of his community and often
volunteers at his local parish and soup kitchen. When not working
in the practice or consulting for MPD, he enjoys playing classical
music on the piano, reading, and teaching his children how to box.

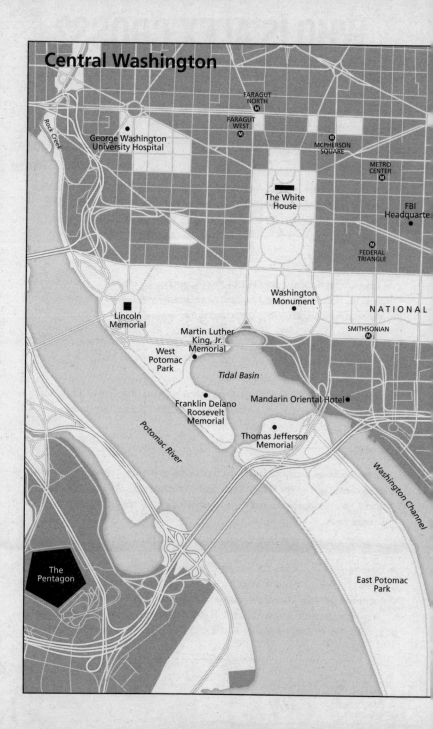

Central Washington

FARAGUT NORTH Ⓜ

FARAGUT WEST Ⓜ

George Washington University Hospital

MCPHERSON SQUARE Ⓜ

METRO CENTER Ⓜ

The White House

FBI Headquarters

Rock Creek

FEDERAL TRIANGLE Ⓜ

Lincoln Memorial

Washington Monument

NATIONAL

SMITHSONIAN Ⓜ

Martin Luther King, Jr. Memorial

West Potomac Park

Tidal Basin

Franklin Delano Roosevelt Memorial

Mandarin Oriental Hotel

Thomas Jefferson Memorial

Potomac River

Washington Channel

The Pentagon

East Potomac Park

Verizon Center

WASHINGTON UNION

Union Station

Metropolitan P.D. Headquarters

United States Supreme Court

Library of Congress

MALL

United States Capitol

CAPITOL HILL

5th Street Southeast

Lincoln Park

L'ENFANT PLAZA

Smithsonian Institution

FEDERAL CENTER SW STATION

CAPITOL SOUTH

Cross family home

EASTERN MARKET

NASA Headquarters

Garfield Park

WATERFRONT-SEU STATION

NAVY YARD-BALLPARK

Anacostia River

1000 yards

1000 metres

Bethesda

Hyattsville

495

CIA Headquarters, Langley

WASHINGTON

66

Arlington National Cemetery

Fairfax

495

Annandale

495

Alexandria

495

Joint Base Andrews

Springfield

Clinton

495

95

Accokeek

Waldorf

95

Potomac River

Quantico

5 miles

10 kilometres

A list of titles by James Patterson appears at the back of this book

Alex
CROSS
Must Die

JAMES
PATTERSON

PENGUIN BOOKS

PENGUIN BOOKS

UK | USA | Canada | Ireland | Australia
India | New Zealand | South Africa

Penguin Books is part of the Penguin Random House group of companies
whose addresses can be found at global.penguinrandomhouse.com

First published by Century in 2023
Published in Penguin Books 2024
003

Typeset in Janson MT Std by Jouve (UK), Milton Keynes.
Printed and bound in Great Britain by Clays Ltd, Elcograf S.p.A.

The authorised representative in the EEA is Penguin Random House Ireland,
Morrison Chambers, 32 Nassau Street, Dublin D02 YH68

A CIP catalogue record for this book is available from the British Library

ISBN: 978–1–529–15990–5
ISBN: 978–1–529–15991–2 (export edition)

www.greenpenguin.co.uk

MIX
Paper | Supporting
responsible forestry
FSC® C018179

Penguin Random House is committed to a
sustainable future for our business, our readers
and our planet. This book is made from Forest
Stewardship Council® certified paper.

Alex
CROSS
Must Die

CHAPTER

1

South Camp Springs, Maryland

ON THAT MID-NOVEMBER MONDAY morning, after nearly three years of careful planning, the forty-eight-year-old man donned latex gloves and scanned the rental-car agreement one last time.

His eyes paused on the flowing signature *Marion Davis* before he stuffed the agreement into an aluminum clipboard storage box, the kind construction estimators use. He set it on plastic sheeting on the credenza in a dingy motel room not far from Joint Base Andrews.

Davis had been there the past three days; he'd told the young woman at the front desk that he was holing up to finish his first movie script. His claim seemed to impress her enough that she agreed to keep housekeeping away, which was good, because how could he have explained the thin plastic sheeting covering every bit of furniture and taped over the floors and walls? Or, even harder to explain, the four large plastic storage bins he'd bought at Walmart and filled with bleach, hydrogen peroxide, and distilled water?

The acrid chemical scent irritated Davis's eyes and nose, but he didn't dare open the windows for ventilation. Instead, he'd kept the air conditioner going nonstop and wore goggles and a KN95 mask. He left the room only in the dead of night, when it was safe to ferry supplies. Now Davis crouched by the closest storage bin, reached with gloved hands into the chemical solution, and pulled out a long belt of .50-caliber bullets bought two years before on the blackest of black markets, this one at a remote ranch in northern Colorado.

He knew from training and experience that a soldier could adjust his aim at a moving target by using this ammunition belt. Every fourth cartridge fired a tracer round that glowed hot orange as it sped through the air.

However, the tracers also revealed the position of the shooter. Davis left in the first four tracer rounds but removed the remaining ones and replaced them with live rounds from a second bleached ammunition belt.

When he was done, he sank the first belt back in the chemicals and went into the bathroom. There, Davis stripped off his clothes and put them in a plastic garbage bag that he closed and sealed with duct tape.

Next, he stepped into the shower stall—all but the drain covered in plastic sheeting—turned on the hot water, picked up a razor, and shaved every inch of skin he could reach, from his already shaved head to the insteps of his feet.

He poured two cups of bleach down the drain when he was finished shaving, turned off the water, and retrieved a large tube of Airassi hair remover. Davis used a sponge on a long handle to smear the stuff on the skin he'd just shaved and all over his back. His eyebrows, eyelids, and ear canals were also dabbed. The cream burned, especially on his testicles, but he waited nearly fifteen minutes before rinsing it off. It was worth the pain to ensure that no FBI crime scene tech would find his hair anywhere.

Davis stepped out of the shower, stood and waited for his body to dry, then applied copious amounts of CeraVe moisturizer, again head to toe, to keep flecks of his skin from shedding. Only then did he step into a white disposable hazmat suit. He pulled the hood over his head and zipped it to his neck.

With the goggles and respirator on, Davis lugged the storage bins into the bathroom and drained them, leaving the various components of his weapon and custom tripod in them. He used two blow-dryers to remove the rest of the moisture and lubricated the parts with oil and graphite.

When he was satisfied, Davis put lids on the bins, tore down the plastic sheeting, gathered everything he had used in the past seventy-two hours, and stuffed it all into four lawn-and-leaf bags. These he sealed with duct tape and put next to the motel room's door.

He pushed back the curtains and saw the rear of the tan utility van. No one else was in the parking lot. But why would anyone be? It was a weekday morning. The kids who lived at the motel were all in school, and their mothers were working or sleeping it off.

Davis opened another bag, retrieved a new Baltimore Ravens hoodie, and put it on over the hazmat suit. A new brown coverall with the logo of the National Park Service went on next. He finished with a pair of glasses with heavy black frames and clear lenses. He added a respirator to cover his face, checked his look, then tugged the mask down around his neck.

All of this had taken several hours. Davis had a great deal of confidence in his preparation, but his heart still raced when he finally opened the motel room door. He quickly moved the storage bins and bulging plastic bags into the rear of the van, near a mountain bike and two blue fifty-five-gallon drums, one strapped to each wall. A laptop computer, purchased the year before from a pawnshop in Kentucky, went in the front seat.

Davis left the key to the spotless room on a chair by the door and drove out of the parking lot a few minutes after two p.m. He felt fully in control of his fate and pleased about the impact he was about to have.

Davis allowed himself a smile, thinking: *Isn't that the way you want to be when you're about to commit mass murder for a righteous cause?*

CHAPTER

2

FOR THE NEXT THREE hours, Davis drove around greater Washington, DC, tossing the trash bags in separate dumpsters. When he was done with that, he went to Thrifton Hill Park, off Interstate 66 in Woodmont, Virginia.

He kept the vehicle running and the air-conditioning blasting when he got out with two magnetic signs reading GROUND CREW below the emblem of the National Park Service system. They were exact replicas of ones he had seen and photographed on a trip to the Shenandoah Valley earlier in the year.

Davis stuck them on the sides of his van, climbed into the rear between the fifty-five-gallon drums, and began assembling a relic left over from Vietnam War days, a Browning M2 .50-caliber machine gun. He'd bought it at the same remote Colorado ranch where he'd bought the bullets.

When he was done putting the Browning together, he fitted a thermal scope on it, then screwed the tripod panhead into the front stock of the machine gun. He bolted the three legs of the tripod to a rotating steel plate mounted on the van's floor and checked the thin hydraulic connection to the tripod's neck.

Earlier, he had screwed a solid steel cylinder, four inches long and a quarter of an inch in diameter, into the rear bottom of the machine gun's stock. That stout nub fit into the receiver of a hydraulic unit that was smaller than a card deck and mounted on a track between two strips of steel that curved from one side of the van to the other. The tracks were screwed tightly into the floor.

The machine gun now stood on its own, fully controlled, barrel cocked slightly upward, the muzzle less than an inch from where the two back doors met.

To finish, Davis attached a small pneumatic vise around the trigger and connected it and the other hydraulic lines and pumps to a palm-size digital control. Davis used the laptop to activate the thermal sight, connected by Bluetooth to the computer, and was soon looking at the scope's reticle and the rear door of the van.

He triggered one of the hydraulic lines and saw the barrel rise as the tripod's neck lifted and extended.

He gave another order. The rear of the gun swept smoothly left and right; he tested the trigger vise and heard the firing pin click. Satisfied, Davis retrieved the ammunition belt and fed it into the receiver, making sure to lay the belt out so it would not bunch or bind and jam the weapon.

Dusk gathered as he put the van in gear and headed east on I-66, then picked up the southbound George Washington Memorial Parkway. Davis turned on his headlights as he passed beneath the Fourteenth Street Bridge and took the exit to Gravelly Point Park, hard by the Potomac River.

He pulled into the nearly empty parking lot and found the stall he wanted. As darkness descended, the last visitors got in their cars and left. Davis called up a public link on the laptop.

Air traffic controllers began chattering to pilots.

Just then a roaring sound came from behind the van. From the north, a United Airlines jet crossed above the Fourteenth Street Bridge, Gravelly Point Park, Davis's van, and a backwater of the Potomac and touched down at Ronald Reagan National Airport.

Davis thrilled at the vibration the passing jet's engines sent through the van and his body. It had been less than two hundred feet above him! He knew this because he had been to the park multiple times over the past three years, purposely going months between visits to study landing patterns and approaches until he felt as if he could put a jet down on that runway himself.

The air traffic control chatter directed the next three planes to approach the airport at the same specific speeds and angles of descent. The wind, they said, was due south, barely eight knots, which made for smooth landings.

The next plane and the one after that came in on the same vectors. Davis fed this information into the laptop just before a police cruiser turned into the parking lot.

He'd anticipated a visit. A cruiser showed up every evening to make sure the parking lot was empty and gated off from vehicles. Davis leaned over and retrieved a sprayer from the floor of the passenger side. He tugged his respirator up so it covered the lower part of his face and got out with a headlamp on his head. The cruiser pulled up. The window rolled down.

"Late night?" the female officer asked.

"On overtime, Officer," Davis said, lowering the mask a little. "They want this place sprayed with insecticide when no one is around."

"You're lucky it's fairly warm and not raining."

"I was kind of wishing for rain so I could go home and see my kids," he said. He unzipped his coverall enough to show the Ravens logo on his hoodie. "Watch the game."

"That's right, Baltimore's playing tonight. You have the key to the gate?"

Davis nodded. "I'll shut and lock it when I leave."

"Thanks," the officer said. She rolled up the window and pulled away.

Davis made a show of leaving the parking lot and trudging down the bike path. The cruiser's taillights disappeared. After a bicyclist passed him heading north, he buttonhooked back to the van, got in, and set the chemical sprayer on the floor. He listened to the next plane land on the same vectors and trajectories and checked to make sure his cell phone was connected to the laptop. Then he sent the computer a command from the phone. Behind him, he heard the gun swivel and adjust for elevation and windage based on the information he'd gleaned from the air traffic controllers.

"Delta nine-four-four, you are clear for landing," a female controller on the laptop connection said. "American eight-three-nine, begin your approach."

"Roger that, National," both pilots said.

Davis got out fast, went around the back of the van, and opened the rear doors. Careful not to bump the barrel of the gun, he eased out the mountain bike, got on it, and pedaled away. By the time the Delta flight landed, Davis was out along the Potomac, listening to the air traffic controllers over his phone and earbuds.

He caught sight of the American jet's landing lights far upriver and stopped the bike south of the Fourteenth Street Bridge. He could barely see the van back in the parking lot.

It didn't matter, and neither did the men, women, and children on the plane. Davis thumbed the screen of his phone to see the feed from the scope.

American 839, arriving from Palm Beach International, was above and behind him over the bridge. The heat signature of the jet was just showing on the gun sight's thermal feed.

Davis activated the firing program and waited for the mayhem to commence.

3

FIFTEEN MINUTES EARLIER, DURING a long, slow banked turn from west to north to east, American Airlines captain Harry Carpenter, a week from retirement, was talking barbecue, his third favorite subject after fly-fishing and college football.

"I'm telling you, the best I ever had was in Chicago," he said to his new copilot, Emma Waters.

"Chicago?" she said. "What about Kansas City or Memphis or Dallas? I always thought those were the hotbeds of the good stuff."

Carpenter chuckled. "Well, the real hotbeds were and are folks' backyards down in the Carolinas somewhere and at cinder-block roadside joints in Mississippi and Alabama, the kind of place that serves you food on a paper plate with a cold can of beer or a Dr Pepper while you sit under the blades of a creaky old fan."

Waters laughed. "Sounds like you've been there."

"Many times," he said. "My old man was a freak for good barbecue, used to drive us all over on the mere rumor of a great rib joint."

"And you found it in Chicago?"

"I did," the captain said and smacked his lips in satisfaction. "Or, rather, Daddy did when he was up there for a convention back in the eighties."

The air traffic controller broke into their conversation. "American eight-three-nine, turn southeast fifteen degrees. Descend to two thousand."

"Looking for that river," Carpenter said.

"Affirmative."

He fed the instruction into the onboard computer and watched gauges as the aircraft followed his commands. "God, I love this. When I started flying this route, you had to come in manual to make sure you didn't hit the Fourteenth Street Bridge. It freaked you out. Now you couldn't hit it if you tried."

As the captain caught sight of the river and lowered the landing gear, Waters said, "You going to make a pilgrimage to this Chicago rib mecca soon?"

Carpenter groaned. "Would that I could, but the great Leon's is no more. My favorite was his rib tips. He'd smoke them and then chop them up into two-inch chunks with a cleaver and dump them in a paper bucket with his sauce, fries, and two pieces of Bunny Bread right there in front of you. Best ribs ever."

"Leon die or give up?"

"Heart attack, I think. It's why now I just sample good ribs occasionally. Otherwise, you end up like Leon, and my old man and I have too much fun to look forward to for that."

"Fun in Boise?" Emma said skeptically.

"I'm telling you, Idaho's a beautiful place. You should see it sometime."

The lights of Washington, DC, and Northern Virginia were brilliant as the plane descended. He could see the bridge and the runway five miles away.

"You deserve it, Harry," his copilot said. "How many years you put in?"

"Twenty-six in the saddle, eight in the air force before that," he said. "Honestly, Emma, I kind of hate flying now. Can't wait to get in my Chevy Trail Boss with Terri and the dogs and light out for Idaho and a better life."

They crossed over the bridge, their landing lights illuminating the north end of the park. As Carpenter was scanning readouts and looking at the runway, he caught the impression of a vehicle at the far end of the empty parking lot. Something hot, orange, and pulsing came ripping out of the vehicle right at them.

Carpenter had flown combat missions in Kuwait. He knew they were machine-gun tracers even before the heavy .50-caliber bullets began to rake the jet.

"Sorry, Terri," he said to his wife before the cockpit windshield blew out.

CHAPTER

4

DAVIS WATCHED THE FIRST tracers and bullets find and chew up the jet's left wing and engine and then saw a rain of 180 .50-caliber armor-piercing bullets smash into the nose, the cockpit, and the forward landing gear.

The plane stuttered in the air, still under computer control and still in full descent as it passed over the parking lot, the van, and the now empty machine gun. The jet wobbled and drifted right, crossing the backwater of the Potomac. The rear gear touched down, and for an instant Davis thought he'd failed, that the jet would land and that he'd had zero impact.

But then the right wing dipped wildly. Sparks flew like thousands of Roman candles when the wing smashed down onto the tarmac, causing the jet's back end to skid violently. The wing broke off entirely, and the fuselage and other wing went tomahawking down the runway.

On the next big impact, the second wing came off. A forward section of the fuselage, including the cockpit, broke away and flew off the runway.

On the third impact, the remaining jet fuel exploded, shredding what was left of American Airlines Flight 839. The wreckage finally came to a stop far down the runway. Flames belched into the night sky.

Davis felt zero regret for murdering however many people he had just killed.

God, I hate Floridians, he thought as he thumbed his phone's screen again. *Old fat-ass do-nothings in wheelchairs. Serves them right that they were the first ones to get what they all deserve. Every single one of them.*

When Davis heard sirens and saw the red flash of fire trucks speeding onto the runway toward the burning mass, he calmly gave his phone and the laptop a final order. Seven hundred yards away, the van blew apart.

Davis biked north. He'd stop when he was two or three miles up the path, pull the chip from the burner phone, break it, throw both items in the river, and move on to safer surroundings.

CHAPTER

5

JOHN SAMPSON AND I were inside a brick apartment building in Southeast Washington, DC, near the border with Fairmount Heights, Maryland, so we didn't hear the machine-gun fire.

But we sure heard the dull thud and roar of the explosion that followed.

"What was that?" a distraught Eileen O'Dell said, her hands trembling. "Oh my God, what was that?"

"Whatever it was, it was far away, Eileen," Sampson said, trying to keep her calm. "I know this is difficult, but anything you can tell us about Trey's routine, especially in the morning, might help us figure out who did this to him."

Eileen's twenty-five-year-old husband, Trey O'Dell, had been shot to death around four a.m. that same day. He was the fourth young man to die in a very-early-morning ambush on the streets of the nation's capital since the beginning of the year. Sampson and I had been assigned to the case of what the media was calling the Dead Hours killings.

John was a senior detective with the Metropolitan Police Department's homicide unit. I used to be with MPD's homicide unit as well, but now I worked as an investigative consultant to both the department and the FBI, where I'd once served as a profiler. I rubbed at the ache in my chest, still getting over a wound that had almost cost me my life.

"I don't know what I haven't told you and the other officers already," the new widow said, on the verge of breaking down again. "Didn't anyone see it happen?"

"No one has come forward yet," I told her. "But you said it was his normal route?"

"Not always, but often enough. He kept a diary of his runs, the routes and everything, you know. You'll see it all on his laptop."

"What about the early hour? Was that unusual?"

"No," she said. "Trey never needed much sleep. He was always up early. And he liked to run before work."

"What's the name of the school where he taught?" Sampson asked.

"Woodrow Wilson."

"Good school," I said.

"He was a good teacher," she said, her voice quivering. "The kids loved him. Everyone loved him. I just don't understand how I can go to bed and he's there and I wake up and the police are pounding at my door and he's not." She started crying again. "This isn't supposed to happen to newlyweds. It just isn't."

I felt terrible. They'd been married in June and moved down from Boston after Trey landed the teaching job.

"You said your mother and sister are on the way?" I asked, handing her a tissue.

Eileen dabbed at her eyes as she nodded, then blew her nose. "Mom and Eva should be here in an hour or so. And Trey's mom and dad after that. How am I going to get through this?"

"With their help," Sampson said.

"They'll hold you up if you hold them up," I said.

She nodded, looking blank and bleary-eyed. "At least they didn't have to see him."

I knew she'd gone down to the morgue earlier in the day to identify her husband. "You were brave, saving them from that."

"Or I'm an idiot," she said. "I don't know if I'll ever forget what I saw."

"You'll never forget him," Sampson said. "But that other memory will fade."

"I hope so," she said as more tears rolled down her cheeks. "I can't take this feeling much longer."

I said softly, "My first wife was murdered, Eileen. It's part of why I do what I do. I can tell you the next few days are going to be rough. But your family is coming, and it takes time, a lot of it, but you will get through this. You will have a life again. You will know happiness again."

She cried harder. "That's the problem. I don't want to be happy again."

Before either of us could answer, my cell phone and then Sampson's dinged with texts telling us to call dispatch.

"I'll take it," I said, walking over to the other side of the simply furnished living area. "This is Alex Cross," I said when the dispatcher answered.

"Drop whatever you're doing, Dr. Cross, and head to Reagan Airport," she said. "A jet just crashed and exploded on the runway. The chief and the FBI want you and Sampson there pronto."

CHAPTER

6

BY THE TIME WE left Eileen O'Dell, promising to check on her later, sirens were wailing everywhere as police and fire crews raced to Reagan National. Two helicopters were in the sky when we pulled out, bubble on, our siren joining the chorus.

Sampson headed west toward the river. The police-radio chatter was all about forming a cordon around the airport and the subsequent traffic snarls that were knotting in and around the Fourteenth Street Bridge.

"I don't know how we're going to get there or why they called us in," Sampson said. "And why the FBI? This is NTSB's show all the way."

"Unless the plane didn't crash on its own."

"I'm not hearing them say that," he said, gesturing to the radio. "And we're driving into a mess."

I put on the AM station WTOP and learned that all air traffic bound for Reagan was being diverted to Dulles International. My cell phone rang: supervising special agent Edward Mahoney, my former partner at the FBI and one of the Bureau's top crisis managers.

"Ned," I said, putting him on speaker. "Did you call us in?"

"I did," he said, panting. He sounded like he was running. "Where are you?"

I told him.

"Don't go to the bridge," he said. "It's a parking lot. Get to the wharf opposite Nationals Park on the Anacostia River. We'll pick you up in ten minutes."

He hung up, and Sampson hit the gas.

Five minutes later, John was running out to the wharf, passing the empty slips of the DC Sailing Club; I followed him, although I couldn't move as quickly, given my recent chest injury. When we reached the water's edge, a big MPD Harbor Patrol Zodiac-style boat was coming hard up the river at us, searchlights on, blue bubbles flaring but thankfully quiet.

John and I looked beyond the boat, farther down the Anacostia and across the Potomac, and saw wind-whipped flames, the flash of many lights, and a great billowing plume of black smoke rising above the runway's south end.

"Reminds me of when the Pentagon got hit," Sampson said. "I thought we were done with that crap."

"We were. And now we aren't," I said.

Mahoney stood in the bow of the approaching police boat, a lean, intense man with a remarkable ability to plan and execute large, complex investigations for the FBI. He was also one of my closest friends, someone I trusted as completely as I trusted Sampson.

I don't think I'd ever seen Ned as sober or grim as he was when we climbed aboard, joining a team of twenty agents from the FBI, NTSB, and ATF.

"What's going on?" Sampson said. "We were told it's a crash."

"American Airlines flight coming in from West Palm Beach. A hundred plus were on board," Mahoney said. "They're searching for survivors. And we're getting unconfirmed reports of gunfire just before the jet went down."

"Unconfirmed?" I said as the boat turned and headed toward the Potomac and the airport.

"Affirmative, but something very big definitely exploded right afterward in Gravelly Point Park, off the north end of the runway."

Sampson said, "I'm calling Willow."

I said, "She's safe with Jannie and Nana Mama at my house."

"Still," he said and he turned away to phone his young daughter, who was in the care of my eighteen-year-old daughter and ninety-something grandmother. His wife had died a while back, and Willow was his pride and joy.

"Terrorism?" I said to Mahoney.

"Looking that way."

I said, "You're running the show?"

"For now. Lucky me."

I sent a text to my wife, Bree, who used to be chief of detectives for MPD and would know well what my life was about to become: a single-minded, all-consuming search for hard evidence amid the chaos, suspicion, and rumor that was sure to whirl around the hunt for the killer or killers of one hundred innocent people.

As we left the Anacostia and headed into the Potomac, the sky began to weep and drizzle, which made the lights and the

23

fire and that black plume of smoke even more surreal and nightmarish.

Big searchlights slashed the river. Above us and circling around the airport were five helicopters. The one closest to us was from a local television station.

Mahoney barked into his radio, "Get the goddamned press back. I want a no-fly bubble around that runway a mile in every direction. If they give you any guff, tell them I'll shoot them down."

CHAPTER

7

THE TELEVISION CHOPPERS HAD backed off by the time the bow of the Harbor Patrol boat nudged the riprap along the riverbank, some three hundred yards from the wreckage. We jumped off one by one and scrambled up the bank to find a hellish scene playing out, the soundtrack a deafening symphony of sirens that seemed to be wailing near and far and coming from every angle.

Five fire engines surrounded the biggest piece of the fuselage. Through hoses, firefighters were shooting foam at it and the scorched tail section. More fire engines were blaring and braying as they and several ambulances sped down the runway from the north toward the mangled nose and forward fuselage.

Two ambulances were already there. EMTs were running to the largest unburned section of the jet. Other EMTs and firefighters were walking both sides of the runway, scanning for survivors. No one was stopping.

"This is going to get rough," Sampson said, gesturing ahead of us at a small human leg clad in denim, the foot in a red sneaker, lying in the low wet grass.

From that point on and with every step we took, the scene turned so horrific and macabre that I could process it only by seeing it as a battlefield rather than a crash site. Chunks of twisted airplane wing, jagged strips of metal, and human body parts were strewn around the runway north and south of where the aircraft had exploded. You could see the scorch line where that had happened.

And still the sirens wailed.

"Goddamn it, I can't think," Mahoney said and barked an order into the radio. Over the next minute, the wails and din slowed and faded until there was only the shouting of the firefighters working on the wreckage. The flames were gone. The plume of smoke was thinning. But the air was still acrid with the smell of spent jet fuel, seared metal, the foam, and charred flesh when Ned gathered us and the top law enforcement commanders.

"We are processing this as a crime scene until further notice," Ned said. "NTSB?"

"Supervising investigator Bob Holland," a man in his forties said, raising his hand.

"Thanks, Bob. You will control the collection of all physical evidence relating to the crash, but your people will work alongside my agents, who will document the remains so we can get them removed, identified, and returned to their loved ones as soon as possible. ATF?"

A tall redheaded woman in a blue windbreaker raised her hand. "Agent Alice Kershaw."

"Glad to have you, Alice. I want your people in that park north of the runway," Mahoney said. "Tell me what blew up out there and see if there's evidence of weapon fire prior to that explosion."

Calvin Stetson, a captain with the Virginia State Police, said, "At least fifteen people who were outside the terminal told us they heard automatic-weapon fire."

"Can a machine gun bring down a jet like that?" Sampson asked.

Kershaw said, "Taliban has brought down jets and choppers with them."

I said, "Why not a surface-to-air missile or something like it?"

Mahoney said, "Because there are hardly any Stingers out there that are not accounted for or destroyed or so old that they can't be fired. The Bureau and DIA are vigilant about tracking them down if they get the slightest rumor of one anywhere in the world. Even the Chinese SA-seven knockoffs."

"But a machine gun?" Sampson asked.

"Easier to find and obtain," Ned said. "Especially if you're willing to skip the federal licensing process and go to the black market."

"Or the dark web," Kershaw said. "There are plenty of heavy guns available if you know where to look."

"We'll figure that out later," Mahoney said, and he clapped his hands. "Let's do this right, people. The victims and families deserve nothing less."

8

WE WERE THERE ALL night while Mahoney's team of investigators grew and fanned out under his direction. Scaffolding was helicoptered in. Within three hours of the crash, a bank of spotlights had turned sections of the runway as bright as a baseball park.

Over the years, Sampson, Mahoney, and I had worked closely on dozens of cases. We were all fine investigators on our own, but together we were far more than the sum of our parts. Knowing that, Ned had John and me shadow him as he moved among agents and officers from seven different law enforcement agencies, listening to their concerns, giving them guidance, and asking question after question after question. He reported in to the FBI director on the half hour.

We heard that the media was giving the crash blanket coverage. We didn't need to hear or see it to know that Washington was on edge and in shock. You could feel it coming off almost everyone who was at the crash site that evening.

John and I stayed quiet for the most part, listening, inhaling information as Mahoney got it. Around ten in the evening, we learned that more than fifty charred corpses remained in the largest section of the fuselage.

Fifteen of those on board, including the pilot, copilot, and the first-class passengers, had been inside the forward fuselage. The violent energy of the crash had snapped spines and skulls.

The rest of the passengers had been cut apart and hurled free as the plane flipped and smashed and broke into fourteen large, ragged pieces. It quickly became clear there would be no survivors of AA 839.

Shortly after midnight, dozens of officers and emergency workers from four different states donned full hazmat gear and began removing the remains that an army of crime scene techs had photographed, bagged, and coded based on their GPS locations. The gruesome job of recovery was so complicated that the last bodies would not leave the airport grounds for another thirty-two hours.

Around three a.m., NTSB supervising investigator Bob Holland showed us bullet holes in the forward foil of the right wing and in the housing of the right engine.

"Fifty-caliber," Holland said. "Looks like he chewed up the left side, nose, and the forward landing gear, which is over there on the other side of the runway."

"How many rounds?" I asked.

"I'm thinking a full belt. Two hundred at close range."

"Lot of destruction fast," Sampson said.

"Enough to say this is now officially a mass murder," Mahoney said grimly.

"You going to announce that?" Holland asked, looking pale.

"In the morning. I want to see what ATF finds in Gravelly Point Park first."

But before we could go there, Ned came under more pressure. A media horde and scores of relatives and friends of passengers on American Airlines Flight 839 had gathered during the night in front of the closed airport and were demanding answers.

Worse, airport managers were demanding to know when flights could resume. Reagan's closure was causing a travel nightmare up and down the East Coast.

After identifying himself, Mahoney had the brutal job of publicly announcing that there were no survivors of the crash, the cause of which was still under investigation. People began to wail and sob. A pregnant woman collapsed into another woman's arms.

"People are saying there was machine-gun fire!" one cable news reporter yelled.

"We're still working to confirm that," Mahoney said. "We'll have more for you later."

"Did the jet crash on its own or was it shot down?"

"We'll know more in the morning," he said, and we left.

CHAPTER

9

IT WAS NEARLY FOUR A.M. when we finally got to the crime scene perimeter around Gravelly Point Park, which had its own bank of lights shining on it; at least fifteen agents in hazmat suits were there, all wearing big headlamps that they trained on a twisted skeleton of charred steel in the parking lot.

"Hard to say what kind of vehicle it was. Probably a van," said ATF supervising special agent Alice Kershaw, who was also clad in hazmat gear. "Looks like he was doing his best to disintegrate whatever was inside."

"Did he succeed?" Mahoney said.

"He blew a lot of it to smithereens, but we're good at putting puzzle pieces together."

"What do you know so far?"

"I don't know how it was detonated yet, but it was a fertilizer bomb. A big one."

I said, "What about a machine gun?"

"There was one here," Kershaw said. "Still is, in parts. My guys found pieces of the receiver and barrel. And fifty-caliber casings, a lot of them in a spray north from the van. They think it's an old Browning M two. Vietnam era."

Sampson said, "Let me get this straight. You think this guy was in the back of the van with his fifty-cal waiting specifically for this flight?"

The ATF agent shook her head. "I can't tell you if he was waiting for that particular plane or not, but I know for certain he was not in the van with the machine gun."

"How?" I asked.

"We've found no body parts here, for one thing. That bomb was huge and threw a lot of metal, but no flesh so far. And we have witnesses who said the bomb went off within seconds of the plane going down, so he had to have been far away when he triggered it. We also found other pieces of the gun that were attached to brackets and fittings that suggest it might have been remotely controlled, probably hydraulically by a computer program of some kind."

She showed us a piece of tripod with melted plastic hydraulic lines fused to it and to part of the barrel, a section of a scorched track that she thought was used to position the rear of the gun, and pieces of the housing of a Dell laptop.

I said, "Did he control the laptop with a phone?"

"Maybe," Kershaw said. "Probably. But I think he would have been too far away to do it by Bluetooth. It would be cellular."

Mahoney said, "Or satellite. Either way, we should be able to find a data record."

"That's out of my wheelhouse," she said and yawned. "We will know after my metal detectors get—" Kershaw paused when a female ATF agent came up with a bent, twisted, and punctured chunk of metal that looked like a crumpled magazine. "What have you got, Burns?"

"Can't get it open, boss, but I think it's one of those thin metal clipboard boxes construction guys carry with their estimate forms inside. My dad used to have one."

"Okay."

Burns turned her flashlight beam on the metal box and into those punctures and gashes, revealing paper inside that had been more baked than incinerated, coal black in places but the rest of it the color of cured tobacco leaves.

"You can read some of what's on it through the big hole there," the ATF agent said and she altered the angle of her flashlight.

We all peered into the hole. Sampson got it first.

"Avis," he said. "The van was a rental."

10

BREE WAS HOVERING IN a groggy, half-awake state just before her alarm went off when Alex came creaking up the staircase of their home on Fifth Street in Southeast DC. He opened the bedroom door and slipped inside.

She came alert and pushed herself up on one elbow. Alex was in the shadows, but Bree didn't have to see her husband's face to know how things had gone. The night was there in his posture.

"It looked terrible on the news," she whispered as he started to take off his clothes.

"Carnage," he said dully. "I've never seen anything like it. You almost didn't know where not to look, if that makes sense. Heartbreaking in every direction."

"Speaking of—how are you feeling?"

"I'm okay. Really."

"Was the plane shot down?"

"Ned will announce it later this morning. Fifty-caliber remote-controlled machine gun and a fertilizer bomb to destroy evidence."

"No one taking credit?"

"Not that we've heard."

Bree pulled back the blankets on Alex's side of the bed. "Come get some sleep."

"I've got to get the smell off me or I won't sleep a wink." He went into the bathroom.

Her phone buzzed. A text from Elena Martin, her boss. At 6:15 a.m.? Bree thumbed the screen. The text came up.

Need you ASAP, Bree. Address to follow. This is urgent.

Bree rolled out of bed just as the shower went on. She went in with Alex.

"Here," she said. She grabbed a large sponge, poured body wash on it, and soaped him from head to toe.

"I can't remember the last time someone washed me," Alex said.

"You looked like you needed it," she said. "Now rinse off and get some sleep."

Alex mock saluted her, then kissed her. "I don't know where I'd be mentally if I didn't have someone like you to come home to."

"Ahh, that's sweet, baby," she said as she washed herself. "I feel the same way."

He got out of the shower, grabbed a towel, and yawned hard. "What's on your plate today?"

"Got to meet Elena ASAP," Bree said. "She just texted me. Said it was urgent."

"Be safe, whatever it is," he said. "Good night, and can you try to keep Ali quiet?"

"As quiet as is humanly possible with your youngest child," Bree said, turning off the shower. She got out and grabbed a towel. "I'll be slinky-quiet going out of here."

"I like you slinky," he said. He trudged to the bed, dropped his towel, and climbed in.

He was asleep five minutes later when Bree left the bathroom after applying her makeup. She tiptoed into the walk-in closet, closed the door behind her, chose one of the navy-blue pant-suits she'd lived in as a police detective, and quickly dressed.

Alex was snoring, a pillow over his head, when she crept out, shoes and bag in hand. She closed the bedroom door and made it down the stairs without a sound.

Nana Mama, Alex's ninety-something grandmother, was already in the kitchen, breaking eggs for omelets. Coffee dripped into the pot.

"Was that Alex just coming in?" Nana asked.

Bree nodded. "He looked like a punching bag."

Nana's face fell. "I hate that he has to see all these things up close. Especially after everything that's happened to him."

"That's the job," Bree said.

"I know. I know, and he's good at it."

"One of the best."

"I worry about the toll it takes on him to be one of the best."

"I do too, Nana," Bree said, hugging her. "We just have to be there for him when he hurts."

Alex's grandmother hugged her back. "Is he hurting?"

"He's sleeping right now," Bree said, pulling away. "But he was, yes."

"What do you want in your omelet?"

"Just having coffee this morning, Nana," Bree said, going to a cabinet for a go-cup.

"You should eat."

Before Bree could reply, her phone buzzed again with an address across the river in Rosslyn, Virginia, and the words Will meet you there in twenty.

Bree's car was parked three blocks away; she decided she'd get there faster if she took an Uber. She ordered it and headed to the door.

"Where are you going now?" Nana asked.

"Just over to Rosslyn."

"When does Alex want to get up?"

"Let him sleep in. He needs it."

CHAPTER

11

ELENA MARTIN WAS PACING in front of a high-rise in Rosslyn, alternately sipping nervously from a coffee and smoking a cigarette.

Bree had never seen Elena smoke before. Or pace, for that matter. Bree's boss, the founder and CEO of the international security firm the Bluestone Group, was ordinarily unflappable and always put together.

Not that morning. No chic Chanel suit. No designer shoes. Elena wore faded blue sweatpants, old running shoes, and a dark windbreaker. Her light brown hair was pulled back in a tight ponytail, and she wore dark sunglasses despite the overcast sky.

Elena checked her watch when she caught sight of Bree. "At least one of you is on time," Elena said. She stubbed the cigarette out in a potted plant.

"Who are we waiting on?"

Two young, well-dressed men came out of the apartment complex. After they were out of earshot, Elena said, "The personal assistant of a dear friend of mine who hasn't been in touch with anyone in any way in three days."

"And that's unusual?"

"In the extreme," Elena said. "Leigh Anne—she lives in this building, which is why we're here—is one of those people who have to be connected. Always. If she doesn't have at least one of her cells on, she feels like she's stranded on a desert island."

"How do you know Leigh Anne's phones aren't on?"

"She's not answering my texts and when I call either number, it goes straight to voice mail, both of which were full as of shortly before that plane crash last night. I heard it, you know. It rattled the windows on my place."

Bree saw her boss's hands shake as she fished in her windbreaker and came up with a pack of Winstons and a lighter.

"I didn't know you smoked, Elena."

"Until last night, I hadn't smoked in fifteen years," she said, looking disgusted as she stuffed the pack of cigarettes back in her pocket without lighting one.

Bree said, "I guess I'm not completely understanding why your friend going silent over a weekend has got you this upset."

Elena tore off her sunglasses. She wore no makeup to conceal the dark rings under her eyes. "Leigh Anne is more than my best friend, Bree. We're like sisters," she said. "Close sisters. We text or talk two or three times a day and have since we were college roommates. Leigh Anne Asher does not go radio silent. Especially on me."

Leigh Anne Asher. Bree had heard the name somewhere but couldn't remember where.

Her boss said, "She's the founder and CEO of Amalgam.

They do IT, huge subscription service, incredible volume of government work. And they're about to go public, which is another reason Leigh Anne would not cut everyone off. This is something she's worked toward, sacrificed for, for more than a decade to achieve. It will make her an instant billionaire."

"Maybe the pressure of that got to her and she needed some space," Bree said.

"No," Elena said. "Leigh Anne is good with the stress. She meditates twice a day, and she's been looking forward to taking a long break after the IPO. She booked a private jet to take us and some other friends to Fiji for three weeks."

"When does the stock go public?"

"Next Tuesday. And we're supposed to go to Fiji three days later."

A freckle-faced redhead in her mid- to late twenties hurried up to them, breathing hard. "I'm so sorry, Elena. The Metro car stopped for ten minutes."

"It's fine. You have the keys?"

"Yes. And I know most of the security guards," the young woman said. She looked at Bree. "Jill Jackson. I'm personal assistant to Ms. Asher."

"Bree Stone. I work for Elena."

"And she used to be chief of detectives for Metro PD," Elena said. "Let's go inside."

Jill Jackson nodded uncertainly and walked toward the front door. "It's worth a shot, I guess, but like I said earlier, she's not living here, she's staying at an apartment in Alexandria. This apartment is still being renovated."

"It's the only place we haven't checked," Elena said firmly.

They went inside. The security guard recognized Asher's assistant and when she said they wanted to check on the renovations, he waved them through. Elena asked the guard when Leigh Anne Asher had last been there. He checked his computer and said at ten in the morning on Friday.

"What time did she leave?" Bree asked.

"We don't track that."

"What about security cameras? Can you take a look at whatever footage you have around that time, three days ago, ten a.m., while we check the apartment?"

"What's going on?" the guard asked.

Bree was about to say Asher was missing when she caught Elena shaking her head. "We're just trying to figure out a few things," she said.

They went to the elevator. Jackson used a key to unlock the penthouse button.

"When was the last time you saw or talked to her?" Bree asked the assistant.

The elevator began to rise. "On Friday, seven in the morning, by phone," Jackson said. "We went through her schedule because I couldn't come in. I had an appointment with my oncologist to get some tests done."

"I'm sorry to hear that."

She smiled. "I'm not. The tests came back negative, so I'm good. No cancer."

"Congratulations," Bree said. "Who was the last person to hear from Leigh Anne?"

Jackson said Chandler Ellison, Amalgam's chairman of the board, spoke to Asher by phone around eleven on Friday morning.

"After she came here?" Elena said as the elevator slowed.

"Apparently," Jackson said.

"Tell me about her," Bree said.

"Leigh Anne? Smartest person I've ever known."

"I'll second that," Elena said. The elevator stopped and the door slid back, revealing a round foyer that was being plastered.

"A genius, then?" Bree said, following them to a door on the far side.

"We hire geniuses every day of the week at Amalgam," Jill said. "From the Ivy League, MIT, Stanford. But Leigh Anne is like no one else at the company. She knows every detail of the business, from the new technology to customer service. Keeps it all in her head. Knows everyone who works at Amalgam by name, and there are five hundred and sixty-eight employees at the moment."

They went through a door and into a cavernous room with dramatic floor-to-ceiling windows that overlooked Roosevelt Island and the Potomac River. "I hate to ask this," Bree said, "but could you ever see her hurting herself?"

Elena said, "Never. Leigh Anne is at peace."

"What do you think?" Bree asked Asher's assistant.

"Leigh Anne is the most chill person I know. And honestly, in the past couple of weeks, I've never seen her so happy."

"How so?"

Jackson shrugged. "She had a lot to be happy about. The IPO. This incredible penthouse to live in. But it felt like it was more than that."

Elena frowned. "In what way?"

"She was glowing. You know, the way you do when you've met someone special and you want to keep it a secret."

CHAPTER

12

CAPTAIN MARION DAVIS DID not wake up until Johnny Unitas leaped onto the bed and landed on his chest.

Captain Davis groaned at his cat. "C'mon, Johnny, there's food in your bowl." Davis's head felt like it was going to explode. And his gut felt turbulent, churning with toxins.

The cat, a Bengal, meowed loud enough for him to at last crack an eyelid open.

Johnny Unitas looked like a miniature leopard as he glared at the captain from two inches away. He meowed again, a high-pitched roar.

"Okay, okay," Davis said, pushing the cat off his chest. "I'm awake."

He tried to sit up. His stomach lurched and soured. His head felt like it had indeed exploded.

The pain turned throbbing and searing. Captain Davis flopped back, panting, disgusted to find his pillowcase clammy and sweat-soaked. His eyes felt like they'd been parboiled. *What the hell did I do to myself this time? I hope I didn't get behind the wheel.*

Meow, Johnny Unitas protested. *Meow. Meow.*

The cat's aggressive voice felt like a saw going in one ear and out the other. Davis pushed off the blankets and sat upright.

He immediately regretted that. The turbulence in his gut turned violent.

Davis lurched to his feet, threw his hand out against the wall to steady himself, then took hurried and wobbly steps across the large master bedroom into a well-appointed bathroom. There he went to his knees and defiled the porcelain throne. The retching went on so long and the aftertaste was so vile he thought that he must have been poisoned.

What the hell did I eat last night? Captain Davis wondered as the dry heaves faded.

Meow. Meow. Meow!

He shut the bathroom door to keep the cat out and managed to get up off his knees and over to the counter, which he held on to with trembling hands. Davis forced himself to raise his head and look in the mirror.

The captain was forty-eight, but that morning he looked like he was pushing sixty. Though his body had retained some semblance of his old athletic form, his hair was thinning and going gray. His eyes were bloodshot and puffy, his skin sallow and waxen.

What did you do to yourself, dude?

Davis tried to recall the previous night and simply couldn't. He remembered going up the steps and entering Bowman's, his favorite sports bar, around noon, but nothing beyond that. A total blackout.

The captain filled the sink with cold water and plunged his face into it. That woke him for good. He knocked back four Motrin and two Tylenol and chased them down with two glasses of water, then donned a Baltimore Ravens bathrobe and opened the bathroom door.

Johnny Unitas was pacing in circles.

"What's the matter? I left food for you yesterday. I know I did."

The cat trotted out of the large master bedroom into the hallway. Davis was about to follow him when he happened to look over at his clock radio, which informed him that the time was 9:45 a.m. and the day of the week was Tuesday.

"Tuesday?" he muttered. He ignored the cat's whines and looked around for his phone. Not seeing it, he picked up a pair of jeans from the floor and rifled through the pockets—empty.

Then he spotted a tan workman's coverall and a Ravens hoodie crumpled on a chair in a corner. Davis liked to tinker with cars and had coveralls like that, but his were blue. And he had several Baltimore Ravens sweatshirts and hoodies, but that wasn't one of them.

And yet when Davis reached into the pocket of the tan coverall, he found his phone, the battery dead. And his wallet and car keys were in the hoodie's pouch.

Meow!

The captain grabbed his charger from beside the bed, went into the hallway, and padded its long length toward Johnny Unitas, coiled at the top of the stairs and ready to bound down. Davis passed three closed doors, acutely and devastatingly aware of how empty his large house was. If he let loose a yell, he was sure it would echo. But the thought of raising his voice made him shudder. He held tight to the banister and went down the stairs to a beautiful foyer with blue-gray slate tiles that always reminded him of Jenna's eyes.

The gauzy image of her had barely begun to form in his sodden brain when the cat meowed and loped away. Davis shook off the memories and followed the cat through a formal dining room into a gourmet kitchen that was neatly arranged—no dishes in the sink, no pots on the red Aga stove. When he looked into the short hallway to the laundry and utility room, he saw Johnny Unitas sitting next to two empty bowls. No food. No water.

"I'm so sorry, Johnny," he said, feeling guilty; he snatched up the bowls and hurried back into the kitchen with them. "You know that Daddy is Johnny's best friend. Yes, he is."

The cat wound through his legs, purring, as Davis poured fresh water and set it down. Johnny lapped it up while the captain got him dry food and a can of tuna.

As the cat gorged himself, Davis started the espresso machine. He made himself a triple shot, carried it to the kitchen table, and sat down. On the wall across from him were three picture frames. Two were empty; the third held a photo of a much younger Captain Davis wearing a flight suit and standing beside a U.S. Air Force F-14 Tomcat.

Waiting for the coffee to cool, he avoided looking at the empty frames and instead stared at his younger, brasher, more confident self, wondering where that man had gone.

"It's Tuesday, Captain Davis," he whispered hoarsely. "Where in God's name have you been the past two days?"

CHAPTER

13

MY CELL PHONE BUZZED and hummed, dragging me from a deep, dark, delicious sleep remarkably free of the nightmare scenes at Reagan National. I cracked my eyes open and looked at the clock radio.

It was 10:10 a.m.

The phone went silent. I shut my eyes and was just starting to drift off when it began to buzz again; it vibrated off the end table and landed with a crack on the floor.

Now it was 10:12 a.m.

Not even four hours of sleep? This is gonna hurt.

I hated when my life got like this, when I had to fight to find scattered bouts of real sleep amid multiple cat naps. But that was the nature of working big cases like the shooting down of American Flight 839.

Your life was not your own. Your life was spent in service to the dead.

47

The cell began to vibrate a third time. I leaned over and snatched it up, figuring I'd see Ned Mahoney's name on the caller ID.

It was John Sampson.

"We've got another Dead Hours corpse. Found about forty-five minutes ago in Marlow Heights."

"Out of the District," I said.

"Maryland state troopers have already asked us in."

"They're sure it's our guy?"

"Same MO. Sheet and all."

"Text me the address," I said.

"ASAP. I'll grab you in fifteen and drop Willow with Jannie and Nana."

I dressed as fast as I could, given that I was still recovering from a chest wound. I heard my cell phone ding with a text, glanced at it, and saw an address on Olson Street in Marlow Heights, which surprised me. I got on my shoulder harness and holster, then tugged on a jacket.

Up to that point, the victims had all been found in and around DC in densely populated inner-city areas with, for the most part, lower-income residents. But Olson Street in Marlow Heights was deep in the heart of suburbia.

Why break the inner-city pattern at death number five?

And why kill again so soon?

The first four killings had all been at least a month apart. The body of Trey O'Dell had been found a little more than twenty-four hours ago.

Over the years, I'd worked my share of serial-killer investigations, and when we saw dramatic decreases in the length of time between slayings, it often meant the murderer was going out of control. That tended to result in even more victims.

But it also meant the killer was ripe to make a mistake.

That thought had me fully awake as I left my bedroom and pounded down the stairs. I found Ali, my almost-eleven-year-old, and Jannie, eighteen, in the front room working on their laptops. Ali's school was closed this week for teacher conferences. Though Jannie had a dorm room at Howard University, she liked to come home to study before big tests. Ali was engrossed in a math lesson, and Jannie sat with her laptop in one of the overstuffed chairs and sighed when she saw me. She'd been doing that a lot lately.

"Dad, I have to study, and Uncle John texted me that—" she began.

"We need your help and he's bringing Willow," I said. Willow's school was closed this week too. "There's been another Dead Hours killing. I've got to eat and get out of here in four minutes."

"Really?" Ali said. "Another one so soon, Dad? That's not good."

"Tell me about it," I said and headed to the kitchen.

Nana Mama was reading in the great room but she struggled to her feet when I came rushing in. "You need breakfast, Alex. I'll make you some eggs."

"Thanks, but no time, Nana," I said. "I'll just grab coffee."

"You and Bree have to learn to eat right!" she scolded.

"Tomorrow," I said, pouring the coffee into a go mug and snapping the lid in place. "Love you. Willow's coming over."

"I figured as much," she said as I went back to the front room.

"Dad?" Ali said.

Outside, Sampson honked. "Come help, Jannie," I said.

Irritated, she put down her laptop. "I don't even have time to study anymore. It's like I'm a full-time babysitter."

"Willow has to do homework too," I said.

"Lot of chatter when she does it," Jannie said, getting up and following me to the front door. Sampson was coming up the porch stairs with his young daughter, who was wearing a puffy coat against the cold and had a knapsack strapped tight to her back.

"Hi, Jannie!" Willow said, throwing her arms up as if seeing my daughter was the greatest thing in life. "I'm back again!"

Jannie couldn't help but smile. "C'mon, we'll get you set up in the dining room."

"You can call me if you need me, Jannie," Sampson said.

Jannie sighed and nodded. "She'll be fine, Uncle John. Go on. You too, Dad."

14

ALI LOOKED UP FROM his math homework when Jannie came back in with Willow.

"Hi, Ali," Willow said, grinning.

"Hey, Willow," Ali said and went back to his laptop.

Nana Mama came in. "Want some juice and peanut butter toast, young lady?"

"Yes, please," Willow said, and she followed Jannie into the dining room.

"Nana?" Jannie said. "Why would Uncle John text me an address in Marlow Heights?"

"I have no idea," Nana said.

Ali got up and went over to her. "Can I see?"

"Why?" Jannie said.

"Because he may have texted a group of people accidentally, including you."

She looked at the screen. "Yup, that's it. Dad got it too."

"I need help, Jannie," Willow said, struggling to get her school bag off.

Jannie set her phone down on the table and turned to help Sampson's daughter. Ali looked at the screen of his sister's phone before it went blank.

"Boy, that is tight," Jannie said.

"Unzip her coat," Ali said, walking toward the kitchen. "That will help."

He heard a zipper unzipping and then Willow laughing. "That worked!"

"Always does," Ali said. "You should know that. Basic second-grade skill."

Willow giggled.

"Nana," Ali said when he reached the kitchen. "I'm going to go out for a bike ride."

"What about math?"

"I finished."

"How long will you be gone?"

He shrugged. "I don't know. A couple of hours. I wanted to stop at Lonnie's house at some point to go over the English homework."

"Have your phone with you," she said.

"Promise," Ali said. He got his jacket and cap from the front hall and went out the back door, then he got his bike from the shed and rode down the alley. He stopped out of sight of his house and locked the bike to a chain-link fence.

As he walked away, Ali called up the Uber app on his phone and entered the address in Marlow Heights. It wasn't that far. He'd be there in twenty minutes, tops.

I'll slip in, take a look around. Get a feel for the crime scene. Slip back out.

CHAPTER

15

ACROSS THE POTOMAC IN Alexandria, Bree Stone made Elena Martin and Jill Jackson put on blue paper booties, head coverings, and latex gloves before they entered the apartment Leigh Anne Asher was staying in while her Rosslyn apartment was renovated.

"I don't know why we're wasting time here," her boss complained as she put on the blue head covering. "I told you, I've already been through the place."

"I have too," Asher's personal assistant said.

"But I haven't," Bree said. "So humor me, and if anything is going to be disturbed, let me be the one disturbing it. If this is a crime scene, we don't want to contaminate it any more than it already is."

She stood aside as Elena used her electronic key to open the missing entrepreneur's flat. It had none of the raw grandeur of the apartment under renovation in Rosslyn. In fact, the place struck Bree as surprisingly ordinary despite the building's tony address. The furniture looked rented. There were very few personal objects to make it homey.

"I get the idea Leigh Anne wasn't here a lot," Bree said.

"She lived at the office and on the road," Jackson said.

"Start calling every hospital in the area," Bree said. "See if she or someone fitting her description has been admitted since Friday."

Then she started methodically going through the apartment, beginning with Asher's bedroom. In one closet, Bree found a business suit and a dress. The rest of the clothes were jeans and white button-down shirts. Even her shoe collection was limited. The other closet held a stack of moving boxes and several large pieces of high-end luggage.

"Something missing?" Bree asked Jackson. "Her overnight bag?"

Asher's assistant's right hand traveled to her mouth. "I didn't see that. You're right. That is where she usually keeps it."

"Okay, then," Bree said. "Something that supports the new-boyfriend angle. Or at least the idea that Leigh Anne left here with an overnight bag, heading somewhere specific."

"Rather than what?" Elena asked.

"I don't know. Rather than being abducted?"

"Oh, dear God," Jackson said. "Thanks for that."

"But it still doesn't explain the radio silence," Elena said.

Bree nodded and crossed the hall to Asher's home office. While the entrepreneur had skimped in the rest of her apartment, she'd spent freely on powerful Apple computers, cameras, speakers, and the kind of overhead microphone you'd see in a radio studio.

"Does Leigh Anne use an iPhone?" Bree asked.

Asher's assistant nodded. "Yes, she's got the latest one."

"You have the passwords to her computers?"

Jackson looked over at Elena, who hesitated and then shrugged. The PA sat in Asher's desk chair and typed something on the keyboard.

The screen shifted to an image of a tropical scene.

"That's Fiji," Elena said, distraught. "That's where we were supposed to go!"

"You may get there yet," Bree said. "Pull up the Find My iPhone app."

"Oh, that's a good idea," Jill said. "I should have thought of that."

She called up the app and found that Asher had indeed linked her phone to it. But when Jackson tried to track it, it blinked for almost a minute before saying, Leigh Anne's iPhone is inactive.

Elena said, "Can it tell us when and where it was last active?"

Bree said, "I don't think so. We'll have to contact the wireless carrier to do that. We'll also need her credit card accounts to check on their most recent uses."

Asher's assistant said, "I can help with that."

"Can you get me into her e-mail?" Bree asked. "Messaging system?"

Again, Jackson and Elena Martin exchanged glances. Elena said, "Bree, we are working for Leigh Anne. She is our client. Are we clear?"

It was clear as day to Bree: Elena was telling her she might see information in the e-mails and texts that was potentially damaging.

They accessed her most recent messages and saw that Leigh Anne Asher had gotten many but hadn't responded to any of them since noon on Friday. The texts from Friday morning, before the silence, seemed routine: reminders and questions going back and forth between the entrepreneur and the various people involved in the upcoming IPO of her company.

"The e-mails?" Bree said.

Jackson called up Asher's Gmail account, which had nearly two hundred unread e-mails. Bree's attention was caught by the subject line of several of them.

She looked at her boss and then at the entrepreneur's assistant, but they both avoided eye contact.

"Leigh Anne Asher's married?" Bree said. "Why didn't either of you mention that?"

Elena said, "I can explain."

CHAPTER

16

OLSON STREET BENDS NORTHEAST past the campus of Stoddert Middle School, which sits a little more than a mile as the crow flies from the southeast boundary of Southeast Washington, DC, where the previous Dead Hours murders had taken place.

A crowd of people had gathered across the street from the chain-link fence at the south end of the middle-school campus, where the grounds narrowed considerably. Lacrosse and soccer goal cages were stored there.

The field's grass had been allowed to grow, making it almost impossible for anyone to see the corpse from the road. But as Sampson and I walked through the wet grass toward the yellow tape around the scene, we saw the body. It was covered in a white sheet and propped up in a sitting position against the school fence.

At the head, two bright blossoms of blood had seeped through the sheet and dripped down the front; it looked like some macabre horror-film costume.

"Same as the others," Sampson said.

I went to one of the Maryland troopers standing outside the tape and showed him my credentials. "We have an ID yet?"

"None on him, Dr. Cross," the trooper said. "Looks like he'd been out for a run. We've got officers canvassing the locals."

"How far do the woods go?" Sampson asked, looking over the school fence.

"Couple hundred yards? There's an apartment complex on the other side."

Two criminalists were documenting the scene with still shots and video. We waited until they gave us the okay to go inside the tape with the Maryland homicide detectives.

One of them, Detective Marilyn Hanson with the Maryland State Police, had the grisly job of lifting the sheet, revealing a chubby, pale man in his mid-twenties wearing a dark blue windbreaker, a bright green reflector vest, leggings, a red skullcap, and Nikes. A Petzl headlamp hung askew from his head.

The killer had shot out the victim's eyes, leaving empty sockets that seemed to gaze at us mockingly.

"Who shoots like that?" Sampson said. "I mean, every time?"

"Someone with serious weapons training."

"And a sheet fetish."

Hanson squinted. "So you think he shoots them, then throws the sheets over them?"

"No bullet holes in the fabric," I said.

"Oh, right. But why the eyes?"

"We don't get it either," I said. "But if I were a young man, I'd think twice about going for an early-morning run around DC until this guy is caught."

Sampson said, "What direction do we think the shooter came from?"

Hanson gestured to a light line in the high damp grass. "Not enough for footprints, though. He was careful to stay on the grass itself."

I thought about that. "So maybe he's more than just trained. Maybe he's a hunter. Or a professional killer."

CHAPTER

17

UP OLSON STREET SEVENTY-FIVE yards from the murder scene, Ali Cross crouched in the shadows thrown by two of the larger trees abutting the middle-school grounds and watched his father, Sampson, and police officers he didn't know gathered around the latest victim in the Dead Hours homicides.

From this angle, he could barely see the top of the sheet, so he turned his attention to the crowd of twenty-five or thirty people who were standing across the street. With his birthday money, Ali had bought a nifty little telescopic lens that magnetically attached to the lens of his phone camera and allowed him to get detailed close-ups. He aimed the camera at the crowd. He'd heard his dad say over the years that some killers, especially serial killers, liked to slip in among the lookie-loos and watch the police reactions.

But the people he was recording on his camera were

women with children, a handful of teenage boys, and two old men, one of them wearing one of those flat Irish caps. He was bent-backed and leaning on a cane, shaking his shaggy silver hair and full beard at something the other old man was saying.

The first old guy started coughing and hacking; he waved dismissively and limped off out of Ali's sight.

Once Ali felt like he'd gotten everyone in the crowd on video, he turned the camera to the police and his dad.

Ali was by nature an inquisitive kid. He often became intensely interested in a particular subject—astronomy, say—and focused on it obsessively for five or six weeks, after which he'd turn to the next new thing that struck his fancy. One of the only subjects he'd never lost interest in was his father's and Bree's work. And Sampson's too. Ali loved to hang around and listen to them talk shop when they thought he was absorbed in a computer game or a Netflix show.

Their world, finding criminals and putting them in jail, never ceased to fire his imagination, so Ali watched closely as Sampson and a female detective began taping off a long narrow area inside the already taped-off crime scene, from the body out past the soccer goals and close to the low chain-link fence that separated the schoolyard from the sidewalk.

His father walked slowly around the perimeter, head down, studying something in the grass.

What is he looking at? Or for? Then Ali got it. *A path to the body from the street. They think the killer shot from the street.*

Isn't that kind of far for a pistol? It was *a pistol, wasn't it?*

Ali remembered hearing Sampson and his dad talking about one of the earlier cases, and he was sure they'd said the bullets were nine-millimeters. He'd looked them up and saw that most guns of that caliber were pistols, although a few were machine guns that the FBI SWAT teams used.

Two people in full hazmat suits exited a medical examiner's van carrying a stretcher. On a whim, Ali climbed the closest tree and got high enough to take pictures of the sheeted body as it was loaded into a black bag. When they lifted the body onto the stretcher, he climbed back down, brushed the bark off his clothes, and checked the time.

He'd been gone from home more than an hour and a half. But his attention was caught by the police officers, who were moving into position under his dad's direction.

They're beginning a grid search, Ali thought, and he grinned. *God, I love this—*

His father was walking his way. Ali ducked down and scooted off, heading north toward the school. He didn't stop or look back until he was beyond the building and unable to see his father or the crime scene. He slowed, his heart pounding.

OMG! Dad would strangle me if he saw me here!

Ali called for an Uber, feeling the thrill of getting away with something and enjoying every second.

CHAPTER

18

CAPTAIN DAVIS SPENT THE morning as he always did after one of these infrequent blackouts: vowing never to drink again, wondering when the trembling in his hands was going to stop, and praying to God he had not hurt someone while he was hammered to oblivion.

The shakes finally settled around noon, during Davis's fourth trip to the sauna in the basement. But he kept chugging water mixed with hydration salts, and he took a fourth cold shower before he felt even remotely normal.

As he dressed in black and red sweats, the captain once again tried to remember what he'd done after going into Bowman's Sports Bar. But he always went to Bowman's on Sundays during the season. Was this a memory of this past Sunday or another one?

Bowman's had the best screens and setup for a football freak like Davis. He adored football. Football had given him almost everything in life, and he still loved watching pro games, especially the Ravens.

But the Ravens hadn't played on Sunday. They were on *Monday Night Football*. And he'd missed the game!

Captain Davis groaned and thumbed the Ravens app on his phone; he was delighted to see they'd stomped on San Diego. That would keep his fantasy teams in tidy shape. Yes indeed. And he'd preset the DVR to record the entire game. He'd watch it that night.

At twenty minutes to two, Davis said goodbye to Johnny Unitas, left his sprawling home in an affluent neighborhood in Falls Church, Virginia, and drove his Mercedes to the Charles School, an elite private institution with a reputation for putting students in the best colleges and student-athletes in the best scholarships at the best colleges. Especially students who played football. The Charles School had one of the best football teams in Virginia. As Davis liked to boast, you'd have to drive at least three hours in any direction before you'd find a team that could rival the Badgers.

Davis pulled his Mercedes into an empty parking spot marked COACH and got out. There was a crispness in the air. Good for football. Good for practice.

He entered the school through the front doors at two fifteen, his normal arrival time. The halls were empty. Sixth period was just getting started.

Davis walked past the school's trophy collection. He normally did not give a glance at his own photographs in the case. But for some reason, he paused and saw a photo of his teenage self in a Charles School Badgers uniform, holding the state championship trophy over his head. Another featured him in a Baltimore Ravens uniform alongside a *Baltimore Sun* article about his decision to return to the air force and leave the NFL after several successful seasons as a backup center and full-time long snapper. The headline read "Captain Davis Reports for New Duty."

"Captain?"

Davis turned to see Nicholas Hampstead III leaning out of his office wearing a bow tie, a crisp white shirt, and a Badgers booster pin and peering at him through horn-rimmed glasses that did little to disguise the bulging bug eyes he had because of a thyroid condition.

"May I see you a moment?" Hampstead said.

It was the last thing the football coach wanted to do, but he nodded and strode toward the headmaster of the Charles School as if he were about to snap a football or fly a combat jet into a war zone and had total confidence in the outcome.

Hampstead, who stood five seven, took several steps back when Davis came in. He motioned for the football coach to shut the door. Davis did, and when he turned around, he found the headmaster staring at him with his arms crossed and a furious expression on his face.

"Didn't know you'd decided to cancel practice yesterday."

Davis held up his palms. "My fault. My cell died and I got food poisoning from a crab boil I went to Sunday. I was on my back and out cold the entire day."

"That's funny, Captain, Coach Penny says he saw you at Bowman's on Sunday."

"I was, for an hour," Davis said. "Then I hit the crab boil. It was ugly. Coming out both ends at one point."

The headmaster looked away, curling his lip in disgust. "This can't happen again, Captain. Our athletes and coaches need a leader who's not drinking his life away. Are we clear?"

"As day," Davis said, making a note to talk with Troy Penny, his offensive-line coordinator, as soon as possible. "Again, I apologize, Nicholas."

"We'll see you on the field, Captain. Shut the door behind you."

19

CAPTAIN DAVIS SHUT THE door carefully. No use antagonizing the man when a little subservience would make him happy.

Nothing made a little turd like Nicholas Hampstead III feel better about himself than having someone who was twice his size and had twice his accomplishments lick his boots.

Just greases the wheels of life, and I'm beyond having an ego about it.

Well, maybe some ego, Davis thought as he set off toward his office in the athletic department. *Can't let Hampstead go too far or you'll have to squash him. I mean, the alumni and the parents know what's best for the school, and that's having the best damn football team in the state.*

"Hi there, Captain," a woman said as he passed the teachers' lounge.

Davis knew who it was without looking. "How are you, Ms. Plum?"

Fiona Plum, AP English and American history teacher at the Charles School, came up to him. "I'm fine now that you've reappeared. Where were you, Captain? Everyone was worried sick."

He glanced over at her. Late thirties, cinnamon hair, creamy skin, quite pretty in her way. She was looking at him adoringly.

Davis said, "Honestly, Fiona, I got food poisoning at a crab boil I stupidly attended when I should have been watching a football game at Bowman's."

Plum nodded uncertainly. "I was there too. Bowman's, I mean. But after you left."

"Oh? That's too bad."

"It was, yes. But I managed. How are *you* managing, Captain?"

People had been calling Marion Davis "Captain" since he'd captained his Pop Warner football team. By the time he enrolled at the Charles School, it was his nickname and aptly so. He'd gone on to captain the Charles School football team and the Air Force Academy team, and he'd been a captain in the air force before joining the NFL.

Funny how things worked sometimes.

"Captain?" Ms. Plum said.

"I'm fine and getting better every day, Fiona," Davis said. "Thank you for asking."

She hesitated. "Then we should go out sometime. Not to Bowman's."

Davis sighed. "Fiona, if I were ready to date, you'd be the first person I'd call."

"Really?" Plum said.

He traced an *X* over his heart. "I'm just not there yet, and it's coming up on the two-year anniversary, you know? Maybe a few months from now?"

The English teacher smiled. "I'd like that. I think you would too, Captain."

"I think I would. At some point soon, Fiona."

She stood there, not quite worshipping him but close.

He said, "Uh, I have to get ready for practice."

Plum startled. "I'm sorry. And I have a class in ten minutes. Bye, Captain."

"Bye, Ms. Plum," he said. He turned and went into the boys' locker room.

Davis went straight to the coaching offices and found Troy Penny, his offensive-line coach, drinking a Gatorade and studying a film of their upcoming opponent on his laptop. "Penny," he said.

The younger coach looked up and chuckled knowingly. "Well, look who the cat drug in. The tomcat, that is. Captain Tomcat."

Davis stepped into Penny's office and shut the door. "Explain that."

"She had you, right? Just wouldn't let you go, and you couldn't let her go either. Didn't care if it was a Monday or not. I know how it is. Same thing with me, first time after me and Nelly split."

"I'm still not following you. Last thing I remember was going in the front door at Bowman's and waving at you."

Penny's face twisted. "You're kidding me."

"Nope."

Penny groaned. "Oh, Captain, my captain, that was a fine brunette you struck up a conversation with. She was laughing. You were laughing and having a grand old time because she was wearing a Ravens tank top that flattered her curves."

"Okay?"

"Then Dallas scored on a fifty-six-yard bomb pass. We all went nuts. When we calmed down, I looked over to see how things were progressing, and you and the Ravens brunette were gone and there was a pile of cash on the table."

Davis shook his head, only vaguely remembering that there'd been a woman, extremely good-looking, and yes, they had been laughing. "But I can't remember leaving with her."

"You did. And I hated having to make something up for Ms. Fiona Plum when she showed up later looking for you. I didn't have the heart to say you'd picked up a serious hottie and hightailed it out of Bowman's. That would have crushed the poor thing."

CHAPTER

20

PADRAIG FILSON LIMPED AND caned down the sidewalk, thinking once again that he was a remarkable angler, better than his own late father.

"A fisher of men, that's what I am," Filson muttered to himself as he hobbled away from the school where the killing had happened.

He crossed Olson Street and entered the parking lot of the Raleigh Court Apartments. Much earlier that morning, he'd parked his blue Dodge Ram there in a section set aside for guests.

Filson almost made it to the vehicle and his medicine before the fit came, as it always did these days. He choked and fought for air, then fell into a hacking that shook his body and almost took him to his knees before the blockage loosened and came up.

He leaned hard on the cane, panting, wanting to spit out

the vile stuff but knowing that could be trouble. The old man shuffled to the SUV, climbed in, and spat a gout of bloody mucus into a fresh Kleenex. He rolled it up, wrapped it in a second Kleenex, and tossed it in a paper bag on the floor of the passenger side. Old habits died hard.

Then he started the car, muttering to his reflection in the rearview mirror, "You think you got Padraig Filson's ticket, Mr. C., but you don't. Not by a long shot. The fisher of men here made fifty K untraceable today, just like he did yesterday. And last month."

Filson lifted the lid on the central console and retrieved a burner phone. He thumbed to a flash photo of the dead man, Bart Masters, up against the school fence with both eyes blown out.

The old man felt nothing as he sent the pic to a number that he'd been texted two days before. He also sent a second photo taken with the sheet over Masters, the blood from his eyes coming through the fabric.

After sending the pictures, Filson texted, Pay in Bitcoin. Same account. Nice doing business with you. More to come.

CHAPTER

21

Alexandria, Virginia

TUESDAY AFTERNOON, NED MAHONEY walked into one of the two massive tents set up on soccer fields less than five hundred yards west of Gravelly Point Park.

The tent was packed with reporters, camerapeople, and grieving family members, all of whom were watching the agent in charge of the FBI's investigation into the crash of AA 839.

I had known Ned for many years. Though he was a deeply caring person in private, he had always been largely unflappable in his professional life. But as Mahoney climbed onto a raised stage of sorts, he looked visibly shaken. And when he spoke into the microphones in front of the lectern, his voice was thick with emotion.

"I want to talk directly to the family members, and then I'll take limited questions from the media," he said, and he cleared his throat. "For all of you who have lost loved ones, I am here to tell you that the FBI will not rest until we've hunted down the perpetrator of this dastardly and cowardly act. He and anyone who helped him will pay for taking your loved ones' lives. I promise you that."

Sampson and I were standing off to one side. I wondered how many people caught the slight shake in Mahoney's hands as he clutched the lectern.

"I want to confirm that the plane was shot down by what appears to be a Vietnam-era fifty-caliber machine gun. We believe the weapon was remotely controlled and that it caused significant structural damage to the wings, cockpit, and landing gear of the jet as it crossed over Gravelly Point Park."

At the words *remotely controlled,* the media started yelling questions.

"I'm not answering questions now," Ned said firmly. He looked straight into the cameras. "We also believe that someone out there knows who was behind this. A relative, a friend, a neighbor must know about someone with a fifty-caliber machine gun and the ability to build a system to fire it from a distance with stunning accuracy. We need your help. If you know this person or suspect that you know him, please call the number on your screen. We have agents standing by to take your calls. And now I'll take some questions."

Mahoney was a master for the next fifteen minutes, answering the questions he could with short, declarative sentences. When he was asked a question he could not answer, he said so and moved on.

Finally, he called on a young man in a ball cap.

"I'm Hector Johnson," the man said, his voice shaking. "I'm not a reporter. My fiancée, Lucinda Grimes, was on the flight.

Her mother and I want to know when her remains will be identified."

Mahoney said, "We will get it done as soon as we can, Mr. Johnson. And I'm desperately sorry for your loss. Just as soon as we can."

A few moments later, an FBI public relations officer ended the meeting with promises of another update later in the day.

John and I followed Mahoney out of the tent and across fifty yards of Astroturf to a second tent. This one had been set up as a command center and was filled with agents from six different federal law enforcement agencies.

Mahoney looked wrung out and beaten up when he got up on a table and called for quiet.

"I want to begin by telling you that the distraught families of a hundred people are grateful that you are on the hunt for the driver of this van. And I want everyone here on the same page with the same understanding of what we know for certain."

A timeline appeared across the top of multiple screens set up around the tent. Below the military time stamp, a grainy video played, showing a tan work van with the logo of the National Park system entering the parking lot at Gravelly Point Park and pulling just out of sight.

Mahoney said, "We have to assume that the unnamed suspect knew that this parking space was in the camera's blind spot, which suggests he had scouted the area multiple times."

The video backed up and froze, showing the fuzzy silhouette of the driver through tinted windows. The image was placed below the 18:44:02 time stamp.

Another image appeared, a police sketch of a man wearing a Baltimore Ravens hoodie and a respirator that partially obscured his features. His eyes, behind safety goggles with heavy frames, were almond-shaped.

Ned said, "You're looking at a rendering of the man Fairfax County Sheriff deputy Iris Blaine encountered last night when she went to lock the gate at Gravelly Point Park. The suspect said he was there to spray chemicals for insect control but wanted to be home watching *Monday Night Football*. She left after he said he had the key to the gate, and she checked the license plate, which was National Park Service–issue."

Deputy Blaine described the suspect as a big man, well over six feet tall and more than two hundred pounds, though that had been hard to judge because of the tan coverall he wore over the hoodie.

"With the mask and the goggles and the hood up, she wasn't entirely sure of his ethnicity, other than that he wasn't pale, and he wasn't Black," Mahoney said. "And before you come down on the deputy for not being more suspicious, let me say she has an exemplary record and is devastated she didn't check him out further. And no, unfortunately, she wasn't running her dash cam."

The sketch was placed beneath the time stamp 19:01:20.

A new video appeared beneath the time stamp 19:59:49. It showed American 839 coming in from the perspective of the airport tower. The landing lights were visible first; they were followed by four orange tracer rounds rising off Gravelly Point at 20:02:02. These appeared to strike the jet; it wobbled across the water, touched down on the tarmac, and lurched to one side, which provoked gasps from me, Sampson, and a dozen others in the tent.

John would later say it was like watching a football player coming down wrong. You just knew bones were about to break and shatter.

On the screen, sparks flew from beneath the jet's nose, and then the entire plane swung hard and started flipping down the runway, shedding landing gear and wings and fuselage pieces and body parts before it exploded in a fireball. The video stopped at 20:02:14.

"Twelve seconds," Sampson whispered in shock. "That's all it took."

I nodded, my stomach sinking. I hung my head at the speed and size of the tragedy, feeling sick and then rageful. *Why would someone machine-gun a commercial jet? Who does this kind of thing? And why? No one's claimed it. Why not?*

Before my brain could start spitting out a laundry list of possible suspects and possible answers to these questions, another time stamp appeared on the big screen above a video feed of the camera that caught the van parking.

At 20:02:01, things started to fly and flash on the surface of the parking lot.

"Those are fifty-caliber casings," Mahoney said. "And here comes the shadow of the plane passing overhead and the brilliance of the crash. Wait for it."

For several moments there was nothing on that camera feed that suggested the nightmare unfolding on the runway other than flashes and flares of light against the glow of the parking lot's sodium lamp. Then at 20:02:16, two seconds after the wreckage of the burning jet stopped moving on the runway, the van exploded and snuffed out the feed.

CHAPTER

22

BEFORE ANYONE COULD COMMENT, Mahoney said, "ATF? What is there to add?"

Alice Kershaw of the Bureau of Alcohol, Tobacco, Firearms and Explosives stood. Another agent brought her a microphone.

She said, "The bomb was sophisticated. The details are in our preliminary report, but the way it was built and triggered and the components used suggests extensive training with explosives in the military or in heavy construction or both."

"U.S. military?" Mahoney asked.

"Can't say yet," Kershaw said. "But the bomb aside, the remote-control system for the machine gun he used was as sophisticated as the bomb. Maybe more."

"Maybe more," Mahoney said. He looked around the tent, then fixed his eyes on me. "Alex? Based on this timeline and what we know, what can we say about him?"

Now I understood why Ned had insisted that I leave the Dead Hours murder scene and attend the briefing. A lifetime ago, Mahoney and I were members of the FBI's Behavioral Science Unit—the serial-killer hunters. I have a PhD in psychology from Johns Hopkins University and I worked for the unit as a profiler, taking clues as they were found and fitting them into an evolving character study that gave us insight into various aspects of the unknown killer's personality, traits, and thinking.

Someone brought me a microphone as I studied the timeline and tried to see it all happening in sequence before I began to imagine the mind behind the carnage.

"He could be part of an organized terror group, but I'm leaning toward a lone wolf," I said. "If he was part of a terror group, I think we would have heard from them in some manner by now. Until that happens, I'm going with a single person acting solo."

"What else?"

"If he's solo, then he could have, as Agent Kershaw said, extensive explosive training with the military or with a commercial blast firm. Unless he was trained in the Middle East?" I said this more to Kershaw than Mahoney.

The ATF agent said, "If he was, he was trained by a top-flight bomb builder. This was no ordinary roadside IED, or at least it carried no signatures that would suggest construction associated with a known jihadist group."

Sampson raised his hand. I handed him the microphone.

"Who's to say this isn't someone who defused bombs for us in Afghanistan or Iraq?" he said. "I mean, it takes one to know one, right?"

"It does, John," Mahoney said. "Point taken. We are looking for someone who knows explosives and is savvy enough mechanically and technologically to rig a remote-controlled machine gun."

I took the microphone from Sampson. "More than rig it. It sounds like he designed and built it, is that correct?"

Agent Kershaw nodded. "We believe so."

I said, "He's more than a bomb tech, then. He's an engineer, probably a design engineer who specializes in robotics or something of that nature."

Mahoney said, "I'm not following you, Alex."

"Well, I can see how a robotics engineer could build a phone-controlled fertilizer bomb. But I can't see a bomb technician being able to design and build a remote-controlled machine gun. Does that make sense?"

Kershaw said, "It does."

"What else, Alex?"

I thought about that. "Again, a loner. Highly educated. Late thirties to early forties. Lives by himself. Secretive. Paranoid. Probably resentful. Obsessed with that resentment and all it entails. Fastidious. Able to design and execute long-range plans. Given that the bomb and the gun control had to be hand-built, I'm thinking that he lives in a rural area where he can do what he does with little chance of prying eyes."

Kershaw said, "I agree with that. And he's patient. Given the size of the bombs, he would have been flagged if he'd tried to buy all that fertilizer at once."

"Unless he runs or works on a big farm somewhere," I said.

"We'd still see a report if it looked out of line," Kershaw said.

Mahoney said, "Are you thinking more of a Ted Kaczynski type, Alex?"

I nodded. "Hyper-smart. Bitterness and hatred stewing."

"Hatred directed at the government?"

"Could be. Or the airline. Or someone aboard the plane. Do we have the manifest yet?"

Ned said, "It's there in your briefing materials. We'll need to start running down each victim's story, figure out if someone hated one of them enough to shoot down an entire jet. And we need to start looking for recent threats against commercial airlines, go through all the social media rantings and ravings, especially from people who are applauding the shootdown."

23

ROUGHLY TEN BLOCKS FROM where Alex, Sampson, and Mahoney were working the AA 839 case, Bree Stone was marching along K Street, feeling like she was being played or at least not being shown all the cards in Leigh Anne Asher's disappearance.

She'd found out about the tech mogul's marriage only because of an e-mail mentioning the prenuptial agreement and something about a name change. It turned out that Asher had been born in Ireland, and Elena Martin, Bree's boss and Asher's best friend, gave Bree some convoluted story about Asher wanting U.S. citizenship under a different name. At that point, Bree had left the apartment, her boss, and Asher's assistant, no longer believing that she was being told the whole truth.

Which pissed her off. She liked Elena. She really did. Bree had been working for the woman for a while now, and she'd thought she'd earned her trust.

Obviously not.

Over the years, Bree had learned that the quickest route to the truth wasn't a straight line. You interviewed everyone surrounding a crime starting on the outside of the circle and spiraling inward, and you found the truth somewhere near the center.

Interview number one, as far as Bree was concerned, would unfold here on K Street, without her boss or the missing CEO's personal assistant shading things.

Bree entered a beautiful old building with a marble-tiled foyer and asked the security guard where to find the offices of the venerable law firm Crebs and Stratton. She was directed to the sixth floor. There, the receptionist laughed weakly when Bree asked to see Rolf Himmel.

"Do you have an appointment?"

"No," Bree said. "And I still need to see him."

The receptionist pursed his lips. "Can I tell him what it's about?"

Bree showed the young man her private investigator's license and said, "His wife's disappearance."

"Disappearance?" he said more soberly, and he picked up the phone.

A few minutes later, a tall, lean man in gray slacks and a crisp white shirt that set off hair the color of tarnished silver came to the reception desk. He had a face as chiseled as a soap opera actor's.

"I'm Rolf Himmel," he said. "You're lucky you caught me here; I was on my way to court. Do you know I've only just learned?"

"What? That your wife's missing?" Bree said.

Himmel glanced at the receptionist, who was trying hard to appear interested in his phone. "Let's go back to my office."

Bree followed the attorney down a dimly lit hallway. Most of the offices on either side were dark.

"Where is everyone?" Bree asked after he'd shown her into a large, well-appointed corner office.

"Construction next door," he said. "Jackhammers involved. Most of the staff are working from home for the next two weeks, but I'm in trial, so here I am. And now I understand Leigh Anne has been missing for days?"

"No contact with anyone whatsoever since Friday morning. I understand that's unusual for your wife."

"Leigh Anne can be needy," Himmel said. "But she's gone radio silent on me before."

"But not on her assistant, Jill Jackson, or Elena Martin."

"Well, they would know, wouldn't they?"

Bree's brows knitted. "When exactly did you last talk to your wife, Mr. Himmel?"

"Rolf," he said and thought about it. "Two weeks ago?"

"I guess I don't understand," Bree said. "Are you married or not?"

"Ahh. Technically, we are, although we're estranged."

"Technically?"

"Yes, like everything about our marriage."

"Do you want to explain that?"

"Not unless it's necessary."

"I'm sure the police or the FBI will ask you, so yes, it's necessary."

The attorney gazed at her a moment, then sighed. "If you repeat this, I'll deny it. I'll claim our marriage was real and based on love at first sight. I'll tell a story of love fading under our crushing workloads, me here, Leigh Anne over at Amalgam. The two of us growing apart. A trial separation at first. Now divorce is looming after the initial public offering. It will be an amicable parting."

Bree didn't take her eyes off him, thinking through what he'd just said. "It was a sham marriage," she said.

"It was a marriage of need and convenience." Himmel chuckled. "And a lot of torrid sex at the beginning. Just to make it look good."

"Let me guess: Leigh Anne needed a green card?"

"She did, but it was more than that. She claimed she needed dual citizenship for tax reasons, which was BS. But I liked Leigh. Wanted to help her out."

"How long ago was this marriage?"

"Almost four years now."

"I don't understand. She was thinking tax haven back then?"

"Amalgam was as sure an idea as they get. Right from the beginning, you knew it was going to be big," Himmel said. "But I didn't understand about the tax haven and did not want to know."

"How long was the marriage supposed to last?"

"Five years, less if the IPO came through early." The attorney was leaning back in his chair, seeming pleased.

"What do you get out of this, Counselor? And don't tell me gratitude."

He smiled. "A significant amount of Amalgam stock, a roll in the hay every once in a while, and Maggie Fontaine's gratitude forever."

"Maggie Fontaine?"

"Leigh Anne's real name. She changed it shortly before she started Amalgam. Said it was time for a completely new beginning."

"And you'll deny all of this if the police ask."

"I will. Actions speak louder than words, and every action we've taken legally says it was a real marriage that soured. End of story."

"Where do you think she is?"

"Honestly? Given how close we are to Amalgam going public? I'm betting she picked up a boy toy and headed off somewhere to blow off a little steam."

CHAPTER

24

AFTER MAHONEY'S UPDATE, SAMPSON and I helped contact the victims' families, looking for any evidence that specific passengers on AA 839 had been targeted.

Other investigators might have wanted to look in more fruitful evidential terrain, but talking to the relatives began to give me a solid understanding of the victims I was serving: A thirty-three-year-old traveling nurse. A young father and his toddler son on their way home from the son's medical procedure. A couple who'd been married fifty years; they were returning from a weeklong trip that had been an anniversary gift from loving family members.

When I got off that last call, I felt like crying myself. I looked up to see Ned Mahoney coming through the tent toward us.

"Leave the manifest work to other agents for now," he said. "I want you two with me."

"Where are we going?"

"An unincorporated area west of Fredericksburg. Hot tip."

Sampson shook his head. "I promised Willow I'd be home for dinner tonight. I haven't had dinner with her in a week."

I could tell Ned wanted to order him to come, but instead he said, "Go. Alex and I will handle it."

"You sure?"

"Work on the manifests until six and then knock off," Mahoney said. "But give me as much time as you can tomorrow."

I grabbed my things and followed Mahoney as he hurried out. I was surprised to find him heading not to the cars but to the field behind the tent.

"I thought we were going to Fredericksburg," I called.

"We are," he said. "In a chopper."

Ten minutes later, we were in the back of an FBI helicopter as it lifted off. The pilot looped around, giving us a clear view of the runway where AA 839 had gone down. The airport remained closed; all traffic had been diverted to Dulles International. Dozens of forensics experts in hazmat suits were still gathering evidence out there.

"They'll be at it for days," Mahoney said grimly into the mic of his headset.

I nodded as we flew south. "Going to fill me in?"

He handed me a file. "The agents combing social media found this guy on an internet chat site known to attract anarchists. He's made threats against aircraft in the past, even talked about machine-gunning a commercial jet out of the sky."

"What about the actual shootdown?" I said, opening the folder. I saw the mug shot and rap sheet of Cameron Blades, a massive, swarthy, bearded man with big bloodshot eyes.

"It's there after his sheet. Blades goes by the name 'Hand of Fate.'"

I turned the pages of the file. Blades had served in Afghanistan as a U.S. Army bomb-disposal technician but had received a dishonorable discharge for repeatedly drinking on duty and getting into violent altercations while on leave. Blades's brushes with the law continued after his discharge, most of them for battery in one form or another. He was also believed to be involved in a gunrunning ring.

"Missing military weapons," I said.

"Keep going," Mahoney said. "Read the chitchat."

I flipped the pages and found a printout of a thread from a chat forum called Silent Warriors. The motto at the top read "Only Dead Fish Swim with the Current."

I scanned the page and found a series of nine posts Hand of Fate had made since AA 839 was shot down. After reading them twice, I tasted metal at the back of my tongue.

"You're right," I said. "This could be our guy."

"Hundred percent."

25

CAMERON BLADES OWNED A dilapidated farmhouse on twenty acres of oak, pine, and overgrown fields in a rural part of Virginia south of the site of the Battle of the Wilderness, one of the fiercest clashes of the Civil War.

Mahoney had the pilot put the helicopter down two miles from the farmhouse in a field by Orange Plank Road. Dusk was coming on.

We were met by FBI special agents Patty Denfeld and Kurt Hawkins, both out of the Richmond office. They'd been keeping an eye on the long gravel driveway that led up to Blades's place, which they said was well back and hidden from the road.

Ned said, "You've met Mr. Blades before?"

"Twice last year," Denfeld said. "After he threatened American Airlines."

"The same airline," I said.

Denfeld nodded.

"What's his beef with them?"

Hawkins said, "They lost his mother's ashes. Even so, he's tightly wound. He never made any stupid moves around us, but I felt like we were poking a rattlesnake every time we asked him a question."

"Capable of shooting down a jetliner?" I asked.

The agents looked at each other.

"He's got a history of violence," Denfeld said. "And he likes guns. Got a bunch of them, mostly AR-style. They're locked up. He's a gunsmith and a welder. But I could see him being good for an illegal machine gun and a bomb or two."

We got in their Suburban and drove down the road in the last good light of day.

"We just going to pull in unannounced?" I asked.

Mahoney said, "I want to stop and take a look at this place, get the lay of the land first."

"We can show you on Google Earth," Denfeld said. "House. Barn. Two sheds."

"I've seen it on Google Earth," Ned said. "Now I want to see it for myself. You, Dr. Cross, and I will walk up the driveway until we can see the house, then we'll call Hawkins forward in the car."

The three of us got out and started up the gravel driveway. We were almost immediately swallowed by a grove of dense pines that made what little light there was gloaming and murky at best. Fifty yards into the forest, we crossed a creek. From there, the driveway got steeper.

Ahead and up the rise, a single light shone through the trees. Denfeld whispered, "There's an ATV trail on the left here. Takes you to a knoll forty yards from the farmhouse where you'll have a better view than you'd have from the driveway."

Mahoney signaled to her to lead the way. We left the relatively even surface of the drive for the rutted ATV trail, which hooked around and climbed to the knoll.

The closer we got, the slower we walked, and soon we were barely creeping along. We saw the silhouette of the farmhouse roof in the dying light, the sagging front porch lit by a single bulb. No light shone in any of the windows.

The wind barely rustled in the last leaves clinging to the oak trees that flanked the farmhouse. The only scents in the air were pine and overturned soil.

Denfeld said, "I'm going to peek up there a little, enough to see the barn. He parks his pickup in front of it."

Mahoney nodded.

The young FBI agent eased up the knoll another five steps. She paused, peered around, then cocked her head toward the barn and took two more steps. She paused for a long moment, and I thought for sure she was going to turn and come back to us. But she took one more step, and her shin hit a fishing line strung across the upper end of the ATV trail.

To our left and right came gunshots, blinding orange blasts that cursed the night.

CHAPTER

26

RATTLED, OUR EARS RINGING, we threw ourselves flat on the ATV trail, digging for our weapons. Lights went on all around the house. A door flew open.

"Whoever the hell you are, you are unannounced and unwanted here!" a man roared. "You're just damn lucky I didn't mix screws and nails into that Tannerite!"

"FBI!" Denfeld yelled, getting to her feet, pistol raised. "FBI, Cameron Blades!"

The rest of us were getting up when she yelled, "Drop the weapon, Mr. Blades!" I ran up the slope to see Blades kneeling on his porch, looking at us over the barrel of a black AR rifle. Mahoney came up beside me, holding his badge up.

"FBI, Blades!" he yelled. "Don't do anything stupid."

"Only stupid ones are you, coming onto a man's place this way. Unannounced, unwanted. What is it with all of you? Don't give a damn about the Constitution?"

"We just wanted to talk, Cameron," Agent Denfeld said. "We should have called ahead or at least come straight up the driveway."

"My fault, Mr. Blades," Ned said. "Can you drop the weapon, please?"

"What, so you can shoot me and make up some damn story about me trying to blow up the FBI?"

I said, "Well, you did just try to blow us up."

"Nah, just trying to scare the bejesus out of whoever's been sneaking onto my place and stealing my shit. That was just Tannerite—makes a lot of noise, but it's a big firecracker, that's all. Bought the cans at a Walmart in Fredericksburg."

"Let's talk about that later, Mr. Blades. Can you please lower your weapon? It will go a long way toward making us ignore the booby trap on your property."

"More like a loud alarm," Blades insisted.

"Just the same," I said as Agent Hawkins came roaring up the driveway in the SUV. It skidded to a stop, and Hawkins got out, his pistol drawn. Blades swung his rifle at Hawkins.

"Don't do it, Cameron!" Denfeld shouted and went straight toward him.

Blades glanced at her, then back at Hawkins, who had his pistol up. Blades's shoulders were dropping when Hawkins fired.

The round hit Blades high in the chest; he fell back onto the porch floor.

Denfeld raced at Blades, screaming at Hawkins, "Why'd you shoot? He was giving up!"

"He was aiming at me!" Hawkins shouted back. "Right at me!"

Denfeld got up on the porch. Ned was calling 911 to report federal agents under fire.

I said, "Stay where you are, Agent Hawkins! Stay right where you are or sit inside the Suburban! Weapon on the hood!"

"I didn't do a damn thing wrong!"

"I didn't say you did. But let's leave the scene as uncontaminated as possible, okay?"

The young agent looked like he wanted to put his fist through a wall, but he placed his pistol on the hood and stood outside the open driver's door as I climbed up onto the porch.

Blades was writhing on the ground. "Oh, that hurt." He moaned. "Oh, that's going to get you yahoos a lawsuit."

Denfeld had put his weapon out of reach and knelt next to him. She unzipped his windbreaker, revealing a combat vest.

"Hit him right in the plate," she said, sounding disgusted.

"That's why you wear them," Blades growled.

Mahoney appeared. "Mr. Blades, I am Agent Ned Mahoney, FBI. I'm in charge of the investigation into the shootdown of the American Airlines jet."

"What?" he said, looking bewildered.

"You threatened to shoot down an American Airlines jet last year."

Blades shook his head. "That was just me being ticked off, that's all."

I said, "On a chat room called Silent Warriors, Hand of Fate celebrated the fact that more than one hundred people died when that plane crashed."

The former army bomb-squad member blinked and said nothing for several moments. Finally, he said, "I frickin' hate American Airlines is all."

"They lost your mother's ashes," Mahoney said.

"Damn straight they did," he said, the anger apparent in his expression. "Cold frickin' swine. Didn't give a damn about the pain it caused me and my sisters. Offered us one ticket voucher. A goddamned ticket voucher for losing our mom's ashes!"

I said, "Cameron, we are going to search this entire farm. An army of FBI agents is on its way here now. Are we going to find bomb components and fertilizer? Evidence that you own a fifty-caliber machine gun?"

The anger in his eyes turned to hatred.

"Cameron?" I said.

"I think I want a lawyer before I say another thing."

27

BREE DIDN'T KNOW WHETHER to trust Rolf Himmel's description of his marriage to Leigh Anne Asher—or Maggie Fontaine or whoever the founder of Amalgam really was.

She took an Uber home. On the way, she called Elena Martin and filled her in on what Himmel had told her about his marriage to the tech mogul.

"All true, but don't quote me," her boss said. "And I didn't understand the tax-haven thing either. But she said it was significant."

"So you knew her originally as Maggie Fontaine?"

"In school, that's right."

It made Bree a little dizzy, but she said, "Okay, different direction before we go to the FBI and the police with what we have. After Jill gets me Leigh Anne's credit card records—"

"She's already gotten into the accounts. Zero activity in the past three days."

"I'll request cell phone records through a friend of mine right now," Bree said as the Uber pulled up in front of her home. "With luck, we'll have them by morning."

"We're going to find her, right, Bree?" Martin said, sounding heartbroken.

"We'll find her, Elena," Bree said, getting out of the car. "I've been looking less than twelve hours."

"Whatever you need. Whatever it takes."

Bree ended the call and walked to the porch, suddenly feeling whiplash from the events of the day. All she wanted to do was lie on her back on a hard floor and let gravity realign her spine and take the tension away.

"Bree!"

She turned to see Sampson trotting up the sidewalk. "I'm late for Willow. Again."

"It's only six thirty," Bree said. "And she'll understand."

"Hope so."

They went in to find Ali and Willow sitting on the couch in front of the TV, riveted by a documentary about an octopus and a snorkeler. The underwater colors were brilliant, other-worldly.

"Is that real?" Bree asked.

Ali stopped the show with the remote. "Yeah, that's real! You've never seen anything like this, Bree!"

"We watched it three times," Willow said brightly. "Dad, the octopus climbs on the man's arm. It knows him."

"Okay," Sampson said.

"We'll watch it when we get home, Daddy," Willow announced, standing up. "I'll get my stuff, and Nana Mama said I could take some cookies."

"Go grab it all," her dad said.

Willow ran into the dining room and started gathering her things from the table.

"You all right?" Sampson said to Bree.

Bree said, "Yeah, I'm just getting thrown around by this missing-person case Elena has me working on."

"Tell me about it," Sampson said. "We're getting yanked in every direction. The Dead Hours and the shootdown. Back and forth all day. Alex and Ned are still at it."

"And probably will be for a few more hours. Can I ask you a question?"

"Sure."

"Why would someone from another country—say, Ireland—come to the United States, go to school at a prestigious university under one name, then change that name and marry someone to get a green card and a path to dual citizenship?"

"Excuse me?"

"I'm told it was for tax issues involved in dual citizenship, but even the fake husband, a lawyer, didn't understand that or why she changed her name before she started her firm."

"That's what's got you? The name change?"

"Among other things. But, yeah, I can't figure that one out."

Willow returned with her coat on and carrying her little backpack.

Sampson shrugged. "Maybe she just didn't like her name—you know, she could have had an ugly name like Brunhilda or something."

"But her name was Maggie Fontaine," Bree said. "I think it's kind of a pretty name. Movie star–ish."

"What's pretty and movie star–ish?" Willow asked, handing her father her backpack.

"A lady's name," Sampson said. "Maggie Fontaine."

"That is pretty," Willow said. "Bye, Bree. Bye, Ali."

Ali did not take his eyes off the documentary. "Bye, Willow."

"Say goodbye to Jannie for me," Willow said.

"We will," Bree promised. "And by the way, I think Willow Sampson is a much prettier name than Maggie Fontaine."

Willow giggled as she and her father went out the door. Bree turned and watched the octopus go darting off through a kelp bed for a few seconds, then headed to the kitchen, hoping to help Nana Mama. The front door opened behind her.

"Bree?"

Sampson was standing there, looking at her. Willow was sitting on the stairs behind him, her back to the door.

"What is it, John?"

"Maggie Fontaine. The name sounded familiar. It *is* familiar. I just checked to be sure."

CHAPTER

28

I GOT HOME AROUND eleven, almost twenty-seven hours after the shootdown and much less than that since the latest victim in the Dead Hours series had been discovered. Climbing up the stairs to our porch, I realized I hadn't even called the Maryland detectives working that case to find out if there'd been an ID on the dead man.

When I got inside, I heard the television playing softly. I found Bree sitting on the couch in front of the TV, holding a pillow to her stomach. Tears streamed down her cheeks. I looked at the screen, which was showing a coral reef somewhere. "What's going on?"

"She's dying," Bree said, her voice racked with emotion. "The octopus."

"The octopus?"

She shot me a mournful look. "You have to watch it to understand."

"I'm getting something to eat."

"There's leftovers in the fridge."

I wandered into the kitchen and found a plate wrapped in foil in the fridge. Nana had put a stickie note on the foil telling me to remove it, put a paper towel over the dish, and microwave it for two minutes. I did, and the kitchen was quickly filled with the smells of garlic and onions and sausage and steamed broccoli with basil. After I took a few bites and drank half a beer, things started to become right in my world again, and I rehashed the day in my mind.

Ned Mahoney had stayed behind to oversee the search of Cameron Blades's farm. He'd sent me home and told me to work the Dead Hours case in the morning and then rejoin the AA 839 investigation in the afternoon. I shut my eyes a moment, telling myself I could do it all, that I could bring equal attention to the people who'd died on the jet and all the men who'd had their eyes shot out in the early-morning hours.

But is that realistic? Both of these cases are all-consuming—

Bree walked into the kitchen, her eyes puffy and red. She sat in my lap, nuzzled my neck.

"Sad?" I asked.

She nodded.

"I'm sorry about the octopus."

"Yeah, but it was beautiful somehow. You'll have to watch it."

"Next time I come up for air," I said.

Bree pulled back and looked at me. I saw deep pain in her eyes.

"This is about more than the octopus," I said.

She nodded. "I have to do something I don't want to do.

Something I have been putting off for the past few hours because it's going to break someone's heart."

"What can you tell me?"

She swallowed. "Elena's best friend has gone missing. That's what she texted me about this morning. Her friend has been out of touch for three days. And John thinks he saw Elena's friend's name, or her former name—it's complicated—on the manifest of the plane that crashed."

"Which would explain why she's been missing."

Bree nodded. "It's going to crush Elena."

"Look, you don't know for certain it's her, correct? Is that what you're saying?"

She puffed out her cheeks. "Not for certain, but Maggie Fontaine is not exactly a common name."

"Then that's what you tell Elena. She deserves to know."

"You think I should call now?"

"I think so."

Bree got out her phone and punched in her boss's number, then put the call on speaker. I held her around the waist as she said, "Elena, is there a chance Leigh Anne kept her Irish passport under her old name? Under Maggie Fontaine?"

"I don't think that's legally possible."

"Forged passport?"

"What? No, I...I don't know. Why would she do that?"

"I was hoping you could tell me."

"Why? What's happened?"

"There's a Maggie Fontaine on the flight manifest of the plane that went down. One of the first-class passengers."

For several seconds, Elena did not reply. Eventually she said, "What seat?"

"Two A. Window."

There was a choking sound, and then Elena said, sobbing, "It's her. That's where she always sits if she can. Always, and...oh my God, I'm sorry, Bree, but I'm going to be sick."

The call ended and Bree sagged against me. "My day sucked start to finish."

"I hear you, baby. Mine wasn't much better."

CHAPTER

29

AROUND TEN THIRTY THE next morning, Sampson and I drove to a meeting with Maryland State Police detectives about the latest Dead Hours victim, who had been identified overnight.

On the way there, my phone rang. It was Mahoney.

"Ned," I said. I put him on speaker so Sampson, who was driving, could hear the conversation. "Find anything at Blades's place?"

"Browning fifty-caliber machine-gun barrel in his shop. Enough to hold him on while we tear the rest of his place apart."

"You think it's him?"

"I don't know what to think at this point, Alex. I was just notified by the lab at Quantico that they were able to bring back some of the writing on the scorched Avis rental contract that Kershaw's people found in that metal estimator's box."

I said, "We have a name?"

"And an address," he said. "Listen, I'm not getting back up there until late afternoon, and that's if I'm lucky. Can you and John go talk to this guy? Get a read on him? I'll send you his info and a picture of the agreement with the signature they lifted."

"We've got a meet on the Dead Hours case in twenty minutes, but we'll check him out right after."

"Let me know."

Sampson was quiet on our drive out to Laurel, Maryland. I asked him how his evening with Willow had gone.

"Great!" he said, but his smile waned almost as soon as it bloomed. "We watched a documentary about this guy in South Africa who snorkels and filmed this octopus every day for a year. I've never seen anything like it."

I laughed. "Bree watched it last night and said the same thing."

He shook his head. "I honestly don't know if I'll ever eat octopus again."

"You love octopus."

"Right? But I feel bad now. They're different. They have serious brains. The damn octopus knew the guy swimming around and befriended him."

"C'mon."

"Watch it."

I promised I would.

Not long after that, we were sitting in a briefing room with Detective Marilyn Hanson and two other officers working the case. They had identified the latest victim as Bart Masters, a twenty-nine-year-old computer engineer and Nevada transplant. Masters lived alone in Marlow Heights about a mile from where his body was found. He'd worked for NASA. Neighbors said they rarely saw the engineer. Masters kept odd hours, often going out to run in the middle of the night, even in the dead of winter.

"You see overlap here, Dr. Cross?" Hanson said. "Among the victims, I mean."

"They were early-morning runners or worked in jobs that had them up and out before three a.m."

"Why does he shoot out both eyes?"

Sampson said, "It has a meaning, no doubt. But what that is and why the sheet with the bloody eyes, we still don't know."

Twenty minutes later, we left the meeting with promises to stay in close touch as our parallel investigations progressed.

I checked my texts when we reached Sampson's car. Mahoney had sent me a JPEG of the writing the FBI lab techs had raised on the scorched car-rental slip. "Marion Davis," I said. "Address in Falls Church." I thumbed the info into the navigator. It came back No such address.

Sampson snorted. "Surprise."

"Hold on," I said. I called up Google on my phone, thumbed in Marion Davis Falls Church, and hit Return. I stared at the results. "Huh?"

"What?"

"There's a Marion Davis, address in Falls Church and…really? He's the head football coach at the Charles School."

Sampson whistled. "That's Captain Davis, then. He went to the Charles School and the Air Force Academy. Fulfilled his commitment to the military, then played in the NFL. Long snapper for the Ravens. Quit football to go back and fly combat missions in Iraq and Afghanistan."

"Says here the Charles School football team is the best in the metro area," I said.

"The best in a good chunk of the mid-Atlantic," Sampson said.

"Captain Davis is a heck of a coach. And a fairly high-profile guy. I can't see him involved in shooting down a jet."

"Still, wouldn't a combat pilot know how to bring a jet down?"

He looked at me. "House or school?"

"House."

CHAPTER

30

MARION "CAPTAIN" DAVIS OWNED an impressive home, a sprawling French Colonial on several landscaped acres.

"If he can afford a place like this on a coach's salary, he sure didn't piss his pro football money away," I said as we drove up around two that afternoon.

We went to the front door and rang the bell. No answer. We buzzed the intercom and got the same result.

It didn't take us long to drive to the Charles School, which had a beautiful campus and an impressive athletic field house.

"Home of the Badgers," I said, getting out.

"The Fighting Badgers," Sampson said.

We heard the whistle, the claps, and the shouting of many voices coming from behind the field house. We walked over there and saw an impressive sports stadium with a scoreboard and a replay screen and seats for five hundred, easy. There were at least fifty players on the field doing ballistic stretches in white practice uniforms.

"Tighten those hip flexors and imagine that you are driving the head of your femur into the turf, gentlemen," a voice growled over the stadium's public address system.

I looked hard at the coaches on the field, but I didn't see Captain Davis among them.

"Switch," I heard someone say. I saw Davis coming out of the field house not far from where we stood. He wore a headset and mic. He was big, around six foot four, and had a good two hundred and twenty pounds on his formidable frame. Even if I hadn't known his background, I would have figured out he was a serious athlete of some kind, the way he rolled loose through the hips out onto the field.

"Ah, jeez, Cap," Coach Davis whined into the mic, "why do we have to do it?" He walked around to the front of the team, pointed at one of his players, and said in his regular voice, "Walker, why do we do this?"

Walker jumped to his feet and said, "Iliacus and psoas muscles can screw you up inside and out."

"Correct—tight hip equals twisted core," Davis said. "We don't want twisted cores. Twisted cores and tight hips get you injuries, and you are no good to your teammates if you are injured. Are we clear?"

"Yes, Captain!" the entire team shouted.

"I didn't hear you."

"Yes, Captain!" they all thundered.

"Good," the coach said. "Now break up for drills. Why?"

"Because repetition is the mother of skill, Captain!" they shouted.

"That's right! Now break!"

The players grabbed their helmets and equipment and hustled to various parts of the field. Soon quarterbacks were throwing to receivers and linemen were hitting sleds.

We climbed into the stands. A handful of fathers were watching from the highest row; lower in the bleachers, a pretty woman with cinnamon hair wearing a Charles School Fighting Badgers hoodie was grading papers. She looked up when we sat down ten feet from her.

"Are you gentlemen scouts?" she asked. "If you are, you need to register at the front office or you can't be here."

"We're not scouts," I said, sliding closer. "We're with the FBI. Or I am."

There was no masking her surprise. "FBI?"

I nodded and showed her my credentials. "We're part of the team looking into the shooting down of the American Airlines jet."

"That involves someone here?" she said. "At the Charles School? Oh my God, Hampstead Three is going to have a fit and a half."

CHAPTER

31

THE CINNAMON-HAIRED WOMAN shook her head in total disbelief. "You can't be serious."

"And yet we are," Sampson said. "Dead serious. What's your name?"

"Plum," she said. "Fiona Plum."

"You work with the football team, Ms. Plum?" I asked.

"I teach AP English and American history. I…I just like football. My father was a fanatic. Nice days like today, I sit out here and get my grading done while I watch practice."

Sampson said, "Tell us about the coach."

Plum stared at us. "You mean Captain?"

"That's right. It's probably just an odd coincidence, but someone named Marion Davis came up in the course of the investigation."

"Well, no one calls him Marion," she said, a little indignantly.

"And he's one of the finest men I have ever known. He's devoted to coaching those boys out there, even though he really doesn't need the job."

"You mean he's rich?"

"As I understand it. Not a crime."

I said in a more soothing tone, "Look, we heard he's a great guy. We're just following up on one of a thousand leads."

"Captain *is* a great guy," she said, her eyes glistening. "He's been through so much, between football and Iraq and Afghanistan and his...I hate that his name has come up in any way. He doesn't deserve it. I hope you're not telling people about this."

"No, no, calm down, Ms. Plum," Sampson said. "We're just checking something out."

She wiped her eyes. "He's a hero around here."

I said, "I'll bet he is."

Sampson said, "And he's coming our way."

I looked over to see Davis jogging off the field. We went down and met him on the track.

"FBI?" he said after we introduced ourselves.

"And Metro Homicide," John said.

"What's this about?" he said, appearing genuinely bewildered.

I said, "The American Airlines plane."

"You mean the jet that went down?"

"Your name came up," Sampson said.

"What? Not a chance. How?"

I said, "The name Marion Davis came up. We're not saying it's you."

"Oh," he said, looking relieved. "Well, it's not."

"Good. So you've never rented a van from Avis?"

"A van? I don't know. Maybe a couple of years ago? At least I think it was Avis."

Sampson held up his phone and showed Captain the picture of the rental agreement and the name and signature the FBI lab had raised on the scorched paper. "That you?"

The coach gaped. "Well, that's my signature. But so what? I rented that van like two Augusts ago."

"Not what the date says."

"I don't care what the date says," Davis said. "Where did you find this?"

Sampson said, "It was among the debris of the bomb that destroyed the machine gun that shot down the jet."

He looked from Sampson to me, incredulous. "No. That is…impossible."

"Can you tell us where you were on Monday evening, Captain?"

The coach frowned, then said, "Yes. I was camped out on my couch with a bucket by my side. I got food poisoning at a crab boil on Sunday and I was home all of Monday recovering."

"Is there anyone who can back that up?" I asked.

Davis hesitated.

"I can," said Fiona Plum, who'd come down to the track. "I heard the coach was sick and I went by his house. He was there."

I said, "You went in and spoke to him? What time was this?"

"Like, five thirty? I mean, I didn't go in. I saw him through the window. He was on the couch sleeping."

Davis looked from Plum to us. "I didn't wake up until halfway through *Monday Night Football*. And the Ravens were playing. Can you imagine it, Fiona?"

"Impossible," Plum said, then gazed at me. "So you know Captain had to have been one sick puppy."

CHAPTER

32

BREE STONE EYED HER boss's haggard face and said, "Are you up to this, Elena? You look like you haven't slept."

"I haven't slept, and no, I'm not up to this," she said. "But it's something I have to do."

Bree put on a disposable mask and handed one to her boss. "You might want it for the smell," she explained.

Martin puffed out her cheeks but put on the mask. They walked inside the Fairfax County medical examiner's building, one of six in the area that had accepted the remains of the passengers on AA 839.

The ammonia-based disinfectant failed to hide the unmistakable scent of widespread death; Bree could smell it even with her mask on. Martin put her hand to her face and shuddered.

"Don't breathe through your nose if you can help it," Bree said, and she went to the clerk at the front counter, whom she knew from her days working homicide. "How are you, Chantal?" Bree said, tugging down her mask.

Chantal Ryder smiled. "God bless, and good to see you, Chief Stone."

"Former chief."

"Heard that," Ryder said. "How can I help?"

"We're here to identify one of the crash victims. Maggie Fontaine. I was told her remains were here."

"If it's her," Martin said. "I'm her oldest friend. She doesn't have any relatives here. Her mother's in Ireland."

"Let me see," Ryder said, typing on her keyboard. After a moment, she looked up and said, "She's here. You're one of the lucky ones. Maggie Fontaine appears to be in one piece. This says she was found still strapped to seat two A."

Behind her mask, Martin choked, then nodded. "That's good. If it's her, I mean."

"Give me a few minutes and I'll have her brought to where you can identify her," Ryder said, typing. "And if it is her, I am deeply sorry for your loss, ma'am."

"Thank you," Martin said. "I mean, if it's her."

"We'll know soon enough," Bree said.

Five minutes later, Ryder led them down a short hall to a small room with green drapes pulled closed over a large window. She drew back the drapes.

Two masked workers in green smocks wheeled a gurney to the window.

"You ready?" Bree asked Martin.

Martin nodded.

One of the workers drew back the sheet. Bree, Martin, and Ryder all recoiled. The body's clothes had been removed. From the chest up, it was hard to tell she was a woman.

"Oh God!" Martin gasped. "Oh God! No!"

Every bone in the woman's upper body appeared shattered. From her neck to her fingers and down the torso to her navel, her skin was grotesquely bruised and swollen, split, and gashed in places. Great hunks of her hair and scalp were gone, as were her ears. Her face was battered beyond recognition.

Martin spun around, tore off her mask, and vomited.

"Did you know she looked like that, Chantal?" Bree demanded.

"No, Chief, I swear!" Ryder said. She triggered the microphone and told the workers to cover the body. "I'm so sorry. There are just so many of them here right now and I can't keep track of their condition."

Bree grabbed a wad of tissues from a box on the counter, went to her boss's side, and rubbed her back while she cleaned her lips.

"Can I go to a restroom, please?" Martin choked out.

"Of course, of course," Ryder said. "Right across the hall. I am so sorry. And don't worry about the mess. We have someone who takes care of these things."

Bree took her boss to the door of the bathroom. "Need help?"

"No," Martin said. "I can handle it."

She went inside and shut the door. Bree closed her eyes and tried—and failed—to will the image of the dead woman out of her mind. She had seen her share of death, of course, but she'd never seen anyone that broken.

Several minutes later, Bree heard the toilet flush, and her boss reemerged, looking somewhat put together and, oddly, smiling.

"Why are you smiling?" Bree asked as they walked back to the clerk's desk.

"I can't identify her," Martin said. "No one could identify someone like that."

"They'll fingerprint her or get DNA samples from her house," Bree said. She looked at Ryder. "Where are her clothes? Effects?"

The ME's clerk typed, then said, "We bagged them yesterday evening. The FBI took them late last night along with the effects of ten others who came in whole."

Bree said, "Any pictures of what she was wearing?"

Ryder frowned. "I'm sure there are but it doesn't look like they've been uploaded to her file yet. I can try to track down who took those—"

"How about a list of what they took from her?" Bree asked.

The clerk brightened. "That I can do. Here it is: 'White blouse, bra, panties, denim jeans, hotel key card, large diamond engagement ring.'"

"That's it?" Bree asked.

"All she wrote."

Elena clapped her hands, threw back her head, and laughed. "It's not her."

"How do you know that?"

"Leigh Anne, Maggie—whatever you want to call her— hated jeans because they made her butt look big. Rolf never gave her an engagement ring, and my bestie was most definitely not engaged."

CHAPTER

33

ALTHOUGH BREE THOUGHT IT was possible that Elena Martin was right, that the woman who'd been in seat 2A on the downed jet was not Leigh Anne Asher, she wasn't completely convinced.

Martin had work to do at the office, and Bree wanted to learn the unknown woman's identity so she could put the Maggie Fontaine inquiry behind her and start looking for Leigh Anne Asher somewhere else. The two women parted ways, and Bree went to a coffee shop and made a list of questions on a notepad:

-Does TSA have a digital image of Maggie Fontaine's ID?
-Where is the FBI keeping other logged evidence from the wreckage?
-Was Fontaine's ID among the luggage retrieved from forward fuselage?
-Are there images of her body in situ?

Bree was a civilian now; she no longer had the authority to get information about the investigation. But she knew Ned Mahoney and Alex could answer her questions.

She checked her watch. Alex was probably still working on the Dead Hours investigation, and she did not want to interfere. She'd wait until he was back on the FBI side of things and ask him discreetly to see what he could find out.

Bree got back in her car and was heading across the Fourteenth Street Bridge into DC when her cell phone rang. Jannie's name came up on the dashboard caller ID.

"Hi, Jannie."

"Hi, Bree. Is this an okay time?"

Bree heard worry in her stepdaughter's voice and said, "I'm all ears. What's going on?"

"Remember I went to that national development camp after I chose Howard?"

"After tying the national high-school record in the four hundred—yes, I think I remember that."

Ordinarily, that would have provoked a laugh and an *I still can't believe it!* from Jannie. But her voice was serious when she said, "I made some friends at that camp. Some good friends, Bree."

Bree frowned, trying to figure out where this was going. "I imagine you did."

"Okay, so I just got off the phone with one of them, and she says—" Jannie stopped.

"Jannie?"

"She's going to call me back. Would you meet with her if she agrees? It's bad, Bree. What's happening to her."

"Of course I'll meet her," Bree said. "What's going on?"

"She's calling." Jannie hung up.

Bree's head spun. What had Jannie gotten herself involved in?

She was almost to the house on Fifth Street when her phone buzzed. She pulled over and checked the text: She wants to talk but she's afraid. She doesn't know what to do.

Bree texted back: Tell her bad things and bad people wither and die when you shine a light on them. Tell her I'll help her if I can.

She got back on the road, reached home a minute later, and found a parking spot at the far end of the block. She was starting to parallel-park when her phone buzzed a third time: She'll meet us. Franklin Park, SE corner, Fourteenth and I, in three hours.

34

LARGELY ON SAMPSON'S INSTINCTS, we'd made headway on the Dead Hours killings. He decided to run the names of the victims through the FBI's criminal databases and came up with three cases that had been sealed and expunged because the perpetrators were juveniles.

What are the odds of that? Five men have been killed so far and three of them had criminal histories lurking in their deep past?

Bart Masters, the dead NASA engineer, had gotten into trouble in Las Vegas when he was in his early teens. Trey O'Dell, the high-school teacher, was roughly the same age when he'd had a brush with the law in Mississippi. Theo Leaver, the second to die, had been in the Kentucky juvenile criminal justice system.

As an adult, Leaver had worked early hours for a regional baking company, driving a delivery van and stocking shelves in grocery and convenience stores in the greater DC area. He had been found in the back of his vehicle, covered with a sheet, gunshot wounds to both eyes.

When we left the Charles School after talking to the captain, we called Eileen O'Dell, the teacher's wife and the woman we had been interviewing when the jet was shot down. She sounded genuinely surprised to learn that her husband had been a juvenile offender.

"No, he never mentioned that, Dr. Cross. Not once. Are you sure?"

"The particulars have all been scrubbed, but we're sure," I said.

"I have no idea what it was about," she said. "I can ask his parents."

"Thanks," I said. "You'll let us know?"

"Of course," she said. "It might be later in the day before I find out. Is this important?"

"It's a long shot," I said. "But let us know."

While John drove us to the FBI command center in Arlington, I called Detective Hanson with the Maryland State Police and told her what we'd learned about Bart Masters, the NASA engineer. She was shocked because she'd checked his NASA security-clearance records and he'd come back squeaky clean.

"No mention of a juvenile record," she told us on speaker. "I would have seen that. Know anyone in Las Vegas PD?"

"I don't," I said.

Sampson smiled. "I do. Detective I met at a conference a couple of years back. She's solid. I'll give her a call, see what she can find out."

John put in a call to the Las Vegas detective, got her voice mail, and left her a message, while I tried to talk to someone in the juvenile court in Louisville, Kentucky. I was told the office was swamped now but someone would get back to me as soon as possible.

We arrived at the FBI command center in the big tent on the soccer field in Arlington and heard and saw a jet come in for a landing over the Fourteenth Street Bridge and Gravelly Point Park, following the same flight path as AA 839. Reagan National was open again, although under heavy guard. Gravelly Point Park remained closed. Virginia state troopers were blocking the vehicle entrance and stopping people on the bike paths.

We found Agent Ned Mahoney wolfing down a sandwich at his makeshift desk amid a whirlwind of activity; there were more than fifty agents in the tent. He saw us, gave us a thumbs-up, swallowed hard, and said, "Just the guys I wanted to see."

Mahoney said that since the shootdown, he had been in close contact with the American Airlines chief of security at the company's headquarters in Dallas; he'd gotten information on present and past employees, especially those who had been fired and might harbor animosity toward the airline.

"We weren't getting anywhere until he thought to look at the washouts," Mahoney said. "People who didn't make the cut during their probationary periods."

"What did you find?" Sampson asked.

"Not what—who."

"Okay, *who* did you find among the washouts?"

"Marion 'Captain' Davis. Turns out the coach has a few skeletons in his closet."

CHAPTER

35

BREE CALLED NED MAHONEY as he was driving me and Sampson to Davis's house in Falls Church. We were hoping Captain Davis would go straight home after he finished coaching.

Ned put her on speaker.

"I'm trying to confirm the identity of one of the victims on the downed jet," she said. "Maggie Fontaine in seat two A. I'm looking for TSA records of the identification she used to board the plane, in situ photos, anything found in the forward fuselage that shows her picture. That can happen, right?"

Mahoney said, "It can. Who is Maggie Fontaine?"

"She seems to be two people, or someone who's trying to be two people," Bree said, and she explained about the disappearance of Leigh Anne Asher.

"We'll try to help you nail her down," Mahoney said, and they hung up.

Captain Davis had just pulled his Mercedes into his driveway in Falls Church when we got there. Ned parked our vehicle across the mouth of the drive.

Davis got out of his car in his coaching gear, and he looked angry when he saw John and me. "What is this?" he demanded. "I thought I answered all your questions."

"You answered their questions," Mahoney said, showing him his FBI badge. "I've got a few of my own."

The coach looked at his watch. "Can't this wait?"

"Would you rather do this here or at FBI headquarters?" I asked.

Captain Davis sighed. "Here. But will you move your car so it's not blocking my driveway? I've got a staff meeting in the field house in an hour."

"I'll do it," Sampson said, taking the keys from Ned.

The coach rested his butt against the trunk of his car, crossed his arms, and looked at Mahoney like he wished they were playing full contact. "Ask."

Mahoney said, "Why didn't you tell Dr. Cross and Detective Sampson that you were once an American Airlines employee?"

He laughed caustically. "Because there's nothing to tell. I lasted twelve days. It just wasn't meant to be. My life as a pilot was done, and it was time to coach."

"American says you were a brilliant pilot with a troubled past who showed up to training with alcohol on your breath multiple times in those twelve days."

Captain Davis took a deep breath and let it out. "I have had a problem with booze and drugs. I'm not proud of it. I still struggle with it because of things I saw overseas."

"Cost you a lot," said Sampson, who'd returned from moving the car.

"More than you know."

I said, "Your girlfriend?"

The anger rose up in him again. He glared at me. "That was an ex-girlfriend. A long-ago ex-girlfriend."

"Antonia Mays."

He nodded reluctantly.

"And she had a daughter, Jenna," Mahoney said.

"You gonna drag them into this?" he said, shaking his head in disgust.

"If we have to," I said. "We can understand you wanting to keep it quiet."

"Look, I had nothing to do with that. Nothing. I started dating Antonia when I played for the Ravens. She hated that I quit the NFL. We had an on-again, off-again relationship for a while, and she was dating someone else when she got pregnant with Jenna. So Jenna wasn't mine, but she was a great kid, and when me and Antonia were done for good, I kept taking care of Jenna. I sent Antonia money every month for her. But Antonia, man, she just had a darkness in her soul."

"Did she support you when you came back from overseas?" Sampson asked.

"Ah, no. She told me I should have stayed in the NFL, made some real money. She hated me, blamed me for everything wrong in her life. Right to the end."

I said, "How long after you were dropped from the American Airlines pilot program did she…"

"Four days. I'd gone down to Galveston to drink to the end of my pilot career with a couple of old buds."

"How'd you hear?"

"Antonia's sister, Lucille, called me," he said. "Told me what she'd done." Davis stared off into the middle distance and shook his head. "It was just shock and disbelief at first. Then it hit me that it was real." He looked at us. "I went to my knees and bawled my eyes out for that poor little girl. I was just gutted."

"But eventually you got angry," Mahoney said.

"Oh, angry enough to tear heads off. And sad enough to blow my own head off. I mean, what kind of woman shoots her seven-year-old daughter in her sleep and then turns the gun on herself?"

I said, "A disturbed one. Was she angry about you getting dumped by American?"

"Of course. Antonia looked for reasons to be angry," Davis said. "About everything. So, sure. It pissed her off. But you know what? The job wasn't going to change my life or hers financially. I made quite a bit of money in the NFL, and I invested it all before I went overseas. I didn't need the job to help take care of Jenna is what I'm saying."

His explanation felt real. The sorrow in his face seemed heartfelt. I think Sampson saw that too, but Mahoney wanted to be sure.

"Mr. Davis," he said. "Captain, I'm trying to believe you here, but do you understand the importance of this investigation?"

"I may have had my bell rung a few times, but I'm not suffering from dementia."

"We want to eliminate you as a suspect once and for all. Will you let us search your house or do I need a warrant?"

Davis thought about it, then said, "Go ahead. I got nothing to hide. I've got a coaching staff meeting to get to. You find something, you know where I'll be."

CHAPTER

36

BREE STONE WALKED THROUGH Franklin Park toward the corner of Fourteenth Street and I. It was chilly, and a blustery wind shook the leaves that were turning color all around her.

Jannie was already at the corner, sitting on a park bench wearing running shorts and a light jacket on which was printed HOWARD UNIVERSITY TRACK. She was sipping a mocha latte that had come from the Compass Coffee across the street. She had two more coffees in a cardboard tray, and she smiled when she saw Bree.

"For you," Jannie said, holding out one of the coffees. "Figured we could all use a warm-up. It's just the way you like it."

Bree took the coffee, tasted it, and smacked her lips. "Perfecto."

"Good," Jannie said.

"How's the life of a college freshman?"

Her stepdaughter shrugged. "Not as much fun as it should

be. But I am learning a lot, and I've made friends with kids on the team."

"And you get to sleep and do your laundry at home," Bree said.

"That too," Jannie said, glancing at her watch.

"Who's the third coffee for?" Bree asked.

Jannie hesitated. "I think she kind of wanted to talk to you anonymously at first. Get your advice on what she should do."

"Fair enough," Bree said and sat next to her stepdaughter. "Picked a major yet?"

"I like understanding how the body works at peak performance," she said. "Physiology, you know? I could see myself coaching or becoming a physical therapist."

"I could see that too. Any guys in your world?"

Jannie shrugged and smiled. "Maybe."

Bree smiled back. "Maybe?"

"Maybe," Jannie said and laughed. "I'll let you know."

"I should hope so," Bree said.

They chatted about the AA 839 investigation and how it was likely to consume Alex's life for some time to come. Bree told her she was trying to determine if one of the passengers on the flight was a woman who'd gone missing the week before.

Another ten minutes passed.

"Maybe I should text her," Jannie said. "She's usually right on time."

"Do that."

Jannie thumbed a text and hit Send. They waited.

"Did she say she was driving straight in from school?" Bree asked.

"No, she came down from Paxson yesterday and rented an Airbnb near George Mason. She said she was going for a light run in some park near where she's staying, then she would take a shower and come straight over. She should be here by now."

"Call," Bree said.

Nodding, Jannie hit Call and put her phone to her ear. Bree could make out a woman's muffled voice and then a beep.

"Hey, it's Jannie. My stepmom is with me and we're waiting. Call me."

Jannie tried twice more in the following fifteen minutes and texted three times. None of the calls or texts were returned. Then she began reaching out to mutual friends. In the next twenty minutes, she spoke to seven different people, and they all said they had not seen or heard from Jannie's friend, although they'd tried to reach her by text and phone.

"This isn't like her," Jannie said. "I mean, really not like her. She's—"

"Give me her name," Bree said impatiently. "And I think it's time you tell me what's happening to her and why she wants to talk to me."

37

CAPTAIN DAVIS HAD UNLOCKED the front door of his house and sped off in his Mercedes.

"What's his play?" Mahoney said. "Letting us go through the house because he's got his toys and stuff stashed elsewhere?"

"Or maybe he has nothing to hide," I said. "Think about it. Where does he get the wherewithal to build a remote-controlled machine gun?"

"Maybe he's got an accomplice who built the gun," Sampson said.

"And the bomb," Mahoney said.

"Still, it's a bold move if he invites us to search his house," I said.

We put on disposable booties, gloves, and caps, entered the grand foyer, and took in the sweeping spiral staircase with a tiger maple banister and dark green granite floor. The high-end finishes carried on throughout the house, with restaurant-grade appliances in the kitchen and tile and stone in every bathroom.

There were four bedrooms, three up and one down that Davis used as an office. That one was organized with military precision and featured little that spoke to the coach's past in the NFL or the air force. Indeed, most of the shelves were empty, and the files in the desk were all from recent months.

"It's like Davis never really moved in," I said.

"Like a visitor," Sampson agreed.

"Computer's password-protected," Mahoney said. "So's the laptop."

One of the upstairs bedrooms was empty. The second held flattened moving boxes. The primary bedroom suite featured a big stall shower and a bed facing a balcony overlooking woods. We did find a row of Baltimore Ravens jackets and hoodies in the closet but not the one the deputy had seen the van driver wearing in Gravelly Point Park.

Overall, the upstairs was as cold and impersonal as the ground floor and the basement, which had been transformed into a sprawling man cave with a large television, movie-theater chairs, and nothing on the wall or floors.

"Like he ran out of ideas on how to spend his money," Sampson said.

"No pictures of the little girl anywhere," Mahoney said.

"There are a couple of empty picture frames on the wall in the kitchen," I said.

"Maybe he can't bear the sight of them," Sampson said.

"Too painful."

"Or too rage-provoking," Mahoney said.

But we found nothing to say that Davis was the man behind the remote-controlled machine gun anywhere in the house or basement, which left the four-bay garage.

We didn't expect to find what we found: five expensive cars

with a complicated hydraulic rack system that kept four of the vehicles stored in stacks of two and a 1963 split-window Corvette up on a lift in the third bay. The fourth bay was empty and spotless.

"This guy doesn't fool around, does he?" Sampson said. "He's got a gizmo and a gadget for everything and his own machine tool shop. That sounds like someone who could build a remote-controlled machine gun."

"Or at least get the hardware to build it," Ned said. "That curved track it was on."

"Maybe," I said, wandering over to the old Corvette, which was in immaculate condition. In front of the car, against the wall, was a steel locker flanked by two obsessively organized workbenches.

I opened the locker and found five mechanic's jumpsuits hanging there, three blue and two tan. One tan suit had grease and oil on it. Another tan suit bore grass and mud stains at the knees. One of the blue jumpsuits had a big stain on the front that smelled like chemicals.

Then I noticed the shoulders and neck of that same blue coverall were bunched up. I reached up with gloved hands and unzipped it, and what we saw pretty much ended our suspicions about Captain Davis.

And confirmed them.

CHAPTER

38

BREE SAT IN SILENCE after Jannie related what her friend Iliana Meadows had told her in strictest confidence.

"And she doesn't know who's behind it?"

"Just that they have the video. She figures it's someone from Paxson State," Jannie said, referring to the college in rural Maryland.

"And the video?"

"She didn't even know the coach had made it."

"But it was in high school?"

Jannie nodded. "When she was seventeen."

"A high-school coach."

"She said that part was consensual, but the video definitely was not."

"And it's not the coach blackmailing her?"

"Not unless he's blackmailing himself."

Bree checked her watch. "And she has that kind of money?"

"Her father was killed in an industrial accident when she was twelve. A jury awarded her and her mother millions."

"Is that common knowledge?"

"No. I knew Iliana for a long time before she told me."

"You said she was down here for a meet?"

"She came down early to familiarize herself with the course. It's at George Mason tomorrow."

"Where's she from?"

"Outside Philly," Jannie said. "Newtown or something. It's close to the city."

"On the Main Line, then," Bree said, shaking her head.

They were quiet for several moments, both scanning the sidewalks on both sides of the street for a girl Jannie said was built like a greyhound and wore her light brown hair pulled back in a long braid. But there was no one like that.

Iliana Meadows was more than an hour and a half late.

"Shouldn't we report her missing?" Jannie said.

"They won't take a report until she's been gone twenty-four hours," Bree said.

"Twenty-four hours?"

"Do you have any idea where she was staying?"

"All I know is it's an Airbnb near George Mason. I think her friend Tina has the address."

"Have you called her mother?"

"Nancy? Iliana says she's not around a lot. She travels and has boyfriends."

Bree thought about everything Jannie had told her. She was getting Iliana's story secondhand, so she knew there had to be flaws in the account. Still, there was no doubt that if even half of Iliana Meadows's story was true, it was a potentially explosive situation.

"Let's try the mom and then the friend who knows where Iliana has been staying," Bree said as her phone began to buzz and chime. She looked at the screen and saw a text from an unfamiliar number that read In situ. AA 839. Interior front near cockpit.

39

WE CAUGHT UP WITH Captain Davis as he was leaving the field house with some other coaches. Fiona Plum walked out of the school building and headed toward him, but we got to him first.

"Find a machine gun in my basement?" he said jokingly. "Here to arrest me?"

"As a matter of fact," Mahoney said, "I hope you're not going to resist and make this all uglier than it has to be, Captain."

"Ugly?" he said. "Resist? You've got to be shitting me. Other than in my F-14, I've never been near a machine gun in my life."

"But you use jumpsuits when you're working on your cars and building your bombs," Sampson said, spinning him around.

"What?" he said. "No, this is not right. You have no evidence that—"

Mahoney said sharply, "We do have evidence, Mr. Davis. One

of your jumpsuits and one of your Ravens' sweatshirts matches the description of the clothing worn by the man who machine-gunned the American Airlines jet. We swabbed both articles of clothing and ran the swabs through a portable analyzer."

I said, "Positive for explosives residue on both the hoodie and the jumpsuit, consistent with the fertilizer bomb that destroyed the van you rented."

"Captain?" Fiona Plum said. She was ten feet away.

Davis's head swiveled to her and he looked pained, chagrined. "It's not true what they're saying, Fiona. I don't know what is happening here or why, but I'm telling you, what they're saying is not true."

The English teacher looked at Davis as if her hero had been vanquished by some dark knight. Mahoney read the high-school football coach his Miranda rights and began to lead him away.

"Hey! What's happening?" several male voices cried.

We looked back and saw coaches running our way. Scurrying toward us from another direction was a pale fellow wearing a bow tie.

"I'm the headmaster here," he declared. "What is this? I want an explanation!"

"Coach Davis is being taken into custody pending a further search of his home," Mahoney said. "No one touch his office. An FBI forensics team will be here in an hour."

"What's he done?" one of the coaches yelled.

"Hates American Airlines," Sampson said, opening the squad car's rear door.

Davis, who was clearly shaken, said, "I don't hate American Airlines." Then he called out to the small crowd as he got in the car, "I haven't done anything but have a little too much to drink.

I promise you all that. I had nothing to do with that airplane coming down. Nothing."

No one said anything for a long moment. Sampson started to shut the door.

"I believe you, Captain!" Fiona Plum called out. "Don't say another thing! I'm calling you a lawyer!"

40

BREE AND JANNIE WENT across the street to the coffee shop and took seats where they could see the corner of Fourteenth and I in case Iliana Meadows miraculously showed.

Jannie texted the friend who knew where Iliana was staying. Bree tracked down an address and phone for Nancy Meadows in suburban Philadelphia. Jannie called the friend, got voice mail, and left a message. Bree did the same with Iliana's mother's voice mail.

Jannie put her phone down, frustrated. "I feel like we should be doing more."

"Sometimes the best thing you can do is wait and get answers," Bree said, finally forcing herself to open the first of three shots an FBI agent named Amelia Franks had sent her of the interior of the forward fuselage of AA 839 before anyone entered to begin retrieving bodies.

The picture had been shot with a powerful flash that threw the macabre scene into a garish light. The hull of the forward fuselage had broken apart in multiple places and had come to rest almost upside down. Most of the seats had been ripped from the floor in the crash and hurled about the interior as it rolled over and over. Some of the victims were still held to their seats by their safety belts. Others had been torn from their belts and tumbled freely along with carry-on bags from the overhead compartments.

All Bree could make out from the picture was a grotesque jumbled knot of bloody torsos, arms, legs, heads, and luggage. There was no one recognizable, and she could not get a good look at the passengers still in their seats and dangling upside down, their backs to the camera.

She opened the second picture, which was not much better. The third, however, was taken by an agent who'd climbed through the blown-out window of the cockpit and gotten the hatch door open.

Five bodies hung upside down from their seats in the first four rows, their arms, hands, and fingers dangling, their faces and upper bodies beaten, gashed, and so swollen Bree doubted their own families would recognize them.

She used her fingers to enlarge the picture and saw past an overweight male in the first-row right window seat to the second-row window. The plane had come apart next to the woman who hung there in a bloody white shirt and jeans, the gashes that had taken large parts of her facial skin and scalp clearly visible.

And there was the big diamond on her left ring finger. A male in a gray business suit hung beside her. He'd been less maimed in the crash. Only the left side of his head had been destroyed.

"Bree?" Jannie said. "I've got the address where Iliana's staying. Tina's going to meet us there. She's driving in from Paxson."

"Let's go," Bree said as her phone buzzed with an incoming text. She got up and saw it was from FBI Agent Franks. She opened it: Still processing luggage, trying to match to Maggie Fontaine in seat 2A.

Thanks, Bree replied as they went out the door. TSA?

When she did not get an immediate reply, she shifted her attention to Jannie and her missing friend, wondering how she'd gotten herself into two missing-person cases in two days. "Address?" Bree asked.

"On Fairfax Boulevard in Fairfax, unit twenty-one B," Jannie said. "I'll pull it up on Waze."

They got in Bree's vehicle, picked up I-66 across the Roosevelt Bridge, drove south past Falls Church to Fairfax, Virginia, and were soon rolling slowly through a condo complex looking for unit 21B.

"Got to be that building up ahead," Bree said.

"Hey, that's Iliana's car," Jannie said. "Right there! The green BMW."

Bree pulled in and parked near the little sedan. It was even chillier here than it was in Washington and the leaves were falling. There were wet leaves on the BMW's windshield.

"She hasn't been out since last night," Bree said. "That was the last rain."

They went to the door of unit 21B and knocked. There was no answer.

"We'll have to search for a manager," Bree said.

"Wait, wait, this is an Airbnb," Jannie said. "Do you have the app?"

She did have the app and signed into it. Jannie had her search the address in Fairfax and quickly came up with the listing.

"Two hundred and ninety a night?" Bree said.

"Look at the contact—there's definitely a messaging thing to the owner and maybe also a phone number or something."

Bree found both and phoned the owner in Reston, Virginia. Margaret Holmes didn't seem interested until Bree explained that she used to be Metro PD's chief of detectives and the young woman who'd rented the condo had gone missing.

"Missing?" she said. "For how long?"

Bree said, "About three hours."

"Three hours? Isn't that jumping the gun a little?"

"I can't get into it, but she was being threatened, blackmailed. That's why she rented the place from you, to get away from that threat. All we want to do is enter and see if she's there."

CHAPTER

41

AFTER A LONG PAUSE, Holmes asked Bree to send a picture of herself and her private investigator's and driver's licenses. Bree did. The owner directed her to a lockbox in a utility closet beneath the staircase and gave her a digital code.

Bree punched the number in, got the key, thanked the woman, and climbed back up to unit 21B, where Jannie was waiting nervously.

Bree said, "I told the owner I would be the only one going in, and I have to video the place as I find it."

"That's okay," Jannie said. "I don't know if I want to go in there."

Bree got out a tissue from her purse and held the door handle with it as she inserted the key in a dead-bolt lock. She turned it, heard it slide, and pushed the door open.

Her phone buzzed with a text. Ignoring it, she turned on her phone camera and started videoing the short-term rental. Nice main room with new furniture and television. Everything neat and tidy. Several textbooks piled neatly on a glass table.

"Jannie?" a female voice called. Bree looked over her shoulder.

"Tina's here," Jannie said. "Iliana's teammate."

"Both of you stay out while I clear it, please," Bree said and she quickly did just that.

No one in the kitchen. Only one of the two bedrooms had been used. The bed had been made. Iliana's clothes hung neatly from hangers. There was a phone charger but no phone. And no sign of a computer anywhere.

Bree called out to Jannie as she returned, "Empty."

Jannie said, "Tina wants to know if Iliana's running shoes are there—Asics. And a blue and gold Paxson State running jacket? She'd wear it in this wind."

Bree pivoted, returned to the bedroom, looked, and called over her shoulder. "No Asics. No running jacket. Ask Tina if she had a laptop."

A moment later, Jannie called back, "Yes, a MacBook with a Paxson Cross-Country sticker on the lid."

"It's not here."

Then she put her phone to her lips. "We are leaving now, Ms. Holmes." She shut the camera app off. Before exiting and shutting the door of the condo, she glanced at her text messages and saw one from Amelia Franks that began Finally.

Jannie was on the landing standing next to Tina Dawson, a tall, fit blonde wearing a Paxson State Track hoodie, shorts, and running shoes. Both girls looked at Bree anxiously.

"If none of her running stuff is in there, she went out for a run," Tina said.

"Hold that thought. I'm trying to do two things at once here."

She stepped aside, opened the FBI agent's text, and saw the image of the Irish passport of Maggie Fontaine used to board AA 839. The photograph was clear.

The woman in seat 2A was unmistakably Leigh Anne Asher.

Her heart sank. Even though she had thought it likely, the evidence was now incontrovertible. Elena Martin's old friend was dead. And she had been engaged. But how could she have two passports under two different names?

She called up one of the earlier pictures Agent Franks had sent. This time she blew up the picture to look at the man with the bashed head hanging beside Asher.

Who are you? she wondered. *Are you just some random guy? Or are you her fiancé?*

"Bree!" Jannie said, snapping her out of her thoughts. "What are we going to do?"

"You said she was going to take a run in a nearby park, right?"

Jannie nodded. "I guess it's part of the race course."

Tina said, "That's what she told me too. Mantua Park. Gerry Connolly Cross County Trail. She said it would be a good place for me to loosen up after the drive down. And I think the trail is part of the course at George Mason. She gave me directions, what trail to take and all."

"You were going to stay here with her?"

"She invited me. Said it was better than the dump Paxson was putting us up in."

Bree said, "Were you two close? Did she confide in you?"

Tina frowned. "We just met like six weeks ago. Confide in me about what?"

"Nothing," Bree said, heading for the stairs. "Let's go look around that park."

"What if she's not there?" Jannie asked.

"We start calling hospitals. And then we call the police."

42

IN A MODEST APARTMENT building in suburban Maryland, Padraig Filson checked to see if the VPN software he was running fully masked the IP address of his laptop. Assured that it did, he typed in commands that bounced his request through six different internet servers around the world before sending it into a virtual universe most people had heard of but never seen.

Filson smiled. *Can you imagine what we could have done with this back in the day? Everything would have gone down so much faster. Easier.*

He looked at the wall where he had thumbtacked a snapshot of a towheaded, freckle-faced young boy grinning through two missing front teeth. Filson sighed, knowing that rewriting the past behind that snapshot was just a pipe dream.

But the future? That could be altered.

Had to be altered, as far as he was concerned.

The boy's life depends on it, Padraig. Get to fishing now. Not much time left.

He turned his attention to the sign-in box in the middle of a blank screen. He used an alias and an unhackable password that a computer nut in Galway had devised for him in return for certain favors.

After a moment, the screen blinked and showed what looked like whole galaxies of stars rushing at him. The experience thrilled him as much as it had the first time he'd gone down this rabbit hole.

God, he loved the dark web, with all its secret nooks and crannies. It was a whole universe unto itself. Here you could get a proper clean gun—pistol, rifle, or shotgun—and bullets matched for accuracy. And garrotes and poisons. All the tools of the trade.

Except one tool, a magical skill that made Filson special in his line of work. No one else on the dark web provided his unique service. He knew. He'd checked.

So today, as he had almost every day since his diagnosis, Filson was going fishing in the deep, stinking pools and rivers of the dark web. He was angling for one of the scum creatures who loved to swim in those places, reveled in them, felt compelled to dive into them no matter how much they tried to repress their inner longings and addictions.

At another time, in another place, and for different reasons, Filson might have trolled for victims on the illegal drug sites that had sprung up in the aftermath of the Silk Road's collapse. But he was focused elsewhere, on the foulest pools and rivers, the ones where the true monsters of society lurked and fed.

Filson typed in more commands, then used another alias and another password to access one of the rankest rivers of them all, one that held some of the most disgusting fish he'd ever encountered. Glancing again at that picture of the young boy on the wall, he felt his anger and purpose grow. "You won't have to deal with these kinds in your life, boyo," he whispered and then returned to his fishing.

Back in rural Ireland, Filson's father had been an avid salmon angler who'd taught his son everything he knew about bringing up big fish from the depths. These fishing techniques worked in the virtual world as well as the real one, Filson knew.

Once Filson was on the site, he accessed an encrypted forum, ignored the new filth posted on its general page, and went to a substring titled Actively Seeking: Mid-Atlantic.

As his father had taught him, he paused to scan the pool he was about to cast into, looking for signs of fish feeding. He read a few of the posts, understood the rude flavor of them, and saw in his mind just the kind of fly that would raise one of these beasts to the surface.

Filson typed, tying his fly with suggestion, innuendo, and lurid description. He finished it with a picture, an image he'd copied from the regular internet, added contact information through an encrypted Tor messaging system, then posted the lure on the dark web forum.

Now all he had to do was be patient.

It was the only way to be when you were trying to outsmart a bottom-feeder.

FILSON STARTED TO LAUGH, but that turned into a hacking cough with phlegm that he spat into a mason jar he kept on the table. Feeling a familiar heartburn building, he left the laptop, went to the refrigerator, and poured himself a glass of milk.

From a cabinet, he got out a bottle of Jameson whiskey and added three fingers of it to the milk. This was the only concoction that eased the burning in his throat and gut.

Ding!

A strike? he thought. *Already?*

Sipping his drink, Filson hustled back to the laptop and saw that, indeed, someone was nosing about his fly. He opened the message, read it, and smiled. He typed an enticing reply.

Several more messages passed back and forth. Filson took screenshots of them all and signed off, feeling like the fly had been taken and the hook was set.

His next fish was firmly on the line.

He quickly signed into another Tor site, pasted the screen-shots into a message, and sent the message to an anonymous address he'd memorized.

As usual, Filson did not have to wait long for the reply: Good criteria. Take him. Same terms. Proofs as well.

After seeing that, Filson signed out of the dark web and closed his laptop.

He and the fish had agreed to meet at three a.m., the dark hour when predators felt comfortable enough to come up into the shallows and hunt.

I am a fisher of men, that's all there is to it, he thought as he left the table and went to the bathroom. He picked up the electric trimmer he'd bought earlier in the day and cut his full beard down to a neat goatee. Then he cut his shaggy silver hair by a good five inches.

Satisfied, he opened a box of henna hair dye, also purchased earlier in the day. He put on disposable gloves and generously coated his hair and goatee with the dye.

Fifteen minutes later, he took a shower and rinsed the dye away. Filson looked himself in the mirror as he dried off and laughed. "You haven't been a ginger in years, Padraig," he said. "It becomes you."

After dressing, he went to a second bedroom. There he unlocked a locker, removed a box, unlocked that, removed another box, and unlocked that. Inside the third and smallest box, cradled in foam, was a weapon Filson had designed and built himself, using an old friend's metal lathes and gunsmithing tools. It had been a simple job, really.

His research had shown that the average pair of human eyes were set roughly fifty-five to seventy-five millimeters apart, measured from the center of one pupil to the center of the other. Filson had used the average of sixty-five millimeters to set the distance between two .25-caliber pistol barrels he then joined to an action he'd designed, milled, and fitted so they operated like side-by-side shotguns, with a single trigger controlling both firing pins. It had a break-action breech as well.

He'd welded a reinforcing rod between the barrels to give them more stability and put a tritium aiming sight on it that glowed even in the pitch-dark. The pistol stock was custom-made, a composite he'd produced with a 3D printer based on measurements he'd taken of his own hand. The butt of it had a hole so the weapon could be hung on a hook.

He picked the gun up and shut the empty breech, surprised once again at how balanced, how right it felt in his hands. Maybe he'd missed his calling. *I could have been a gunsmith,* Filson thought.

He looked over at his reflection in a mirror on the closet's sliding door. He ignored the dye job and studied his ravaged eyes and face, then took a long swig of the milk and whiskey, feeling it fire his tongue and cool his throat and gut.

Filson laughed at his reflection. "Nah, Padraig. No gunsmith. You were born for this life, weren't you? You and your mad fishing father before you."

Then he raised the double-barreled pistol and aimed the glowing green tritium sight at the reflection of the bridge of his repeatedly broken nose. When he squeezed the crisp trigger and heard the firing pins snap, he broke into a cackle that soon had him coughing harder than ever.

CHAPTER

44

Fairfax, Virginia

BREE, JANNIE, AND TINA DAWSON stood on the west side of Mantua Park at the entrance to the Gerry Connolly Cross County Trail, almost directly across the street from the Airbnb the missing Iliana Meadows had rented.

Bree had her phone out with the Google Maps application up. She looked at Tina. "Give me the directions she gave you."

The cross-country runner got out her phone, found the text. "She says, 'Enter across from condo. Trail follows Accotink Creek. Cross Barkley Drive. Go south to Prosperity Avenue. That's a mile and a half. Turn around. An easy three miles.'" Tina choked a little. "Then she say, 'Have fun! See you soon! We'll order out!'"

"Don't worry, Tina," Bree said. "We'll find her. She's probably just sprained an ankle or something."

They entered the park and took the trail down along Accotink Creek. It was pretty there that crisp autumn early evening. Many of the trees on the slopes along the creek and trail were in full fall color.

A steady wind blew, rustling the leaves and deepening the chill as they walked, looking up the trail and at the hillsides flanking it. They encountered a few runners and two moms hiking with babies on their backs.

They stopped all of them and showed each one a picture of Iliana. "She'd be wearing a jacket like this one," Jannie said, pointing at Tina's.

None of them had seen the cross-country runner or anyone with a similar jacket.

A few hundred yards on, a branch of the trail turned north toward Arlington Boulevard. Somewhere up there in the trees, a dog was yapping. The main path extended east and south toward Barkley Drive. They followed it, with Jannie and Tina calling for Iliana.

There was no response. They reached the intersection of the paths and Barkley Drive, which was busy with traffic. The trail disappeared into the woods south of it.

Bree said, "You know what? I'll take the trail from here south to Prosperity. You two go back, see if we missed anything, then get in Tina's car. You'll come get me."

Tina looked upset.

"What's the matter?" Jannie asked.

The young woman said, "I have nowhere to stay tonight. I told Coach I was going to stay with Iliana."

Bree exchanged glances with Jannie. "What coach was that?"

"Thayer," she said. "He usually sets up our lodging."

"You'll stay with us tonight," Jannie said. "We're not far."

Tina hesitated. "You're sure?"

"Absolutely," Bree said. "Wait until you taste Jannie's great-grandmother's cooking."

The young woman smiled. "Okay. I'd like that. It's been a while since I had a home-cooked meal before a race."

"Call me on my cell if you find anything on the way back," Bree said, then hustled across Barkley Drive.

The light was more slanted in these woods, the trail more heavily used. Bree saw five times as many people using this section, and she decided that if something had happened to Iliana, it had to have been back there, across Barkley, on the trail north and west to Pickett Road.

She jogged back, crossed Barkley, and was puffing when her cell phone rang. "Jannie?"

Her stepdaughter was on the verge of crying. "We found her jacket, Bree."

"Don't touch it," Bree said, quickening her pace. "I'm on my way."

"Why would it be here like this?" Jannie said. "Down in the creek?"

"Get back on the trail and wait for me!"

She caught up to Jannie near the spur trail that ran north to Arlington Boulevard. Her stepdaughter was crying hard.

Somewhere, that dog was still yapping.

"It's bad, isn't it?" Jannie said, gesturing down into the creek bottom where a blue and gold Paxson State jacket was caught on an exposed tree root next to a culvert that ran under the spur trail. "I don't know how we missed it the first time, but Tina saw it when we were coming back."

"Where is Tina?" Bree asked, getting out her phone to photograph the jacket.

Jannie gestured toward the spur trail. "She said she wanted to know what that dog was barking at, and—"

Over the yapping and from the woods west of the spur trail came a cutting scream of horror and loss.

CHAPTER

45

CAPTAIN DAVIS INVOKED HIS Miranda rights and refused to answer any more of our questions until he'd spoken with an attorney. We had forty-eight hours to hold him without charges while FBI criminologists pored over everything in his residence, looking for additional evidence.

The U.S. attorney who had jurisdiction over the case was getting bombarded with calls from people complaining about Davis being taken into custody and the subsequent search of his house. Rebecca Cantrell called Ned Mahoney, John Sampson, and me to her office in Arlington after we'd left Davis at the federal holding facility in Alexandria.

A short, pretty brunette in her late forties, Cantrell had worked multiple terrorism cases while an assistant U.S. attorney in New York. She had a reputation for being extremely thorough.

"You're sure you've got Davis cold?" Cantrell asked after she'd waved us into chairs in front of her desk.

"Residue of explosive components on the coverall and hoodie," I said.

"From a nitrate bomb," Sampson added.

"He's a high-profile suspect. We're accusing a former NFL player and war hero of killing a hundred people. What's the motive?"

"We don't—"

"Rage," Mahoney said. "His ex-girlfriend killed her daughter and herself after Davis flunked out of an American Airlines pilot program."

"What?"

"True," I said. "Davis was very close to the daughter. Treated her like his own."

"Right to the end," Sampson added. "And he claims he had enough money from football he didn't need the job."

"So the motive is shaky," Cantrell said.

"With all due respect, I don't think a grand jury will see it that way."

"With all due and deep respect, Agent Mahoney, I'm the grand-jury expert here and if we're going to destroy a man's reputation in public, I'd like to do it with utter confidence in his eventual conviction on all charges."

"That could take time. Longer than forty-eight hours."

"I think I can keep him in custody a bit longer based on the explosives residue. But for now, we'll stick to that window, which should give me enough time to proceed to arraignment if I choose to."

I said, "What will make you confident enough to charge?"

"All open angles closed," Cantrell said. "All other known suspects eliminated."

Mahoney said, "We're still working on Cameron Blades, the guy who threatened American Airlines after they lost his mother's ashes."

"He had fifty-caliber-machine-gun components?"

"Affirmative. And no federal firearms license for them, according to ATF."

The U.S. attorney sat back in her chair. "Any chance they were collaborating? Davis and Blades?"

"I suppose, but we've seen no evidence of that."

Cantrell pressed her fingers into a steeple and thought for several moments. "Okay," she said finally. "I want you three to change tack, be my devil's advocates."

"How so?" Mahoney said, looking uneasy.

Cantrell sat forward and slid a manila folder across to us. "Someone used a machine gun to shoot at a single-engine plane last year about thirty miles west of Fort Bragg," she said. "Didn't take it down because the plane was too far away, but the fuselage had several bullet holes, and people in that area said they heard the automatic-weapon fire coming from a remote part of a national forest."

"That didn't come up in our records," Mahoney said, frowning and opening the file.

"NTSB handled it and came up with nothing," Cantrell said. "But there's a sheriff's detective down there who contacted us and said we need to look at a few things she believes may be connected to the downed jet. Look, any good defense attorney is going to find this eventually, so let's do the work before they do. Mahoney, I'd like you and Dr. Cross to fly down there ASAP and hear her out."

Before we could reply, she turned to John. "And Detective Sampson, I know you're the sole caretaker of your daughter, so I won't ask you to go out of town on short notice. But I've spoken with your chief, and in addition to your work on the Dead Hours killings, we want you to check out the alibi that this teacher, Fiona Plum, gave Captain Davis. And check the security cameras at that sports bar he claims he went to."

Sampson nodded. "He says he got sick eating crab after the sports bar."

"Check that out too," Cantrell said.

CHAPTER

46

BREE TOOK ONE LAST look at the corpse of Iliana Meadows before walking away from the scene with Fairfax County Police detective Marcia Creighton.

When Detective Creighton showed up as one of the responding investigators, Bree was instantly relieved. She and Creighton had known each other for years, having worked several cases together that crossed district and state lines.

Ahead of them and down the spur trail, other detectives were talking to Tina Dawson and Jannie. Dawson had a space blanket around her shoulders, the shock and horror she'd felt at her discovery now replaced by trembling disbelief.

Jannie wiped at tears with her sleeve as she answered a detective's question.

Creighton stopped twenty yards away and said quietly to Bree, "Looks like the victim was hit from behind, blunt force."

"Sharp-edged weapon, though, the way it caved in her skull," Bree said. "A rock?"

"Or a tree limb with a broken piece coming off it. The ME will give us more when they look at her, but I saw no signs of sexual assault."

"No," Bree said.

"You know what Jannie and Tina are going to say?"

"Iliana told Jannie that someone was blackmailing her over a sex video her high-school coach had shot of the two of them together."

"When she was underage?"

Bree nodded.

"She have any idea who the blackmailer was?"

"No. The demands came to her and her high-school coach by e-mail. They wanted fifty thousand dollars the first time. The second time—evidently two days ago—they wanted a hundred grand."

"How does a college freshman come up with fifty K?"

Bree explained about the father dying in the industrial accident.

"And the coach?"

"I've got nothing firsthand."

Creighton rubbed her temples. "And Dawson knows nothing?"

"She and Iliana weren't that close. Or anyway, they weren't BFFs," Bree said.

"But the victim invited her to stay the weekend?"

"As I understand it," Bree said. She explained that Meadows had texted Jannie earlier in the day to set up a meeting with Bree. "I was supposed to advise her on what to do next."

"Where's the mom in all this?"

"Nancy Meadows. I left her a message earlier. No response. She evidently flits about the world with various boyfriends."

"I'd like the three of you to come down and give formal statements at Chain Bridge Road," Creighton said.

"We can drive ourselves?"

"I'll have cruisers take you, if you don't mind."

Bree understood. The detective wanted to check their stories, see if everything had played out the way they'd said.

"I don't mind," Bree said. "Our car's next to Iliana's green BMW, across the street in the apartment parking lot. And by the way, I videoed the apartment as I went through it. Her running shoes, jacket, and laptop were missing. I'll forward the video to you."

"Her phone wasn't on her either," Creighton said. "And you knew to come down this trail how?"

"Iliana texted Tina about it, said that she could get a loosen-up run in here."

"Thanks, Bree," the detective said. "I'll be along soon."

Creighton went back up the spur road to the murder scene. Bree waited for Jannie and Tina Dawson to finish talking to the other two detectives, and then they walked up the hill together to the cruisers waiting on Pickett Road.

"Why can't I drive myself?" Dawson asked.

"It's standard operating procedure," Bree said. "They'll bring us back. Do you want to call someone?"

"The coaches. They'll want to know."

"They will."

"How do you tell somebody something like this? I've never…" Tears rolled down her face and she put her hand to her mouth. "Oh God, it was awful."

Jannie hugged her. "You tell them you're okay and that you found Iliana and you're talking to the police."

Dawson had calmed down by the time they reached the cruisers. The detectives took them in two separate patrol cars, Jannie and Tina in one, Bree in the other.

Three junior detectives were waiting for them when they arrived at Fairfax County Police headquarters. They brought them to separate rooms and heard their stories.

About an hour later, Bree signed her statement and left the room. Jannie was sitting on a bench, waiting.

"How did it go?" Bree said, taking out her phone and seeing several texts.

Jannie shrugged. "I just told them what I knew, which was not much. They wanted to see our texts and I showed them. They seemed frustrated that Iliana hadn't had her phone with her."

"I'd be frustrated too," Bree said, opening a message from Alex. "Huh. Your father is on his way to Fort Bragg, North Carolina, with Ned. Something to do with the downed jet."

"Does he sleep?"

"Sometimes I wonder," Bree said as the door to a room opened and Tina Dawson came out. Her eyes were puffy and her voice was thick when she thanked the detective.

"All I want to do is sleep," Tina said. "And I haven't eaten a thing since, like, breakfast."

Bree glanced at her watch. It was getting late. "We'll get the cars and go straight to our house," Bree said. "Nana Mama's cooking up a storm, I'm sure."

"And you can use my brother Damon's room tonight," Jannie said. "He's down at Davidson."

"Thank you both," Tina said as they exited the police headquarters. "I don't know what I would have—"

"Tina!" a man called as they went into the parking lot.

Bree turned to see a tall, lean, balding man in his late thirties and a seriously fit brunette of roughly the same age hurrying toward them. They both wore Paxson State windbreakers.

Tina burst into tears and ran at them. "Coach!"

The man slowed. The female coach went to Tina and held her tight as she sobbed. "It was…she was just dead, Marie. Just lying there dead."

47

EVENTUALLY TINA AND THE coach broke their embrace. Tina went to the other coach, hesitated, then hugged him too.

"I'm Bree Stone," Bree said, shaking the female coach's hand. "This is my stepdaughter, Jannie Cross."

The woman did a double take. "Jannie Cross?"

"Yes, Coach," Jannie said.

"Marie Neely," she said, pumping her hand. "I'm the women's cross-country coach at Paxson. This is Rick Leclerc, men's track coach at Paxson."

Leclerc's big hand swallowed Bree's, but like Coach Neely, he seemed more interested in Jannie than what had happened to one of their top athletes. Bree found this odd enough to study the coaches closely.

Shaking Jannie's hand, he said, "Coach Neely and I both think your race to tie the high-school four-hundred-meter record was one of the best performances we've ever seen."

"At any age or level," Neely said, nodding. "You have some future ahead of you, young lady. Howard is lucky to have you."

"Thank you, ma'am."

Bree said, "Don't you want to know what happened to Iliana Meadows?"

Both coaches paled. "Of course," Coach Leclerc said, holding up his beefy hands. "Please."

Before Bree could reply, Coach Neely said, "I'm sorry. I'm confused. How are you and Jannie involved in this?"

Tina said, "They were both there with me, Coach. In the woods. We went there together to look for her. Iliana."

"Okay?" Leclerc said.

Without giving away certain details, Bree explained that earlier in the day, Iliana had arranged to meet her and Jannie in DC. When she didn't show, they'd come out to the Airbnb apartment Iliana had rented for the George Mason race and found it empty, her running gear gone.

Tina explained about the text she'd gotten from Iliana, describing a route for a light workout. She said, "We went in there because they had waited more than an hour for Iliana in DC, and she's not like that, Coach."

"No, she isn't," Coach Neely said.

"Definitely not," Jannie said.

Tina went on. "And, I don't know, we all missed her jacket when we went one way down the trail, but you could see it in the creek near this culvert coming the other way. And then there was this dog barking and..." She started crying again. "I went up there. Her head was, like, caved in, Coach."

"Oh God, you poor thing," Neely said, showing genuine pity as she took the girl in her arms again.

"Her mom doesn't even know yet," Tina said, sobbing.

"We'll make sure she knows," Coach Leclerc said. "I'll track her down."

"We've left messages already," Bree said.

"Oh? And how exactly are you involved?"

"Jannie and Iliana became good friends at a training camp," Bree said. "Good enough friends that when Iliana found herself in trouble, she reached out for my advice through Jannie."

Neely's brows knitted. "What kind of trouble?"

The men's track coach said, "And why would she seek you out, Ms. Stone?"

Jannie said, "Iliana knew my stepmom used to be the chief of detectives with the Metropolitan Police Department."

"I work privately now," Bree said, studying the coaches.

Coach Leclerc cleared his throat. "What kind of trouble was she in?"

Bree said, "Did you know she'd rented an Airbnb rather than stay with the team?"

Coach Neely said, "Not before you mentioned it a few minutes ago."

"She said she'd told a Coach Thayer about her plans."

Leclerc nodded. "He'd be the one. Works in the Paxson athletics department. Sets up all road trips. Good guy."

Neely said, "And you still haven't told us what kind of trouble Iliana was in."

Jannie's voice sounded a little hoarse when she said, "She was being blackmailed over a sex video shot by her high-school coach of the two of them together."

"What?" Coach Neely said, her hand going to her mouth.

"Steve Hawley?" Coach Leclerc said, sounding appalled. "That's not right. No, that can't be true. I know him. Hawley's a stand-up guy."

"Not this time."

CHAPTER

48

Accokeek, Maryland
2:42 a.m.

PADRAIG FILSON DROVE HIS motorcycle, headlights off, onto a wooded farm lane near the entrance to Piscataway National Park, killed the engine, and removed his helmet. Earlier, he'd cut his hair short on top and tight across the sides. The goatee was down to a trim mustache. The dye job had turned his hair a dark ginger.

Filson waited for his eyes to adjust to the dim light. He heard the breeze moving the leaves but nothing else for almost ten minutes. Then the distant hum of an engine came from the south.

That was a surprise. He'd figured the fish as a city type. Members of this species often were because it was easier to get lost in crowds.

But as Filson's father used to say, "You catch fish where you find them feeding."

The vehicle got closer and closer until it stopped roughly one

172

hundred yards away, at the entrance to the park, which featured a working colonial farm. Filson waited until he heard a car door shut, then went to his saddlebags and retrieved thin leather gloves, a computer tablet, a white sheet still in the wrapper, a black ski mask, and the double-barreled pistol.

He hung the gun on a hook he'd sewn inside the left front of the long duster coat he'd worn against the chill. He put the sheet, the tablet, and the ski mask into a deep, wide pouch pocket he'd sewn inside the jacket's front right panel.

The man buttoned a single button on the duster, donned the gloves, and limped across the road. He relied on scouting he'd done earlier online with Google Earth, found the boundary fence, climbed it with some difficulty, and dropped over into the national park.

He skirted around the closed ticket office, saw the expected paved walkway ahead, and stopped. The park was closed, but he wasn't taking any chances.

And there was the fish, shuffling in the shadows beyond the single security light, a good fifty yards back from the entrance. The fish was nervous, wanting to be cautious but failing.

How could he be in control?

Filson knew the fish was trapped in a trance of longing and obsession, unable to resist coming to the surface to see if the fly was something real and satisfying.

Filson tugged the ski mask on, put the computer tablet under his arm, and stepped out where the fish could see him. He walked directly toward him, mindful that there were probably security cameras. Although at this point, Filson was almost past caring. Besides, they wouldn't see much of him with the ski mask on.

But the fish noticed him and stopped shuffling.

"I hoped you'd show," Filson said. "This is a rare thing I'm offering you."

"I'm here, aren't I?" the fish said. "Show me."

Medium build, nervous voice, and now that Filson was getting closer, he could see the guy was soft-handed. He figured the fish for a desk jockey—an accountant or an actuary or an IRS agent. Someone with a soul-sucking job like that.

Filson reached the shadows and stopped a good ten feet from the fish. He got out the computer tablet and called up a video he had ready. "You're not a cop, are you?" Filson asked.

"No," the fish said sharply. "You?"

Filson laughed. "Hardly. Even if I were, being in possession of what I'm about to show you would get me crucified."

"I know what it's like. Now show me."

Filson flipped the tablet around to face the fish and pressed Play, but he also started recording a new video with the camera. He tuned out the squeals of terror, struggle, and bondage on the video and focused on what he was seeing in the light thrown from the tablet screen: the fish's goggling eyes, his flaring nostrils, the thin lips slightly apart and gulping for air.

Filson waited for the big scream, then turned the video off. He placed it on a tree stump so the camera could keep filming. He wasn't surprised when the man stepped toward him and said breathlessly, "You said it's close. This place."

"Twenty minutes away, tops."

"And that's the one? In the…"

"Or your money back."

"How much?"

"How long?"

"Two, three hours?"

"Six thousand for three hours."

"Six thousand?"

"It's the going rate when they're that age."

There was a long silence as the fish fought the line and the hook. Then he said, "You take Bitcoin, right?"

"I do," Filson said and got out his phone. "Here's my Venmo. You'll pay before you play at the site."

"After inspection."

"After inspection."

"Then we have a deal. Gimme the Venmo."

Filson gave him the account name and watched the fish thumb it into his phone. Then he reached inside the duster and drew out the double-barreled pistol.

"You perverted piece of dung," Filson said, aiming the glowing tritium pin at the bridge of the fish's snout at point-blank range.

"No! Plea—"

Filson didn't give him a chance. He pulled the single trigger and blew out both goggling eyes.

The fish flopped, dropped his phone. Filson turned off the tablet's camera. He hung the double-barreled gun back on its hook, then went over and picked up the phone.

The crypto app was still up. He typed in $10,000 in Bitcoin and sent it to one of his anonymous accounts.

Then he wiped the phone clean with a camera cloth, put large disposable gloves over his leather gloves, and tore off the ski mask. Next, he pulled out the sheet, removed the wrapper, and draped it over the dead man's head. Filson pressed the fabric into the eye sockets until the blood came through, then sat the fish upright, his back to the boundary fence.

He retreated a few steps, picked up the tablet, and took several photographs of the scene. Satisfied, he turned and left, not giving the fish a second thought. *Got what he deserved, the creepy bastard,* Filson thought. He felt a rumble in his stomach.

Ah, Jesus, he thought. *Not now.*

Filson tried to swallow against it, but there was no controlling his body these days. He broke out in a cold sweat and then projectile-vomited up his dinner, lunch, and whatever was left of breakfast.

Racked by dry heaves so powerful he thought he'd fall over, Filson knew he'd just made a huge mistake, the kind that a careful, disciplined man always feared. He'd left a trace of himself behind. A big one.

And there was nothing he could do about it now.

CHAPTER

49

Fort Bragg, North Carolina

SHORTLY AFTER EIGHT THE next morning, a young FBI agent named
Sherry Beaufort from the Bureau's Raleigh office picked me
and Mahoney up at Fort Bragg. We'd caught a late military
flight out of Joint Base Andrews and spent the night in guest
quarters on base.

Agent Beaufort drove us thirty miles northwest to the small
town of Albemarle, where we were met by Detective Melanie
Toof of the Montgomery County Sheriff's Department. Detective Toof was one of the more physically formidable women I'd
ever seen: at least six feet tall, broad-shouldered, and muscular,
with short sandy-blond hair.

"I thought someone might finally show up from DC," Toof
said after we'd introduced ourselves. "Told my husband the
same thing when that plane got shot down."

"We didn't have this incident in our files," Mahoney said.

"Don't doubt it," Toof said. "Doug Ferris? The guy they sent out from the NTSB? He was a dipshit if ever there was one. Pardon my French."

"French pardoned," I said. "You're saying there's more to the investigation?"

Mahoney said, "First tell us what Ferris did find."

The detective said the federal aviation investigator looked at the fuselage of the Cessna 130, noted three holes consistent with .50-caliber rounds, and spent the rest of his time grilling the pilot about where he'd really been when the plane came under fire.

"The low-altitude radar at Charlotte was acting up that day, which meant they weren't picking Lunt up on most of his flight path," she said. "Ferris got it in his head that Lunt hadn't known where he was going, went by Fort Bragg, and got shot at. His superiors saw that and talked to folks at Bragg, who denied it up, down, and inside out. Lunt denied it as well. Then Ferris got popped for an opioid addiction. NTSB buried the report, fired the junkie, and never got around to putting anyone else on the case."

She was smiling.

I said, "But you kept looking into the case, didn't you, Detective Toof?"

"Yeah, I kept looking," she said, and she gestured for us to get in her Jeep Cherokee. Mahoney told Agent Beaufort to follow, which she wasn't happy about.

Toof drove us east out of Albemarle on Highway 27, explaining that Chris Lunt, a part-time resident of Charlotte, North Carolina, kept his private plane at a strip north of the city. Lunt spent his summers flying tourists around Denali National Park and his winters doing the same in the Florida Keys.

"Spring and fall, he's here flying the Cessna," Toof said. "I guess what I'm saying is he's a pilot's pilot, so he knows where he is in the air, you know?"

"I get it," Mahoney said. "Is he here? Lunt?"

"Visiting his mom in Arizona, but he said you can look at the plane if you'd like. He hasn't flown it since."

"We might do that," I said. "Tell us about Lunt knowing where he is in the air."

Toof said, "He knew where he was when he was shot at." She crossed a bridge over the Pee Dee River and pulled off the road. We all got out.

"Lunt says he was four miles north of this bridge, about two thousand feet up, early morning. Little foggy, you know. He picks up tracers coming at him from his ten o'clock about a mile out, then he gets hit by three rounds. He goes into a dive and does evasive maneuvers to get the hell out of there."

"He reports it to air traffic control in Charlotte?" Mahoney asked.

"Within seconds of him getting out of range. Gave his GPS position then too."

I asked, "Did he know where the shooter was?"

"Lunt and I worked at that, factoring in his speed, the dive, the GPS location at that point, the altitude, and the weather conditions," she said, moving back toward the squad car. "That got me close, but I went up there and found exactly where the shooter was. The gun, anyway. I'll take you there."

50

DETECTIVE TOOF DROVE US farther east on the highway, then turned north on Liberty Church Road, a two-lane paved affair that headed north through dense woods that were part of the Uwharrie National Forest. Here and there we saw small farms, homes, and cabins; inholdings, Toof said.

About twenty minutes later, we headed back west toward the Pee Dee River. We ended up taking a dirt road that climbed through denser forest and up a ridge.

She pulled the Cherokee off the road just shy of the top of the ridge and onto a two-track that led to a house of sorts, built out of big steel shipping containers, twenty-four of them by Toof's count. Beaufort got out of her car and followed us.

Six stacks of two containers each were set in a two-by-three pattern that formed the middle of the structure. The other twelve boxes were stacked three high and two deep at either end of the first twelve, and all featured slit windows.

The double door dead center of the structure was shielded by a plate of steel three inches thick, ten feet high, and six feet wide. It was welded to two stout posts driven into the ground about three feet from the door.

"It's like a fortress," Mahoney said.

"That was the idea," Toof said, getting out of the car.

"Prepper?" I asked as I got out.

"Big-time prepper," she said.

"Is that police tape?" Mahoney asked, gesturing at the front doors.

"We're getting a little ahead of ourselves, Agent Mahoney," she said. "I want you to see where the shots were taken first. I think it's important you understand that before I explain what happened here."

"Okay," Ned said. "Where were the shots taken?"

She pointed behind the mini-fortress to a gray cliff rising above the far trees. "Up there."

A half hour later, Mahoney, Toof, Beaufort, and I were hiking our way up the last switchback before the ridgetop and the cliff.

"You think someone dragged a fifty-caliber machine gun up here?" I asked, breathing hard and telling myself I had to get a run in one of these days.

"No," the detective said. "I think they brought it up on the back of a side-by-side ATV that belonged to Leslie Parks, a conspiracy-theory-spouting wack job who bought the land and built the fortress of solitude down there that, among other things, gave him private access to a whole lot of remote national forest where he could shoot to his heart's content."

"You said you thought *they* brought it up," Mahoney said. "Parks and who else?"

"I'm getting there," she said as we crested the ridge and followed her to the edge of the cliff, which was perhaps sixty feet high and looked west toward the river about a mile away. She stopped and said, "Lunt was out there flying at one o'clock."

"Quartering to," Agent Beaufort said.

Mahoney and I looked at her.

Beaufort said, "That's almost the same angle the jet was shot at, sir."

Toof shook a finger at her. "Smart girl. Exactly my thought."

"Okay," Mahoney said. "So where exactly was the machine gun?"

The sheriff's detective grinned again. "I came up here, you know, and I was looking for spent fifty-caliber rounds and I was finding nothing."

"How long after the shooting?" I asked.

"Took us three days to figure it out," she said. "So, four days, but again, I was looking for spent brass and finding nothing."

"Get to it, Toof," Mahoney said.

The detective got a sour look on her face. She walked along the cliff about ten feet, squatted, and dusted aside the leaves and debris there, revealing four bolts in a square pattern, each about a foot apart and sticking up out of the granite.

"The gun was here," Toof said.

Mahoney came up beside her. "You think they bolted the gun down on those?"

"No, they bolted the frame and curved carriage of that same remote-control system I read was used to shoot the jet down."

Ned squinted at the bolts skeptically until Toof showed him a time- and date-stamped photograph of the bolts as she had first found them. Through the middle of the bolts and a few inches to either side, there was a wide U scuffed and scratched in the dirt.

"Look like the shape of the system he used?"

Mahoney nodded thoughtfully. "It does."

"Where do we find Parks?" I asked.

Detective Toof sighed. "You can't. He's dead. Official cause was suicide, but I believe he was murdered. And if I'm right, the guy you're after for the downing of the jet and the guy I'm after for killing Leslie Parks are one and the same."

CHAPTER

51

Accokeek, Maryland

JOHN SAMPSON PULLED OFF the road near a Maryland State Police cruiser with the lights on and several other unmarked squad cars as well as a Ford F-150 with the emblem of the National Park Service on the door.

Sampson got out and showed his credentials to the young trooper at the front gate. "Detective Hanson called me."

"She's waiting for you in there, sir," the trooper said. "Watch your step on the walkway. Someone got sick up there. Probably the groundskeeper who found him."

Sampson frowned. He went around the gate and up the little rise, smelling something sour and then seeing what looked like vomit with dirt and pine needles thrown on it. Looking past it, he spotted four people in Maryland State Police windbreakers, including Detective Marilyn Hanson, who was squatting about ten feet back from the latest Dead Hours victim while a photographer recorded the scene.

Detective Hanson saw Sampson and walked over to him. "Thanks for coming on such short notice."

"I'm actually used to being called in a lot earlier on these cases."

"A park groundskeeper found him. ID says Henry Pelham. Business card says he's an accountant for a firm in Waldorf. His phone is missing."

"Security cameras?"

"One looking at the road over the front gate, another behind us a good fifty feet. We've called the superintendent to get access."

"Who puked?"

"The trooper says it was here when he arrived. I think the groundskeeper saw the body and did it. Or the trooper. This is his first homicide."

"Really?" Sampson said, then went back to the vomit.

He used a stick to move the coagulated stuff around, seeing chunks of what looked like sausage and strips of lettuce. After pushing the sausage aside, he saw something that made him stop and call over Detective Hanson.

"How old's the groundskeeper?"

"Thirty?"

"Blood clots," Sampson said, gesturing at three of them in the vomit. "Unless the park worker or your young trooper has an ulcer or some kind of cancer, I'd say the Dead Hours killer just left us a big DNA present."

Hanson agreed and immediately sealed off the area. Because the murder was clearly the Maryland State Police's jurisdiction, Sampson left soon after, promising to speak with Hanson once she had a chance to dig more into the life of Henry Pelham, accountant.

He drove north to Alexandria and was soon parking in front of the Charles School. He went to the office and spoke at some length about Captain Davis with Headmaster Nicholas Hampstead III.

"Everyone loves Captain, but I always thought there was something off about him," Hampstead said, flicking at a speck on his trousers. "And he definitely has a drinking problem. He rarely lets it get in the way of coaching, but it did happen the day the plane was shot down."

"He was sick from a crab boil."

"So he says," the headmaster said. "I believe he was with his cronies drinking at their favorite watering hole, Bowman's. The big sports bar."

"I know it," Sampson said.

"Davis lives there most Sundays and has to be driven home most Sundays."

"By whom?"

"Coach Penny, I imagine. Troy Penny, his assistant and now the acting coach."

"I'd like to talk to him. To Coach Penny."

Hampstead checked his watch. "He should be ending a gym class about now, and he has the next period free. Try his office in the field house."

Sampson walked over to an impressive athletic facility that contained a lap pool, indoor practice space, and a weight room that looked like it belonged at the University of Notre Dame, not a high school. He found Troy Penny looking at film.

The coach jumped when Sampson knocked. John showed him his badge.

"I know who you are, and I don't want to talk to you," Penny said.

"This is a mass murder investigation," Sampson said. "You have to talk to me."

Penny crossed his arms. "There's no way Captain Davis shot down a jet."

"That's exactly why I'm here," Sampson said, coming in. "The U.S. attorney has asked me to play devil's advocate, to tell her every reason why we should not think Captain Davis is responsible. So tell me why we were wrong to arrest him."

"He's a war hero, for God's sake. And he played in the NFL!"

"So did OJ. But it's true Davis is a war hero."

"Damn straight. What he gave up going? What he did over there? Hero."

"When was the last time you saw Davis before the plane was shot down?"

"Bowman's Sports Bar," Penny said. "Sunday, one in the afternoon."

"Before he went to the crab boil?"

"Honestly, I got no idea on the crab boil. But if he went to one, he wasn't alone."

"Who was with him?"

"I've never seen her before, but mmm-mmm, she was something. She must have recognized Captain from his Baltimore Ravens days. I mean, she was wearing a Ravens tank top herself. They were drinking, carrying on, and next thing I knew, they were gone. I figured they were on a one-way street to the sack and that's where he was the next two days."

"Why didn't anybody tell us this before?"

Penny looked chagrined. "Sorry, Detective, I wasn't asked, and, well, I didn't come forward with it because I didn't want it to get around to this teacher friend of mine who has a mega-crush on the coach."

"Fiona Plum?"

"That's the one." Penny sighed. "Sweet woman. Fiona would lie down and die for Captain and I don't know if he even sees her half the time."

"Describe the woman who was with Davis at the bar."

"Late thirties, super-attractive, brunette, built like Captain likes them. And big brown eyes like Antonia. In fact, she could have been Antonia's sister."

"Antonia Mays? The ex-girlfriend who killed herself and her daughter?"

"Yeah, Jenna Mays," Penny said, shaking his head. "Captain loved that little girl. And you know what? No matter what he says, he still loved Antonia. He just couldn't live with her, you know? It's a sad, sad thing."

CHAPTER

52

Albemarle, North Carolina

MAHONEY, AGENT BEAUFORT, AND I followed Detective Melanie Toof back down the ridge as she told us what she knew about the late Leslie Parks.

"There's more rumor than fact," she said. "I'll give you the facts first and then the gossip, if that works."

"It does," Ned said.

Detective Toof said Parks was born in Little Rock. He was an only child. His father was a well-to-do dentist. His mother died when he was eight. His father died in a car accident when Parks was nineteen, and he inherited a large gun collection and a sizable amount of money.

"Enough to make him shiftless," Toof said. "He quit school, partied. A lot. And here's the thing I don't understand. At some point in the next three years, he comes in contact with

189

a couple of ex–Special Forces guys, and suddenly he's in the Middle East."

That caught our attention. "Doing what?" I asked.

"Gunrunning. All legit at first. He and the two Special Forces guys formed a company the U.S. DOD contracted with to get weapons to the Kurds and other rebel groups in Syria."

Agent Beaufort said, "So Parks would have had access to heavy machine guns?"

"I assume so," Toof said.

We had reached the bottom of the ridge and were walking through a pine forest back to Parks's fortress when Mahoney said, "You said he was legit *at first.*"

"Correct, and this is where it gets a little hazy," she said. "One of Parks's private convoys was attacked in an ambush on a remote route in northern Syria shortly after they crossed in from Iraq. His partners were killed in the firefight." Parks was shot twice, Toof said. One bullet hit him in his right arm and shattered his elbow. The other laid a quarter-inch crease down the left side of his head. "CIA Ground Branch guys found him and got him out," Toof said. "They patched him up in a military hospital and then deported him because the entire shipment had been lost to some Iranian-backed militia group. Not only that, the DOD sued him for his profits on the missing weapons. A couple of million, I think."

Agent Beaufort said, "That's kind of harsh. I thought he was working for us."

"For us and for himself," Toof said. "But again, your instincts are excellent. Parks thought what they did to him was more than harsh, especially on top of wounds that left him with chronic arm pain, migraines, and a tendency toward rage, paranoia, and the occasional end-of-the-world diatribe."

We emerged into the clearing where Parks had built his steel house.

"Which brings us to the fortress of solitude," Mahoney said.

"Why the police tape if it's been ruled a suicide?" I asked.

"That's my doing," she admitted. "The estate's tied up in probate with distant cousins fighting over twenty million, so no one can touch it until that's resolved. And I still think his death was a murder."

She led us to the front door and used two keys to open the locks, explaining that Parks had taken a lot of money left over from his inheritance and the early success of his gunrunning company and bought the twelve acres and the shipping containers about a year after he left the Middle East. "He had crews in here for almost three years, excavating, making it just the way he wanted," she said and pushed the door open.

I'd expected to find Parks's fortress a dim warren of small musty rooms stuffed like a pack rat's nest with supplies. Instead, he had cut out the floors and some of the walls of the containers to create a large living space with vaulted ceilings and skylights that were made of bulletproof glass.

The place was decorated spartanly with steel furniture and fixtures. One of the chairs at the table was turned over on its back. There were bloodstains on the floor and on the wall beyond the chair.

"He died right there?" Mahoney asked.

She nodded. "Twelve-gauge buckshot to the throat. Almost decapitated him."

I said, "The throat's not usually the target in a male gun suicide."

"Exactly," Toof said. "They usually put it to the mouth or the side of the head."

"And every once in a while, under the jaw," Agent Beaufort said.

Mahoney said, "That can't be the only reason you think he was murdered."

"It's not," the detective said. "We'll come back after you see the armory and the practice range. They matter."

CHAPTER

53

DETECTIVE TOOF LED US past pantries with floor-to-ceiling shelves filled with canned and dry goods into the three-story west wing of the fortress.

Having seen the shooting slits in the walls, I figured we were climbing up the spiral staircase rising from the floor. But Toof went to the far corner and waved her hand across a motion sensor.

A large plate in the floor slid back, revealing a shiny metal chute.

"It's a spiral slide to the lower level," she said. "Don't worry, there's a way out." With that, Toof got into the slide and pushed off. She disappeared around the bend.

"I'd rather go down another way," Mahoney said, but he got in and slid out of sight.

Agent Beaufort went next, and I followed, going down a full corkscrew that spit me out into a foam pit.

"It's the only thing I like about this place," Toof said, then she took us through a door and turned on a light revealing a space about half the size of the living area upstairs.

Mahoney and I both gasped. The walls on three sides featured floor-to-ceiling lockable rack systems bulging with guns, sporting and military.

"His father started the collection with the rare hunting rifles and shotguns," Toof said. "The rest belonged to Leslie, and he had federal firearms licenses for all of them."

She walked us over to the fourth wall, which was mostly covered in sports paraphernalia, collectibles, and photographs of Leslie Parks with various athletes. An elaborate shooting bench faced the only blank space on the wall.

Toof flipped a switch, illuminating a hundred-yard tunnel with a bullet backstop at the end.

"He used to shoot in here all the time, and no one knew that was possible," she said. "Well, the contractors knew because they built it."

I left the shooting range and walked around the room, looking at what had to be hundreds if not thousands of weapons, wondering what possessed someone to buy this many guns. Then I realized the collection was probably all he'd had left of his father and kind of understood the compulsion.

I returned to the sports wall and was looking at the various signed and framed hockey, baseball, and football jerseys when Mahoney said, "Why isn't Parks's death a suicide? No note?"

"No, there was a note," Detective Toof said. "It said, 'I hate who I have become.'"

"And?"

"I talked to his PTSD counselor, who described Parks as suffering a mild case compared to a lot of his clients."

"Lot of people with mild symptoms kill themselves," I said, still looking at the photographs, many of them taken at major sporting events, the World Series, the Super Bowl, and so forth.

"One hundred percent," Toof replied. "But those people didn't have an Iraqi refugee living with them around the time of their deaths, a refugee who has not been seen or heard from since someone with a machine gun on the ridge above us tried to shoot Chris Lunt down."

"Name?"

"Ibrahim. No surname. Multiple people saw Parks driving around with the guy in the month before his death. Two older women down the road who share mailbox space with Parks said he stopped there to get his mail and introduced the man as Ibrahim, an old friend from his time working in the Middle East.

"And the only neighbor who ever socialized with Parks said the man was introduced to him as Ibrahim, an old friend from Parks's days in Iraq and Syria, a refugee who was looking for work as an engineer in the Raleigh area."

Mahoney and I exchanged glances at the Iraqi's profession. Ibrahim was an engineer. Someone who could design and build a remote-controlled machine gun.

Mahoney said, "Why do you think this Ibrahim killed Parks? I mean, is there a fifty-caliber machine gun missing here?"

"Maybe."

That answer made me turn away from the wall.

"Maybe?" Ned said.

"You tell me," Toof said and went to a device mounted on the rear wall of the room. "It's a retina-scan control for that." She was pointing at the floor and a round galvanized steel lid, like the one that covered the corkscrew slide.

"I had to have welders come up and cut it open just the other day. I don't know what all is down there. I took one look, saw what I saw, came straight out, and contacted the FBI and the U.S. attorney's office overseeing the case."

"Smart," Mahoney said. He helped her push the hatch lid aside, revealing a straight steel ladder dropping into darkness.

Toof got on the ladder, climbed down several rungs, and reached under the lip of the hatch. She flipped a switch that lit up the space beneath her and climbed down to a concrete floor.

Mahoney went after her. I followed, with Agent Beaufort behind me.

The room was as large as the one above it but had a much lower ceiling and smelled faintly of gun oil and cleaning solvent. Most of the shelving was stocked with ammunition of various calibers. Hundreds of thousands of rounds.

By the time I'd gotten down the ladder, Mahoney was with Toof over at the base of the far wall. They were looking into an open, weathered wood crate some six feet long, four feet deep, and three wide. The lid lay beside it.

"Could that hold a big machine gun?" Toof said.

"You've touched it?" Mahoney asked.

She shook her head. "I saw it. I backed out. I called."

With gloved hands, Mahoney lifted the lid and turned it over. Something that looked like a serial code was stenciled on the wood. There was nothing on any of the sides of the crate, so he had me help him turn it over.

"Damn," I said. "There it is."

Stenciled on the bottom of the crate was the same serial code along with the blurred words BROWNING ARMS CO., USA, .50 CAL. AUTO RIFLE, FEB. 1967.

"This entire fortress is a crime scene," Mahoney said.

"I knew it!" Detective Toof cried. "I knew it was him!"

Mahoney made for the ladder. "We need a forensics crew in here."

"Agent Mahoney?" Agent Beaufort called from deeper into the room. She stood next to three olive-green boxes, one with an open lid. "You're going to want to see this."

Mahoney, Toof, and I walked over. The open box was empty except for what looked like a small rusted missile cradled in foam.

"That's a Stinger," Mahoney said. "One of ours."

"Looks old," I said. "Too old to work."

"Maybe that's why only the launcher's missing," Beaufort said.

Mahoney went to the two other boxes, lifted the lids, and went pale. "Son of a bitch," he said. "Son of a son of a bitch."

In both boxes, shoulder-mounted rocket launchers lay in protective foam. But the rockets and their explosive tips were missing.

CHAPTER

54

JOHN SAMPSON RAPPED FOR the fifth time on the front door of Bowman's around eleven that morning, a solid hour before the sports bar was due to open. Sampson figured the manager or someone would be around already, and he was right.

A big dude in a Washington Nationals T-shirt finally came to the inner door, shook his head, and yelled, "We're closed! Still!"

Sampson held up his badge, and the dude sighed and opened the door.

"I'm Tommy Bowman," he said. "The owner. What's this about?"

"John Sampson, DC Metro Homicide on loan to the U.S. attorney here in Virginia."

"Homicide? Here?"

"No, sir. I just need to take a look at your security tape from last Sunday noon. Check out someone's alibi."

Bowman hesitated. "So we—my place and my staff, I mean—have nothing to do with this, whatever it is, right?"

"As far as I know, Mr. Bowman," Sampson said.

"C'mon in, then," he said. "Anything for law enforcement."

Bowman led Sampson to his office, which was spartan and tidy with two desks and two computers. He gestured to one of them.

"I'll feed the tape to you there, if you don't mind," he said. "I've got a couple things I have to attend to."

"No worries," Sampson said, sitting down.

Bowman went to the other desk and computer, typed instructions on his keyboard, and said, "Coming at you." He crossed to Sampson, shook the mouse, and accepted an airdrop message he'd sent. A fairly large file downloaded and opened.

"That's from eleven on," Bowman said. "We open early on Sundays during football season."

"Because some fans want to watch the pregame shows with a cold one or a Bloody Mary," Sampson said.

"As long as someone else drives," Bowman said. "We watch our patrons. We're known for it."

"Good to hear," Sampson said. "Thank you."

"Anytime," Bowman said and went back to his desk.

Sampson thought about what Captain Davis's assistant coach had said, about Davis being at Bowman's around one p.m. He called up the feed on the saloon's front door and fast-forwarded it to 12:45.

He found Coach Penny and Davis on the recording at 12:49 p.m. Sampson switched to the restaurant's internal security cameras and watched them go to a high table in front of three big screens.

Many people in the bar seemed to know the former NFL

player; they gave him high fives as they passed. Sampson sped up the feed a little, making sure to keep track of Davis and Penny as the games began and the waitress brought their drinks, beers for both.

Sampson kept waiting for Davis to encounter the mystery woman, which he did at 2:12 that afternoon. Coach Penny was standing at another table talking to two women and a guy when she appeared on the video.

She was as Coach Penny had described her. Or at least she seemed to be; it was hard for Sampson to tell because of the camera's high, wide-angle perspective, looking down from the ceiling in a corner of the room.

But the woman was wearing a Baltimore Ravens tank top and she was certainly turning heads as she crossed the room. She paused every now and then to scan the bar as if she was looking for someone.

The third time she paused, Davis was no more than five feet away. If she was targeting the football coach, she didn't show it. Indeed, Davis seemed to initiate conversation with her. After a few moments, she threw her arms wide and hugged him.

They chatted animatedly. Coach Penny kept talking with the three people at the next table as he watched the game, occasionally glancing at Davis. When Penny got up and went to the restroom twenty minutes later, the mystery woman and Captain Davis moved to another table and ordered more drinks.

They partied for a good hour, during which she got up to use the restroom twice and Davis got up once. During his absence, she checked her phone and sipped from a cocktail. At one point, she reached across the table for a napkin, picked it up, dabbed at her cheek with it, then crumpled it and set it aside.

Something about that looked strange, so Sampson rewound

it and replayed the feed a couple of times. He noticed that her hand passed directly over Davis's glass as she reached for the napkin. The film didn't have enough resolution for him to see if her fingers had parted as they passed over the glass.

But that could have been a drop, right there. If it was, she's good at this. She's played this game before. And she keeps her head tilted down all the time. I haven't gotten a clear look at her yet.

About fifteen minutes after his return from the restroom, Davis and mystery woman were getting snuggly. She said something to him. He roared with laughter. He threw down cash and they got up. Davis put his arm around her, and she held tight to his waist. Next, Sampson picked them up on the front entrance camera, walking away.

They stopped halfway down the parking lot and kissed. Then they got in a white Jeep Grand Cherokee, the woman at the wheel. The vehicle started, drove forward, turned left, and took the exit farthest from the bar. Sampson rewound the feed from the front door again and used a zoom tool to look at the Jeep as it made the left.

Davis appeared to be slumped against the passenger-side window. Or had he just turned around to face the mystery woman? Sampson couldn't tell.

He was, however, able to zoom in and read the SUV's West Virginia license plate. He wrote the number down, feeling like he was finally getting somewhere.

Sampson thought about everything he'd seen and then realized there was one angle he hadn't examined. Still using the front-door camera feed, he reversed the film and slowed it to a crawl at 1:12 p.m.

The Cherokee entered the parking lot by the same west entrance it later left from. The driver got out; she wore a

Baltimore Ravens cap low over her sunglasses as she walked directly toward the front door and the camera. If she'd continued in that manner, Sampson would have had nothing.

But before she reached the front door of the bar, a red Corvette convertible sped by and passed so close to the mystery woman that she jumped back.

The sunglasses fell. The hat was knocked askew. She threw her arms wide and apparently yelled at the car going deeper into the lot. Then she tore off her hat, swung a mane of thick brunette hair around, jammed the hat back on, and retrieved her sunglasses.

Her face was hidden again as she entered Bowman's. But Sampson believed he had what he needed.

He reversed the feed slowly and stopped it at the moment when she was swinging her hair and her entire face was revealed.

"Got you," Sampson said.

CHAPTER

55

AROUND NOON, BREE SAT down to eat lunch with Jannie and Nana Mama. Ali had gone out on his bicycle. Tina Dawson had decided to spend the night with her team rather than at Jannie's house.

"She's running in the race today? Shouldn't she go home after experiencing something like that?" Nana Mama asked.

"You mean finding Iliana?" Bree said. "I don't know. Jannie? What do you think?"

Jannie thought about it. "I mean, if they were best friends, it would be a little weird, I guess. But they only met recently, and Tina's like I am."

"And how's that?" Alex's grandmother asked.

"Athletically competitive, Nana," Jannie said. "And focused."

"Oh, I get that," Nana said. "People are all pulled in some

203

direction or another. Some competitive. Some not. Some book-ish. Some not. Some good with numbers."

"And some not!" Jannie said, laughing as she held up her hand.

Her great-grandmother smiled. "And some are pulled to teach. And still are."

Bree studied Nana Mama. "You miss it? Teaching?"

Alex's grandmother had spent decades teaching high-school English, and she'd been the vice principal of a local high school. "Of course I miss teaching," Nana said. "It was my calling. It still is."

Bree noticed that she said this not with gloom or melancholy but with kind of a glow about her.

Jannie said, "Nana, you teach me something every day."

"Me too," Bree said.

The older woman shrugged. "It's not enough for me to cook and chat with each of you as you come and go about your busy lives. I still have too much energy, too much to give. And I feel like it's all bottled up inside of me and going to waste."

This kind of surprised Bree. It wasn't often you heard a woman in her nineties talk this way. But then again, Alex's grandmother was no ordinary woman.

Jannie said, "Well, you could find another way to teach. You know, where you don't have to go to a school."

At that, Nana broke into a wide grin and chuckled. "That is exactly right. I'm going on Zoom and maybe YouTube."

"To teach what?"

"High-school English," she said. "It's what I do best. I've already spoken with the principal at my old school. She was happy to hear that I was willing to talk online about various books on juniors' and seniors' reading lists. If it works out, I'll offer my services to the entire district. Or whoever wants to listen."

"Wow," Bree said, sitting back. "Well, good for you."

Jannie's brows knitted. "Does this mean no more great food?"

"It means I may need help making great food once in a while."

Bree smiled. "That can happen. Have you told Alex about this yet?"

"Not yet," she said. "But I am still capable of making my own decisions, you know. I haven't taken to wandering around the neighborhood in my nightie or anything."

Bree and Jannie burst into laughter. "No," Bree said. "You're a long way from that."

"Well, good," Nana said. She smiled broadly, and then her eyes went to the clock on the far wall. "Don't you have to leave for that race?"

"Oh God," Jannie said, jumping up. "Will we make the start?"

"We'll try," Bree said. "After we clean up for Nana."

CHAPTER

56

Arlington, Virginia

SAMPSON FOUND U.S. ATTORNEY Rebecca Cantrell at her office that afternoon. She was dressed down in jeans, running shoes, and a snug red fleece top that set off her dark brown eyes and mahogany hair.

"You have more time to work on this, Detective Sampson," Cantrell said, waving him to a seat in front of her desk.

"I think I've found enough already," he said.

"To do what?"

"Let Captain Davis go."

"What?" the U.S. attorney said, sitting forward and looking skeptical.

He described going to Bowman's and seeing the security recordings, then showed her the pertinent clips, including the possible drop of a drug into Davis's drink, the suggestion of Davis slumped in the front seat of the Jeep Cherokee, the West

Virginia license plate, and the video still of the woman with her hair in the wind and her face exposed.

"I'm not convinced on the drop of the drug," she said.

"I'm leaning toward it. The license plate was stolen two days ago. Belongs on a Ford pickup truck registered to a college kid from Seneca Rocks, West Virginia."

Cantrell thought about that. "You think she stalked Davis? That he's the fall guy and she's part of the frame?"

"I'm saying I'm not buying the crab-boil story, and the mystery woman is why."

She sat back in her seat and for the first time Sampson noticed just how striking the U.S. attorney for the Eastern District of Virginia was.

Cantrell did not seem to be aware that he was studying her. "We also got a report from Quantico on the signature on that fragment of the van-rental agreement found in Gravelly Point Park. There's something off about it."

"Is it a forgery?"

"You could argue duress or forgery. Which means any good defense attorney is going to bring it up in court."

"You've still got the bomb residue," Sampson said.

"Do I? Defense will argue that this mystery woman at Bowman's could have planted it, in which case she's an accessory before and after the fact."

"And a hundred percent connected to the downing of the American Airlines jet."

Cantrell nodded, considering something. "You know, we could have found her DNA on that jumpsuit with the bomb residue on it. But we didn't. In fact, we didn't find anybody's DNA besides Davis's, and it's all near the collar, the wrists, and the ankles."

"As if the DNA was planted."

She smiled sourly. "That's the way I'm leaning."

"Nothing else?"

"Mahoney just called me," she said, and explained about the dead gunrunner, his friend Ibrahim, and the missing .50-caliber machine gun and Stinger missiles.

"But we were told those missiles were all accounted for."

"We were told wrong."

"But unless you have a link from Leslie Parks and Ibrahim to Captain Davis, what do we really have on him?"

Cantrell brooded on that for a few moments before conceding, "Not much that wouldn't get tossed out in court."

"Then you don't have much of a choice, do you?"

"No. I'll call the holding facility and have him released."

"Sorry to disappoint you," Sampson said, getting to his feet.

She got up as well and gazed into his eyes with curiosity. It made him feel a little awkward. "No disappointment whatsoever, Detective," she said. "I asked you to do a job and you did it extremely well."

Sampson did not break eye contact. "Need any more work like that done? Or do I go back to my other cases?"

Cantrell studied him a moment longer, then looked away and laughed. "I'm trying to figure out some way to keep you around, but I'm failing, I'm afraid."

"Oh," he said. "That's good."

"That's good?" she said, looking at him with amusement.

"I think so," Sampson said. "Because once I'm no longer on official loan to you, it isn't a conflict of interest for us to go have a late lunch somewhere."

Cantrell took a step back, but the amusement mostly remained. "You're asking me out on a date, Detective?"

"I don't know you well enough for a date. It's just lunch. Unless you're taken?"

"Taken?" She laughed. "I'm taken by the job. By this investigation."

"All the more reason to go out to lunch with me."

She looked at him, a little puzzled, a little pleased. "But why?"

"I don't know," Sampson said. "I'm usually fairly shy, but I was just sitting there, and, I don't know, I felt compelled to ask you."

"Compelled?"

"That's what it felt like."

She squinted one eye. "Age? Marital history? Kids?"

Sampson said, "Forty-six. Widower. A seven-year-old daughter, Willow."

Cantrell's expression melted a little. She said, "Forty-eight. Widow. Never had the pleasure."

They stood there and stared in silence at each other for several long moments.

"Well, Rebecca?" Sampson said finally.

She smiled a little bit more. "Okay, John. I'll go have a late lunch with you. But we talk about the case."

"And nothing else."

CHAPTER

57

Fairfax, Virginia

BREE AND JANNIE HURRIED toward the field for the NCAA cross-country race at George Mason University.

"We missed the start." Jannie groaned.

"No one cares about the start," Bree said. "Only the finish."

Jannie frowned. "I care about the start."

"I'm talking ordinary spectators," Bree said. "Oh, there's Detective Creighton."

The Fairfax County detective saw Bree and they walked to each other.

"Anything?" Bree asked.

"Murder weapon," she said quietly. "Like you thought. Sharp rock."

"Where was it?"

"On the bank by the jacket. Covered with blood and brain matter."

"Nothing else?"

"A few things I'd like to keep close to the vest, though the Airbnb owner needs to hire a new maid."

"How's that?"

The detective's nostrils flared. "The shower in the smaller bathroom had dirt and hair in it. And the toilet in there looked like it hadn't been cleaned in weeks."

"Lovely," Bree said. "Where next?"

"I'm heading to suburban Philly to talk with Iliana's high-school coach," she said. "Steve Hawley."

"You might also check out this coach at Paxson State," Bree said. "Thayer. He supposedly knew she was renting the Airbnb."

The first group of women runners appeared.

Jannie cried, "Tina's right there with the top girls!"

"Nice, but I've got to go," Creighton said. "Good seeing you, Bree."

"I'll be in touch," Bree said, and she turned to watch with Jannie as the knot of the five leading women came unraveled in the last two hundred yards.

Tina Dawson held her own and finished third. Coach Neely and Coach Leclerc were thrilled and gave each other high fives, but Bree didn't think Dawson was all that happy as she came up to them.

"That looked great," Jannie said.

Tina smiled briefly. "Thanks. I really thought I had them. The leaders."

"Still a podium. You'll get them next time."

Coach Neely came over and said, "I think you were running for Iliana out there."

"I was," Tina said. "Definitely."

But again, it was half-hearted.

Bree and Jannie congratulated them all once more and then started back to the car. They were just exiting the campus when Jannie pointed across the street at a blond woman, walking away, head down, shoulders heaving.

"Bree, that's her, Nancy," Jannie said. "Iliana's mother."

They ran across the street, dodging a few cars, and down the block to a parking lot. They caught up to the dead girl's mom as she was opening the door to her car.

"Hi, Mrs. Meadows," Jannie said. "It's me, Jannie Cross."

The woman stared at her in some bewilderment before nodding. "I remember you. Always kind to Iliana. She liked you very much."

"And I liked her. She was such a good person. I'm so sorry for your loss."

"I am too," Iliana's mother said and started to blubber. "I only just got back from Italy. I talked with her on the phone, and now she's gone. Just gone."

Bree caught a whiff of alcohol on the woman's breath. "Mrs. Meadows? I'm Jannie's stepmother. Are you all right to drive?"

"Not really," she said. "I plan on sleeping in the car awhile before I drive home. I haven't slept in...I can't remember."

"You're sure?"

"I am," she said, sliding into the front seat. "I just want to take a nap and then try to find the strength to arrange the funeral of my only child."

Bree didn't have it in her to ask about Iliana's high-school coach, the alleged sex tape, and who might have had access to it. Instead, she said, "Jannie mentioned that Iliana had good coaches in high school. Shouldn't they be notified?"

"Of course," Mrs. Meadows said, nodding and yawning.

"Steven Hawley and Lily Christopher. I'm sure they'll be crushed. And now, I do have to sleep."

She shut the door, put her sunglasses back on, and lowered the seat.

"Steven Hawley and Lily Christopher," Jannie said as she and Bree walked away. "I know them. They were coaches at that training camp where Iliana and I met."

CHAPTER

58

Albemarle, North Carolina

NED MAHONEY WATCHED AS the first crew of forensics experts prepared to enter the late Leslie Parks's fortress around three that afternoon. They were all wearing hazmat suits to prevent further evidence contamination inside.

"I want you to focus on the suicide area and the empty crates in the subbasement," Mahoney told the criminalists. "That's where I think we're most likely to pick up Ibrahim's fingerprints or DNA, but I want the entire place dusted and examined while we continue the search."

"Who's been inside already?" the head forensics tech said.

"The four of us," Detective Toof said. "And the county medical examiner and the two guys from the funeral home. Otherwise, it's been sealed."

Mahoney said, "You were the one who found Parks, correct?"

Toof nodded. "I went up to look for machine-gun casings on the cliff and knocked when I came back down. There was no answer. I tried the door. It opened. Parks was sitting right there. Been dead for days. I called the ME, who saw the shotgun and the note and immediately ruled it a suicide. But here, check the writing."

She went to her phone and pulled up a picture of the suicide note. "See? It looks shaky, forced."

I studied the six-word explanation for Parks's death: *I hate who I have become.*

The writing *was* shaky. "Then again," I said, "he was about to kill himself."

"He didn't," Toof insisted. "Ibrahim killed him. I mean, we know he stole the machine gun and the missiles, right?"

Agent Beaufort said, "Unless Parks was so upset about giving Ibrahim the weapons that he blew his own head off."

That annoyed Toof.

"Either way, Ibrahim is now our prime suspect," Mahoney said. "Let's go back in and search the bedrooms and the offices, see if he made a mistake."

"Parks left three computers—a laptop in the bedroom and two desktops in the office," Toof said. "Should be some good stuff there."

"Show me," Mahoney said. He looked at Agent Beaufort. "Start with the bedrooms. Be thorough. If you find something, get me."

The young FBI agent beamed and nodded. "Right away, SAC."

I put on blue booties, a mask, and gloves and followed them back inside. Toof and Mahoney went to secure the computers and Beaufort left to search the bedrooms, and I decided to explore the upper three floors of the wings at either end of the all-steel structure.

I'd seen the slit windows from the exterior but found them on all sides of the long rectangular and empty rooms on the upper two floors in the west wing. Each slit was equipped with openable windows made of bulletproof glass.

I could almost see Parks up here, imagining society falling apart and his fortress under attack. Extremely effective defensively, the slit windows would have allowed the gunrunner and his allies to shoot down on anyone crossing the open ground surrounding his redoubt.

I returned to the east wing, climbed up, and saw the upper two floors were similarly designed and equally empty, so I decided to go back to Parks's gun room. It seemed to be the only place in the house where he revealed anything about himself.

Staying out of the way of the crime scene techs, I walked around the armory, amazed again that a single person could own so many weapons. I didn't know much about valuable guns, but I vaguely recognized names like Purdey and A. H. Fox on the fine shotguns and Zeiss and Leica on the telescopic sights of the hunting rifles.

But I knew next to nothing about modern military weapons and skipped them, heading again toward that rear wall where Parks had hung various pictures and sports collectibles. I found where I'd left off earlier in the day and was soon looking at several rows of framed photos that began with the gunrunner at the Olympic Games in London and then one of him in Fenway Park on the Green Monster with a beer in one hand, his arm around a swarthy guy with a beard and sunglasses.

It had a date on it. The picture had been taken quite recently, back in September. *How long ago did Toof say the neighbors saw Ibrahim? Could this be the same guy?*

I was about to go upstairs and tell Mahoney about the photograph when I happened to glance down.

The picture below and left of the Fenway Park shot had been taken in Honolulu eight years before. It stopped me cold.

59

UPON CAPTAIN DAVIS'S RELEASE from the federal lockup in Alexandria, his attorney told him that his home was still an FBI crime scene, so he should rent a hotel room with room service in DC and lay low until the media calmed down and the facts came out to fully exonerate him.

Furious at having been jailed and having his good name smeared, Davis had almost followed through on the advice. Instead, he decided he had to retrieve his car and get a few things out of his office at the Charles School.

When he arrived in an Uber, however, he found his car gone and a football game under way. He could hear the crowd roaring and then the announcer crowing, "Touchdown, Clint Maxwell! Touchdown, Charles School, on a bull-like five-yard run!"

Despite his foul mood at finding his car gone, Davis grinned and had to fight not to run to the stadium and join the celebration over Maxwell's touchdown. He'd been working with the sophomore fullback on keeping the ball tight to his body so he wouldn't be stripped of it, and here he was, scoring against one of their fiercest rivals in a goal-line situation.

Davis sighed and went into the school and down a deserted hallway, heading for the field house.

"Coach Davis?" Nicholas Hampstead III said. "What are you doing here? Where do you think you're going?"

Groaning internally, he turned to face the headmaster. "The feds released me for lack of evidence."

Hampstead looked annoyed. "Well," he said, "that's all well and good for you, but I have recommended, and the board concurs, that you be terminated. Your services are no longer needed or welcome at the Charles School. We just can't have that kind of negative publicity; it will do irreparable harm to our stellar reputation."

Davis felt like decking the little puke but he kept his cool and said, "Again, I was released for *lack of evidence.* And now you can count on a lawsuit for wrongful termination. I'll be seeking damages that will make your stellar bug eyes pop right out of their sockets."

Hampstead's shoulders tensed. "Get out. I have a thyroid condition."

Davis heard a door shut somewhere. "Who cares, bug eyes? I'm going to my office and getting my things."

The headmaster sputtered, "That office was sealed by the FBI, and you are leaving. Now. You are no longer the football coach of the Charles School, and I will call the police and have you forcibly removed if I have to."

Davis caught a flicker of motion down the hall beyond

Hampstead and saw Fiona Plum standing just inside the front doors.

"See you in court, bug eyes," Davis said and he brushed by the little man, heading toward the English teacher and the front door.

"We'll countersue," Hampstead called after him. "For damage to our reputation and brand."

The former coach raised his middle finger overhead and kept walking.

"Captain?" Fiona Plum said, smiling nervously as she looked past him at the headmaster glaring her way. "When did you get out?"

"An hour ago," he said, brushing by her and exiting through the front doors.

She followed him. "I'm so happy. I knew that attorney was good."

Davis, still furious, stopped halfway down the front steps of the school and looked at her. "The U.S. attorney released me for lack of evidence. My attorney had nothing to do with it."

"Oh," she said, her face falling. "Of course."

He felt bad, but he wanted to punch something. "Look, Fiona, I really do appreciate you finding her for me. She's smart and you are...something else for sticking up for me."

Fiona Plum raised her chin a little. "I believe in you, Captain."

"I know you do," he said, and hesitated. "Someone's been trying to frame me, Fiona, and I don't get it. Why me?"

A police cruiser came into the parking lot. "He called the cops," Davis said, and he started walking. "That little bug-eyed freak." He waved at the officer in the cruiser as he passed him, saying, "Just leaving."

The cop nodded. Fiona Plum ran after him. "Where are you going?"

"To get a drink and then a hotel room because my house is a goddamn crime scene, Fiona."

"Don't go to a hotel room," she said. "We'll rent you a car and you can stay at my place. I have an extra bedroom, and you know what? You deserve a drink after what you've been through. I think we both do."

Davis turned to her and saw the way she was looking at him.

He finally surrendered. "Okay, Fiona. You're on."

CHAPTER

60

JOHN SAMPSON AND REBECCA CANTRELL walked to a nearby café and sat outside next to a heater. Despite their different stations in life, he found her easy to talk to.

After ordering, they spoke about the missing machine gun, launcher, and missiles in North Carolina and about the police sketch artists that Mahoney had working with Parks's neighbors to come up with a likeness of Ibrahim.

"The entire focus is on finding this guy now?" Sampson said.

"Has to be," Cantrell said, nodding. "Unless there are third parties we don't know about, he's the only one who had access to a Vietnam-era Browning fifty-caliber."

"What I want to know is what he's got planned for the Stingers."

"If they work," she said. "They're notorious for degrading over time."

"So we're praying for duds?"

"We're determined to find Ibrahim before he even thinks of trying to fire one," she said firmly. "And we will."

Sampson got a text from Willow asking when he'd be home. He told her around six thirty. She was at Alex's house with Nana Mama and Ali.

Even though they'd promised to keep the conversation focused on the AA 839 case, Cantrell asked about Sampson's daughter. He told her how she loved ballet and summer camp and going to Alex Cross's house to hang out with his family.

"You light up when you talk about her."

"Willow is easy to light up about." That led him in a roundabout way to talking about Billie's sudden and tragic death from a heart attack brought on by complications of Lyme disease and how it had hit him like a sledgehammer.

"Ronny died just over three years ago. Drunk dump-truck driver T-boned his car on the way home from work. He died instantly. My entire life outside my job was gone."

"I'm sorry to hear that. Billie passed in the ER where she worked. I miss her."

"What was the best thing about your Billie?"

"How resilient she was and how much she loved our life together. You?"

"Ronny's vision and his genuine compassion for people. And the way he made me feel in his arms."

Sampson saw the sudden glassiness in her eyes and felt a wave of longing for Billie's touch and smell.

Cantrell said, "But enough about—"

The waiter arrived with their lunches. At almost the same time, their cell phones rang. She looked at her screen. "I have to take this."

Alex was calling Sampson. "Me too."

"You've heard about what we're onto down here?" Alex asked when Sampson answered. "About the dead gunrunner and the missing weapons?"

"And Ibrahim," Sampson said. "The U.S. attorney just informed me."

"I'm sending you two pictures. Guy on the left at Fenway in the first pic is Leslie Parks. Guy on the right could be Ibrahim."

"And the second pic?"

"Speaks for itself. Got to jump. I'll call back." Alex hung up.

Cantrell was listening to her phone intently. "You're sure?" the U.S. attorney said, briefly closing her eyes and shaking her head. "Okay. Let me know if there's more."

She ended the call and looked at Sampson as his phone buzzed with the arrival of the pictures. "We may have screwed up a little," she said as he opened them.

He looked up. "How's that?"

"Captain Davis," she said. "After he came back from the Middle East, he spent six months as an air force–army liaison at Fort Bragg, North Carolina, which is not far from where Mahoney and Cross are. Thirty minutes, tops."

Sampson nodded. He looked at the pictures and felt his stomach sink. "I may have screwed up big-time," he said, and showed her a picture of Leslie Parks taken at the Pro Bowl with his arm around the shoulder of Captain Davis.

Cantrell immediately got to her feet. "We have to go."

"We haven't eaten."

"We'll box the food and take it," she insisted. "I need you back on Davis. Now. Which means you're back working for me, and this late lunch *is* a conflict of interest."

Sampson smiled. "Promise me you'll fire me when this is over so I can at least get to know you better?"

Cantrell dipped her head to one side and smiled back at him. "The second we catch Davis and Ibrahim, you are getting tossed overboard."

"Can't wait to hit the water," he said.

CHAPTER

61

CAPTAIN DAVIS RENTED A Chevy Cavalier, then followed Fiona Plum to her house. She gave him the fifty-cent tour of a little bungalow she'd bought and renovated the year before.

The modern kitchen opened to a nice living area with lots of books and a small television that looked rarely used. There were three bedrooms upstairs. She showed him the room with the bunk beds for her nieces, who often visited, and the guest bedroom with a queen bed.

"You'll stay here," she said. "Bathroom is across the hall. I'm all the way back."

"Thank you, Fiona," he said, putting the clothes and toiletries he'd bought on the bed. "You're a good person. A very good person for helping me in so many ways lately."

She beamed. "I do not abandon friends in need. Never."

"Well, I'm glad. Shall we celebrate my release from jail and coaching?"

"Your release from jail," she said. She turned and started back down the stairs. "Once the board members come to their senses, you'll be right back on the sideline for the Fighting Badgers."

"Maybe," Davis replied, following her. "But maybe it's time I see what my record at the Charles School is worth."

Plum hesitated at the bottom of the stairs. "What? Schools in this area? Our league?"

"If I thought they had the kind of potential I'm looking for," he said. "But maybe I've been thinking too small. Maybe I should be talking to Division One colleges. Or even the pros. I still know a lot of people."

"I'm sure you do," she said, entering the kitchen. "What would you like to drink?"

"What do you have?"

"Anything your heart desires," Plum said and she opened a cabinet that was well-stocked with liquor.

Davis gaped.

"What?" she asked.

"I don't know," Davis said. "I guess I didn't expect that from you."

Plum laughed. "I like to be surprising. I put myself through school bartending."

Davis examined the contents of the cabinet for a moment, then said, "I should probably just have a beer."

"A beer?" she said, sounding slightly insulted. "C'mon, where's the adventure? Coach Penny says you're a bourbon man."

He smiled. "Coach Penny talks too much, but yes, I like bourbon now and then."

"You're lucky," she said and opened another cabinet, revealing at least fifteen different kinds of bourbon. "I inherited this collection from my dad after he passed." Plum pulled out a medium-size glass jug that was half full. "This was his favorite. Single-pot from a distiller in Alabama who has also passed."

Davis hesitated, then said, "I'll give it a try."

The English teacher found two cut-crystal glasses, got two large cubes from the freezer, and poured a finger of the liquor over each. She handed him a glass, raised hers, and said, "Congratulations on being released, Captain."

"Thank you," Davis said and took a sip. "Wow, that is good. Starts out with a smooth burn and finishes caramel."

"Uh-huh," Plum said, sipping hers. "And makes you want more."

"That could get dangerous," he said.

"Maybe that's the idea," she said, then laughed and turned away.

Davis smiled, thinking that he had never seen the teacher like this. She wasn't her normal staid self; she was free and relaxed. Plum opened the fridge, looked over her shoulder, saw Davis watching her, and laughed again.

He drank more of the bourbon and reached for the jug. "May I?"

"Please do," she said. "I'll get us something to nibble on."

Davis popped the cork and poured more bourbon into his glass. "What do you do around here other than read?"

When Plum turned away from the fridge, she had several kinds of cheese in her hand and a frown on her face. "You have something against reading?"

"No, no," he said and compulsively took another sip. "I was just wondering."

She put the cheese down. "I listen to music. I garden. And I am learning to take care of the house with all the tools left by the last owner."

"Really," Davis said, interested. "Where are they?"

Plum gestured to the door behind Davis. "Down in the basement. An entire shop next to the laundry, plus all the gardening equipment they didn't want to take with them to Florida."

"Where's the garden?" he asked.

She gestured across the living area to two curtained French doors. "A lot of work, but I love it."

The booze was hitting him. The teacher's face had flushed, her pupils were slightly dilated, and she had this happy-go-lucky air about her. *This could work out after all.* "Show me your garden," he said.

"Tomorrow."

"C'mon," Davis said in a kidding tone. "I just…"

"What?" she asked.

"I loved the way you looked just then, talking about your garden. I want to see what you look like out in your garden."

Plum grinned at him. "But it's cold and dark out there."

"No lights?" he said.

"No, there are lights."

"Then it's just a matter of the right jackets, hats, and a little more of your daddy's favorite to take with us." He poured himself more bourbon and gazed at Plum with arched eyebrows.

She laughed and looked wildly happy. "Yes, please. I'll get my jacket." She hurried from the room.

"Perfect," Davis said, and poured two more fingers of bourbon in her glass.

CHAPTER

62

MARION DAVIS WAITED FOR the dose he'd slipped into Fiona's third drink to take full effect, then left her sprawled on her belly across the bed, face over a bucket in case she vomited. With the drug in her, she wouldn't crack an eye open for another twelve hours easy.

Davis had seen the drug work time and again. It was what he used at critical moments when he needed to silence someone close and get work done without any possibility of interruption.

He went out to his car and retrieved two rectangular hard-sided cases that could have held rifles or guitars, though they held neither. He went straight to the basement door off the kitchen and opened it. He flipped on the lights, climbed down the stairs, passed the laundry room, and went through a man cave of sorts to a door on the far side of it.

He opened it and entered a long, narrow space with an equally long bench against the left wall. He found a pull cord and switched on a bank of overhead lights.

Davis gave the extensive tool collection a sweeping glance. Satisfied, he opened the first case. The shoulder-mounted stock, shooting mechanism, and sight of the Stinger were all snuggled in cavities in the foam he'd cut with an electric knife.

He opened the second case, brought out the two warheads, and began to methodically take them apart according to diagrams he'd brought with him.

Davis had always taken things apart. Some of his earliest and fondest memories were of dismantling devices and then putting them back together or modifying them.

Indeed, everything in Davis's recent life had followed from that first love of all things mechanical and technical as well as the deep and secret hatred he felt toward the United States and Americans in general.

He'd seen up close what their corruption had done to Afghanistan.

To Iraq.

To Syria.

Their unrelenting sleaze had turned Davis radical eventually, made him willing to speak and act one way, while believing the exact opposite in his heart. The clerics had a term for it—*taqiyya*—a special dispensation for acting in secrecy, for taking on false identities, and for engaging in deceptions and destruction in the name of a greater good.

Davis had been cloaking his true aims for more than a decade by then, first with the US military, and then stateside with all the people who mattered, the people in power. Never slipping. Never letting on who he really was deep inside.

And planning, he thought as he got the rocket casing off the missile, exposing the primitive electronics and crude circuit boards. *Always planning.*

Davis accepted the fact that it had been his old friend Leslie Parks who first taught him the importance of working out contingencies before entering questionable legal terrain and therefore possible law enforcement scrutiny.

Planning and story, Davis thought as he retrieved a sensor and meter from the other end of the bench. *Just like old Les Parks always said, you know your story going in and you stick to it. Once you've put the story together, you never waver.*

It's what worked for Parks, wasn't it? That son of a snake bluffed and lied and corrupted his way to millions and a life of complete and total paranoia.

Davis lifted his head, smiled in satisfaction, and thought, *I'm grateful I got to end that life before it went on much longer.*

Then he touched the sensor to a circuit inside the Stinger and saw the needle on the meter swing positive.

Deeply, deeply grateful.

63

AROUND EIGHT THE NEXT morning, John Sampson, holding his coffee, pulled over, glad to see that Marion "Captain" Davis's rental Chevy Cavalier was parked in Fiona Plum's driveway.

Rebecca Cantrell had exercised her authority as a U.S. attorney to track Davis's credit card transactions soon after her late lunch with John had abruptly ended. Overnight, she got Avis to activate the GPS transmitter in the rental car. Sampson had dropped Willow with Nana Mama, Bree, and Jannie early that morning, and the transmitter had led Sampson straight to the English teacher's place.

Cantrell's plan called for Sampson to sit on the coach while her team dug into his relationship with Leslie Parks. Drinking more of his coffee, Sampson thought, *Is Captain Davis Ibrahim? Is that possible?*

He called up the pictures Alex had sent him the day before

and studied the bearded, swarthy man at the Red Sox game with the gunrunner. *Or are you Ibrahim?*

Flipping to the photo of Davis with Parks at the Pro Bowl, he wondered at the odds of the two of them connecting. And then he realized that Parks had to have met or known Davis before he left the NFL and went to Iraq.

But had the relationship continued in Iraq and later, after Davis was assigned to Fort Bragg? As everyone had noted, the military base and Parks's prepper fortress were less than thirty miles apart.

But was Davis there in North Carolina the day the machine gun was fired at that plane? Was he there the day Parks died? Did the coach blow the man's head off?

These kinds of questions swirled around Sampson's mind as he finished that first cup and mentally prepared for a long sit. Still, Davis had to come out sooner or later.

Unless Davis and Fiona Plum were shacking up? Plum didn't seem like his type, based on the pictures of the woman with whom he'd left the sports bar the week before. Then again, Sampson had never expected to be attracted to an alpha female like Rebecca Cantrell, and yet there it was, out of the blue.

He thought about the U.S. attorney and wondered if someone of her stature and responsibility had time for a relationship. *Do I? I don't see Willow enough as it is, and with Alex working full-time with the FBI at the moment, the Dead Hours investigation is mine alone.*

He set the empty cardboard coffee cup in a holder, took the full one beside it, drank a little, and realized that if he and Cantrell were meant to be, it would naturally evolve on its own. That's how it had been with Billie. Unexpected and easy.

If this is right, it will be like that, he thought, and scolded himself for mooning over a woman he'd not even had an entire lunch with yet. *But she said she'd fire me as soon as she could, right?* A light rush of anticipation went through him like a welcome shiver. *Maybe Alex is right. Maybe I can be happy again with someone.*

He'd no sooner had that thought than the front door to the teacher's bungalow opened. Fiona Plum came out carrying a book bag over one shoulder and pulling a carry-on suitcase with rollers.

Plum slammed the door behind her, went to a white Kia sedan, put the suitcase in the trunk, then leaned against the car and hung her head a long moment.

What's going on? What's she doing? Is she sick?

The teacher raised her head at last, got in the driver's seat, and backed the car out. Sampson's car had tinted windows, but he still slid down a little in his seat as she passed.

He got a good look at Fiona, who was normally very put together and bright-eyed. Her eyes were puffy and glazed. Her skin was sallow, and her mouth was open. She was chewing the air as if she was fighting off the urge to cry.

Sampson looked at his phone, saw the icon representing the rental car still blinking on the map of the teacher's neighborhood, and made a split-second gut decision to abandon his eyes-on surveillance of Captain Davis for the time being.

He started the car, turned it around, and sped after Fiona Plum.

CHAPTER

64

CAPTAIN DAVIS FELT LIKE someone had swung an ax through his skull. He knew this feeling and didn't want to open his eyes to figure out where he was, much less determine the amount of time he'd lost in the blackout.

When he heard a door slam, his eyelids fluttered open, shut, fluttered open again, then stayed open as he fought for focus. He didn't recognize his surroundings at first, then realized he was curled up naked in a bottom bunk bed, the one the nieces used when they visited Fiona Plum.

How the hell did I..., he thought. He heard a car start and pull away, then a squeal of tires. *Oh no, what did I do?*

Davis sat up and almost puked but pushed the urge down. After the room started to spin a little less, he got to his feet, wobbling, wondering where his clothes were.

There they were, folded neatly on the bunk above him, beside a note written in a fine hand:

Captain,

You behaved terribly and said horrible things. Given that, I thought it best if I go to my sister's until you find yourself another place to stay.

A lot of people care about you, Captain. A lot of people love you, including me. We are deeply worried about you, but we will not aid and abet your self-destruction. I know how to drink responsibly, and you do not. Get help. Get sober. And replace your addiction with faith. It's the only thing that works.

If you don't, then goodbye, Captain. I will always remember you as that better man.

Sincerely,
Fiona Plum

Davis's hands shook as he read the letter again. He thought of the way Fiona had looked at him in the parking lot the day before and how she'd said she never abandoned her friends. He read it a third time and began to cry.

No matter her quirks and over-earnest personality, Fiona Plum was a good and decent woman, the kind he should have had the good sense to latch onto. The truth was he'd always kind of looked down on her, considered her a poor naive woman.

And he had seen things, hadn't he? Too many things.

But it didn't matter how naive she was. If he came to his senses…

Captain Davis read the letter a fourth time, his mind flashing with images of missiles launched by his hand, their contrails leading to some Stone Age village, then exploding in dark mushrooms of destruction and ribbons of flame.

Through his tears, he stared at Fiona's final sentences.

We are deeply worried about you, but we will not aid and abet your self-destruction. I know how to drink responsibly, and you do not. Get help. Get sober. And replace your addiction with faith. It's the only thing that works.

Davis hung his head, seeing those images again, those mental recordings of missiles rocketing from his fighter jet, their vapor trails a promise, then the explosions and the craters and the wounds and the wounded and the dead.

Gripping his head now, trying to squeeze the memories back into some dark box in his mind, Davis knew that this dear, sweet teacher was right in everything she said in her letter. He needed help, and that was the problem.

No one can help me. No one can absolve me of the guilt for what I have done.

Not even Fiona Plum.

CHAPTER

65

SAMPSON FOLLOWED THE ENGLISH teacher's Kia to a small blue Cape in the Groveton neighborhood of Alexandria. Before she could get out, he was at her door, showing her his badge.

Fiona Plum looked dreadfully hung over. When she saw him, he thought that she might be sick.

She lowered her window, said, "I don't want to talk to you."

"You have to talk to me. It's a murder investigation. Where's Captain Davis?"

"I left him passed out naked in my niece's bunk bed. He's got more issues than I can handle at the moment."

"Such as?"

"He drinks too much. I drink, but he drinks way too much."

"Did he say anything while he was drinking?"

Plum stared through the windshield. "He said a lot of things. I have no idea if any of it is true."

"Let me figure that out."

"You really have it in for him, don't you?"

He sighed. "Honestly, Ms. Plum, I don't have it in for anyone. I just want justice. If he's guilty, I want to nail him. If he's innocent, I want to see him stay free."

The English teacher drummed her fingers on the steering wheel, still gazing off into the distance. Finally she said, "He evidently had to kill a lot of people in Iraq and Syria. As a pilot, I mean. Whole villages, I guess."

"That would affect a man."

She nodded.

"Maybe make him angry."

Plum glanced at Sampson. "He's angry about a lot."

"His ex-girlfriend?"

"Ex-girlfriend and her daughter. You know why he says she did it?"

"Because he lost his chance at a job with American Airlines?"

The English teacher shook her head bitterly. "Because he'd killed so many people and the psycho girlfriend found out and it drove her even more insane. Enough to kill her own daughter and herself."

"That doesn't make much sense."

"I'm just telling you what he said. She was seriously mentally ill. Finding out snapped her."

Sampson watched her cheek twitch. She put her hand to her mouth. "That man is suffering," Plum said.

"Violent?"

"No…I mean, no," she said. "I think he's just consumed by sorrow and anger."

"At who?"

"Himself. His commanders. The government. You. The police. The FBI. The headmaster at the Charles School. Me."

"You?"

Tears dripped down her cheeks. "He's angry at me for loving him. Says I have no idea who he is. And you know what? I guess I don't, which is why I left to come to my sister's."

"You letting Davis stay at your place?"

"I left a letter telling him to leave. He was still passed out."

"Did he mention anyone named Ibrahim?"

"No."

"How about Leslie Parks?"

She shook her head. "Why? Who are they?"

"People of interest."

"If he knows them, he never mentioned them to me."

Sampson felt his phone buzz. He ignored it a moment. "Are you going to be all right?"

Plum barely nodded. "Funny how one night can shatter a dream."

"Knowing what you know now, is he capable of it? Of shooting down a plane like that?"

She dropped her chin a little. "Before last night, I would have said no. Emphatically no. Now? I…I guess I can't tell you how deep that black hole in his heart is."

Sampson patted the roof of the car. "I'm sorry, Ms. Plum. And thank you for the talk. I think your sister and nieces are up there waiting for you."

The English teacher looked toward the house. The drapes were open, and her sister and her sister's daughters were looking out in concern.

Sampson returned to his car. As he did, he pulled out his phone and saw an alert from the software tracking the GPS signal from Davis's rental car.

He swore, jumped in his car, and spun it around.

66

CAPTAIN DAVIS WAS ON the move, already a mile and a half from Fiona Plum's house, getting on the George Washington Parkway, heading north.

Sampson threw a bubble on the roof of his car and lit up his sirens. He raced east until he reached the parkway and accelerated north, hoping to close the five miles that separated them—

He looked at his phone, saw Davis was getting off at Reagan National Airport. What was he doing there, of all places?

Sampson stomped on the gas and was trying to figure out how best to handle the situation when the signal from Davis's car slowed to a crawl. He was going to catch up.

But two minutes before he reached the west entrance to the airport, the signal stopped. He shut down his sirens and the bubble, looked at the screen. Davis was at 2500 National Avenue, parking garage A.

The Avis car-rental return.

Son of a bitch, he's ditching the car, Sampson thought. He grabbed his radio, called dispatch, and asked them to send airport police to the Avis return and get eyes on Davis. Then he texted Rebecca Cantrell, asking the U.S. attorney to alert him if Davis tried to rent another car at Avis or another agency.

Traffic began to move. And then it stopped.

Sirens suddenly began to wail. Dispatch called Sampson to tell him someone had just called in a bomb threat to the airport and all police were responding.

Did Davis do that?

He could see parking garage A ahead of him, no more than two hundred yards away. He put the bubble up again and turned on his sirens.

Sampson drove up on a lawn, got around a knot of vehicles, went back onto the road, and made it to the entrance to parking garage A. He drove straight to the Avis rental return, spotted the Chevy Davis had been driving, and jumped out of his car, holding up his ID to a guy checking returns. "Where did the man driving this car go?"

The guy shrugged. "Terminal? He left his phone."

As Sampson ran toward the exit, he said, "Do not touch it."

"What about your car?"

"I'll be back!" he yelled.

A minute later, he was running down the aerial walkway, scanning the people in the terminal. The scene had become angry and chaotic now that airport police were pushing the crowds back until the bomb threat could be cleared.

Captain Davis was a big guy. He would stand out. And

Sampson was tall enough to look over the top of a lot of people. But he wasn't seeing Davis in the crowd, and he didn't see him when he got past the first line of airport police and scanned the passengers exiting the planes.

He looked everywhere for the former NFL long snapper. But after thirty minutes, Sampson had to admit defeat.

Davis had shaken the tail. He was in the wind.

67

BREE CHECKED THE CLOCK in the kitchen. Alex was supposed to land at Joint Base Andrews in less than an hour.

Though he hadn't been gone that long, she felt like they hadn't connected beyond quick conversations for the past week, and between the Leigh Anne Asher case and the death of Iliana Meadows, she had a lot to talk over with him.

Jannie hurried into the kitchen and whispered, "She's about to go on!"

Bree hurried after her stepdaughter into the dining room and stopped where they could both see into the front room. Nana Mama stood in the center of the room facing Ali's laptop, which he'd set on the mantel above the fireplace. Someone had removed the shade on one of the table lamps, so it threw a nice warm light on Nana's face and the simple dark blue dress and pumps she wore.

"Ready?" Ali said.

Nana Mama nodded.

Ali said, "Remember to look at the camera. That way they'll all think you're looking right at them."

"Got it," she said. "Let's go."

Ali hit a key, and the Zoom room began to fill with the faces of teenagers, some looking at Nana Mama curiously and others completely bored or studying their phones.

"Hello," Nana said. "My name is Regina Cross, but you can call me Miss Reggie. Pay attention, now. I am older than you think, so I can't promise I won't keel over and go toes-up in the few minutes they've given me to talk to you."

Several of the students laughed. Others sat up in their chairs.

"How many of you are seniors?" Nana Mama asked.

Half the students raised their hands.

She held up the novel *The Color Purple* by Alice Walker. "Who has done the assigned reading?"

Many young women held up their hands. Only a handful of the young men did.

"Matthew Gundry," Nana Mama said, picking one boy who was slouched down, staring dumbly at the screen. "Have you even started it?"

Gundry sat up, shrugged. "Didn't see the point."

"Really? I see the point of this book in every one of you — you're all tired of your situation; you feel like you have no say in your life, that you're helpless, that your life is unfair somehow. Isn't that about right, Matthew?"

Gundry's brow furrowed. "I mean, yeah, I guess. Who doesn't want their life to be better somehow?"

Many of the other kids on the screen were nodding.

Nana Mama said, "Those of you who have read Alice

Walker's masterpiece: Celie's life is a lot worse than yours, correct?"

All the readers in the class agreed.

Nana Mama picked one, said, "Tell us, Cheryl Walsh."

Walsh pushed her glasses farther up the bridge of her nose and said, "Way worse, Miss Reggie. People treat her horribly. I mean, what Celie goes through is, like, not to be believed. One terrible thing after another."

"And how is the book written?"

"Like, it's Celie writing these letters to God because no one else listens to her?"

"That's right—Celie has no voice except in those letters. But despite everything she goes through, she manages to retain her humanity, her inherent goodness, doesn't she?"

The ones who'd read the book nodded.

Walsh said, "In the end, it's like she outlasts every bad person and every bad situation, and gradually, she's the one who comes out of it better. Comes out on top, I mean."

"And she stays true to herself, and she's at peace because of it," Nana Mama said.

The students who'd read the book all nodded again. All the students were listening intently.

"There are many lessons in this book," Nana Mama went on, holding the novel up again. "Too many to talk about in the short time they've given me to speak with you today. But the one I hope you learn well is that no matter your circumstance— even if you're trapped in a life of real violence and misery, as Celie was—you can endure, and you can come out of it a better person."

She paused, then took a step toward the camera. "Is that the kind of story you might be able to relate to, Mr. Gundry?"

The kid who'd been slouched down tried not to smile. "Yeah, maybe."

"Then do me a favor—read the story before we meet again. If I don't keel over and go toes-up in the meantime, I'd love to hear what you have to say about it. Especially the knife-fight scene."

"There's a knife-fight scene?" Gundry asked.

"A good one," Nana Mama said. "Lots of blood. You'll tell us all about it. And now it's time for Miss Reggie to say good-bye. Until next time—keep reading. I promise it will change your life."

She nodded to Ali, who signed her out of Zoom.

Bree and Jannie began to clap.

"That was awesome," Ali said. "I want to read that book."

"Next year," Nana Mama said, and she smiled at Bree and Jannie. "Okay?"

"More than okay," Jannie said. "You were fun, Miss Reggie. They liked the keeling-over-and-toes-up line."

Nana Mama laughed.

Bree said, "You were relatable because you related to them."

"That's right," Nana Mama said. "And I let them teach each other. It was always my secret weapon and that has not changed a bit. No one wants some old person lecturing them about what to think."

"That's true," Jannie said.

Bree's phone rang. She looked at the caller ID. "I have to take this," she said, turning toward the kitchen. "That was great, Nana. I think you're a YouTube star in the making!"

CHAPTER

68

WHEN BREE ANSWERED HER phone, Elena Martin said, "I haven't heard from you."

"Because there hasn't been a lot to tell," Bree said, walking into the kitchen.

"And you've been looking for things to tell me?"

Bree thought that was an odd thing to say. "Well, I mean, we have a positive ID, Elena. We know it was Leigh Anne in that seat no matter what country issued her passport or how disfigured her body was."

Her boss was quiet a beat, then said, "But there's more."

"Okay…"

Martin cleared her throat. "A member of the Amalgam board—anonymous for the moment—contacted me because of my relationship with Leigh Anne. Turns out the FBI has been investigating Amalgam."

"What?"

"I swear to God, I just found out. Leigh Anne said nothing."

"Did she know?"

"Evidently. And she decided not to file a notice of the investigation with the SEC until something definitive turned up."

"So that the IPO could go forward."

After a pause, Martin said, "The more I learn, the more I realize that my best friend not only had a secret life—she liked to play right at the edge of the law."

"What was the thrust of the investigation?"

"That's fuzzy, but my understanding is that some of the funding sources during the early financing rounds were, uh, sketchy."

"Sketchy?"

"That's how the board member described them," Martin said. "Seems Leigh Anne's chief financial officer had connections through offshore companies based in the Bahamas with some very shady characters. Russians."

"And Leigh Anne looked the other way?"

"That's what they want us to find out. The board is going to stall the IPO until we can do a thorough investigation into all aspects of the company's early funding and Leigh Anne's death."

"A terrorist shot her out of the sky, Elena," Bree said, getting irritated. "I do not believe your friend was the specific target."

Martin's voice was cold when she said, "The board still wants to know why she was on that plane and why she disappeared under such strange circumstances."

"That I can work on," Bree said.

"Thank you. Call me if you need me." She hung up.

Bree rubbed her brow, knowing she'd been a little curt with

her boss. But Elena had a tendency to spout theories based on little or no evidence.

Jannie came into the room. "I'm going back to the dorms. Have you talked to Detective Creighton?"

"Not today," Bree said. "I'll try to give her a call later."

Alex's daughter crossed her arms. "I just hate the idea that Iliana's death is going to fall through the cracks, you know?"

"It won't. I promise."

Jannie nodded and left.

After Bree finished a report on everything she'd found about the late tech entrepreneur, including Elena Martin's disclosure of the federal investigation into her financing sources, she called Creighton.

"Chief," Creighton said. "I'm driving, but I was about to call you."

"Tell me."

"I just left Iliana's high school," she said. "Nice place. Nice people. I did the interview with Hawley in front of the principal. He denied the affair with Iliana at first. But when I told him we knew about the blackmail, he broke down. Not that it matters, but he said the affair was consensual."

"It's what Iliana told my stepdaughter as well."

"The principal is furious. He wants the guy locked up. Hawley is toast."

"What about the blackmail?"

"Hawley was contacted anonymously in an e-mail by people who said they had the video he'd taken and they'd ruin his life if he didn't give them fifty thousand in Bitcoin."

"Did he?"

"After they proved they had the video. Took a second mortgage on his house. Bought Bitcoin and sent it."

"Is he married?"

"Yep, and Hawley's wife doesn't know any of this yet."

"Bad night coming."

"He brought it on himself. This is what happens."

"Where next?"

"Going to Paxson State to talk to her teachers and coaches."

"Try her roommate as well."

"She's high on my list."

69

NED AND I ARRIVED back in DC around one and went straight to a conference room in Rebecca Cantrell's offices in Arlington to meet with her, Sampson, and top agents assigned to investigate the downing of AA 839.

I'd thought Cantrell would be very pissed off when Sampson told her that Captain Davis was in the wind, but she was only mildly irritated.

"He'll pop up," she said. "We're watching his credit cards and bank accounts."

John said, "Fiona Plum told me that when Davis was drunk, he talked about having to blow up entire villages in Iraq and Syria. He was thrown out of the American Airlines pilot program for drinking. But he evidently believes his ex-girlfriend killed herself and her daughter because of what he had to do over there."

The U.S. attorney narrowed her eyes. "How's that?"

"That's what he told Plum. In any case, she said he's angry. Very angry."

"Noted," Cantrell said, and she looked at Ned and me. "And in North Carolina?"

Mahoney said, "We've got army investigators looking into the connections between Davis, Leslie Parks, and whoever this Ibrahim guy is. We know now that someone in Parks's fortress wiped down the guest bedroom and poured bleach down the guest bathroom's drains."

"You got nothing?"

"No," I said. "They've identified multiple different sources of DNA inside the fortress, especially around the gun room and subbasement."

Ned added, "Which is where we believe this Ibrahim may have made a mistake."

"Quantico have the samples?" Cantrell asked.

"Already in analysis."

"Good, then you're all free to focus on this until we get results or Davis surfaces," she said, clicking a key on her laptop. Three photographs of three different men in robes filled the screen on one wall of the conference room. They were all candid shots, two taken on the street, one at a café.

"A gift from the CIA," the U.S. attorney said. "All three of these men worked with Leslie Parks during his gunrunning days. After Parks left the Middle East, the two men on the street in that picture went to work for the U.S. military and eventually got permission to immigrate here. The one in the café there, the guy smoking the hookah, is Sami Abdallah."

Abdallah, she said, had been taken hostage and disappeared for almost a year after Parks's weapon caravan was attacked and seized. He surfaced in the town of Qa'im on the Iraq-Syria border claiming that he'd been held prisoner by a pro-Iranian militia group but escaped. "He sought asylum, and we gave it to him three years ago," she said, hitting another key on her laptop. The screen changed to an image of Abdallah's green card.

"Turns out he's right here in the area," she went on. "Lives near that mosque in Gaithersburg with the imam that's always screaming persecution and oppression."

I said, "Is he a member of that mosque?"

"He is," she said. "The FBI's counterterrorism division has been keeping an eye on him and several other young men who live with him and attend the mosque. About three weeks ago, we lost the intercept on Abdallah's phone. Or, rather, he stopped using the phone in favor of another one. An Orion."

"Whoa," Mahoney said. "Where'd he get something like that?"

I wanted to know the same thing, because an Orion encrypted phone was impossible to intercept and cost tens and sometimes hundreds of thousands of dollars. Our government gave them to diplomats and others who needed to talk securely.

"More important," Sampson said, "what's he doing with it?"

"Exactly, John," Cantrell said. "I suggest you three go and ask him."

CHAPTER

70

ACCORDING TO THE LATEST intelligence from the FBI's counterterrorism division, Sami Abdallah and three other men from the Gaithersburg mosque rented a small house in a loose group of manufactured homes, barns, and outbuildings set well back from a road west of town near Seneca Creek State Park.

Satellite images of the place showed it was surrounded by woods on three sides and a cornfield on the fourth. It looked as if it had once been a working farm with several families all living in the same area.

"Do we know who's living in the other homes?" I asked when we gathered an hour before dark in another agricultural field about two miles from Abdallah's place.

"They're all owned by a single absentee landlord," Mahoney said. "I talked to him in Florida on the way up. He calls the place Little Baghdad because his renters are all Iraqi refugees.

He says there's a family called the Shariffs—a mom, dad, and triplet girls—living across the way from Abdallah, who has two roommates. There are three more refugees living in the double-wide beyond Abdallah's place, all males. He's never had a problem with any of them, but then again, he hasn't been there physically in more than a year."

Mahoney, who was a master at dealing with these kinds of situations, had decided to bring an additional eight FBI agents as well as a drone and a drone pilot. He sent two agents to each of the three wooded sides of the compound. The remaining pair went into the cornfield, which remained uncut.

The pilot launched the drone at the same time Mahoney, Sampson, and I drove off to talk with Sami Abdallah. The drone flew high over the compound, and Mahoney watched the feed on an iPad. He saw the three little Shariff girls and their mother in their yard. One of the girls was on a swing set. The other two were riding tricycles.

At the rear of the compound, a man was raking leaves near the manufactured home. There were two cars and no one visible outside Abdallah's place.

Mahoney had the drone go to infrared and saw there were three people in Abdallah's home, one in the Shariffs', and two in the manufactured home. There were also two people in the barn on the east side, the side closest to the cornfield.

"Full house plus two," he said, then called the drone pilot on his jaw mic to tell him to keep the eye in the sky circling until we were done.

"Roger that," the drone pilot said.

The sun was sinking low when Sampson drove us down the gravel road that wound back through trees losing their leaves. A deer bounded past us just before we emerged into the clearing, maybe a hundred feet from where Mrs. Shariff was watching her girls playing tag.

She caught sight of us immediately and called her girls to her side. They hugged her waist as we passed. She clutched her headscarf and watched us, stone-faced, until we pulled up in front of Abdallah's house, which sat catty-corner from hers.

A slate walkway wound between two large oak trees to stairs and a front deck.

"Hands resting on the grip of your weapons, gentlemen," Mahoney said and climbed out of the front passenger seat. I kept track of the woman and the girls as Sampson and I exited the car. As Ned had directed, I immediately put my hand beneath my coat and rested it on the grip of my Glock 17.

Before we made it to the front deck, the door opened. Sami Abdallah stepped out and shut the door behind him.

Bearded and wearing a skullcap, he sported a dark sweater over a long white tunic, black pants, and black leather soft-soled shoes. "Yes?" he said. "Who are you?"

"FBI, Mr. Abdallah," Mahoney said, showing him his badge and identification.

Abdallah smiled. His upper right canine was black. He had a gold cap over the opposite canine. "What can poor Sami do for the FBI?" he asked in thickly accented English.

"For one, you can tell us where you were last Monday night."

"Easy one," he said. "Right here with my roommates watching *Monday Night Football*, Baltimore Ravens versus San Diego Chargers. Ravens punished!"

Sampson said, "You're a football fan?"

He flashed the gold tooth and the rotten one again. "Love it. Love the Ravens and the Washington, DC, football club and Tampa Bay."

I said, "Ravens fan. So you must know Captain Davis."

The smile faded. "Davis? No."

"Long snapper," Sampson said. "Left the NFL to fly for the air force in the Middle East."

Abdallah shook his head. "No, I do not know this one."

"He was just in the papers and on the news. We were holding him on suspicion of being involved in the downing of the American Airlines jet."

The smile was back as he shook his head again. "I have learned not to read or watch the news too often. It affects my mood."

"But you heard someone machine-gunned that jet as it was landing at Reagan National," I said.

"It was hard not to hear that," he said. "But again, why are you here?"

Mahoney said, "Checking out some loose ends."

"Like?"

"Like your relationship with Leslie Parks back in Iraq."

Abdallah's expression hardened. "That relationship was abandoned. When the caravan was attacked and they took me, he could have paid a ransom, but he did not. I spent a year in captivity because of Parks. I hate the man. Where is he?"

"North Carolina," I said. "Dead."

His eyebrows lifted. "Dead? I hope it was a difficult death."

Sampson said, "Someone blew his head off with a shotgun and tried to make it look like a suicide."

He considered that. "Well, of course there would be violence involved. It traveled with Parks. Trouble. Violence. But I have not seen him in years. He's involved in the plane coming down?"

Mahoney said, "Supplied the machine gun."

Abdallah paused, then said, "Any more loose ends I can help with?"

"Did you know someone named Ibrahim when you worked with Parks?"

Something flickered in his eyes before he said, "Not that I remember. That it?"

"Just one more thing. The information that travels over an Orion encrypted phone is fully secure, but did you know that when you or someone else in your house uses an Orion, it attracts attention from people like us?"

We all watched him. He was cool, I'll give him that.

"I have no idea what this Orion thing is," he said with a dismissive wave of his hand. "But maybe my roommates do. Should I get them?"

"Please," Mahoney said.

Abdallah pivoted, opened the front door, and called, "Racif, Badawi, the FBI, they want to talk to you."

Someone grumbled inside just as one of the FBI agents in the cornfield barked through our earpieces, "Armed subject! AR rifle, body armor, exiting rear of east-side barn, aggressive posture, heading your way."

All three of us dropped into crouches, drew our guns, and moved to cover just as someone inside Abdallah's house opened fire with an automatic weapon, blowing out the window glass.

CHAPTER

71

I LUNGED HARD BEHIND one of the oaks, heard slugs slamming into the tree. Sampson and Mahoney got behind the other tree, John high and looking to his right, Ned low and looking left.

The moment the shooting stopped, we all leaned out and fired multiple shots toward the window. Sami Abdallah was crawling off the deck, trying to get out of the line of fire.

In our earpieces, the drone pilot said, "You've got two more armed men, automatic weapons, leaving the mobile home."

"All agents engage," Mahoney said. "Repeat, all agents engage."

I caught movement in the growing shadows to my right and saw the guy who'd left the barn, complete with body armor and a light machine gun, running my way, his weapon at port arms. I twisted toward him and slid down the tree until I was almost lying on the ground.

Two automatic rifles started shooting at us from inside the

manufactured house, short, disciplined bursts. I ignored them and the woman screaming behind me, focusing on the guy running my way. The second he was inside forty yards, I opened fire, double-tapping him to his left leg and groin. He screamed and went down, dropping his rifle.

One of the automatic weapons in the house stopped. The other sprayed my position wildly, which caused the woman to scream even more.

Before I could turn to see what was happening with her, there was a barrage of shots toward the manufactured home, then reports of two bad guys down, one by the cornfield and another at the rear of the property.

That left four by my count. We could hear shouting from inside the house, and I heard the clanking sound of men trying to seat new clips in their weapons and not doing it well.

Sampson heard it too, charged around the oak toward the deck, and fired through the blown-out window. Mahoney was behind him, shooting at another window.

I heard a man shout in agony and then the woman was screaming again, this time calling for help in English. I spun around and saw Mrs. Shariff on her knees next to two of her daughters, both of whom were lying on the ground.

They're hit!

More shots went off behind me, all from Sampson and Mahoney; all of them, it turned out, connected with the throats and foreheads of the two gunmen trying to reload unfamiliar weapons under pressure.

There's still two of them left, I thought, running toward the mother and her two wounded children, expecting her husband to come out the front door at any moment, blazing at me and possibly hitting his wife and daughters.

But the door never opened, and I saw no one. I arrived at the poor woman's side and saw that both little girls were unconscious. One had been hit in the chest and was laboring to breathe. The other had been shot through the right thigh. Bone stuck out. Blood spurted.

"Help," their mother whimpered. "Help them. I don't know what to do."

I tore off my jacket and pressed it against the girl's leg wound as shouts went up. I looked over my shoulder to see Sampson sprinting after Sami Abdallah. He tackled the man and drove him facedown into the dirt.

Mahoney ran to me as I moved to the second girl. "Both roommates dead," he said.

"We need multiple ambulances," I said, then realized I could hear sirens in the distance. I squatted by the second girl, pulled her jacket and her shirt open.

I recognized what was going on when I saw the wound in her chest and heard the sucking sound it made whenever she breathed. "Mahoney, give me your windbreaker."

Mahoney looked at me quizzically but took off the FBI windbreaker and handed it to me. "Good. Now I need a knife."

Ned handed me a pocketknife.

"Wait, what are you doing?" her mother cried.

"Saving her life," I said. I took the blade and used it to slice the jacket in two. I pressed one half of it against the wound and wrapped the other half around the girl's slim torso to keep the makeshift chest seal in place.

By the time the ambulances came, the girl's breathing was less labored. The front door opened. Mr. Shariff stood there holding his third daughter, who was unhurt but crying. He was wailing in anguish. "We are not like them! We are not part of this!"

I looked over and saw three of the other FBI agents coming toward us with two cuffed men in body armor.

Mahoney shook his head, said, "I'm sorry, sir, but everyone in this compound is under arrest until we can search it and figure out exactly what has been going on here."

CHAPTER

72

IT WAS WELL AFTER midnight before we reached DC. John Sampson went straight to my house to pick up Willow.

Mahoney and I went to FBI headquarters. We wanted to interrogate Sami Abdallah, the two men in body armor who'd given up rather than fight, and Aden Shariff, the father of the wounded girls. However, Abdallah and the other two men, Kourie Mustapha and Umar Hassan, immediately invoked their right to remain silent and asked for lawyers. Mahoney threw them in separate cells to let them stew before fulfilling their demands, and we turned to Mr. Shariff.

He was sleeping, head down on the table, when we entered the interrogation room around two a.m. Shariff came groggily alert. "My daughters?" he asked, searching our faces. "Maya? Aleah?"

"They're both going to make it, Mr. Shariff," I said, sitting down opposite him and pushing a cup of coffee across the table. We'd decided I would play good cop during the talk and leave the heavy lifting to Ned.

Shariff's tears came again along with a wide smile. "This is true?"

"As far as we know, sir, yes," I said.

He shut his eyes blissfully. "Then all is good."

Mahoney said, "We read you your rights, Mr. Shariff. Do you wish to talk to us?"

Shariff's bloodshot eyes opened again. "Or what? You torture me?"

"We don't do that kind of thing here," I said.

"Americans did in Iraq."

"Not us," I said. "In this room, you have rights. We want to talk to you, but we cannot force you to help us understand why your girls were shot this evening."

He said nothing for several moments, just stared at the table.

I said, "I sense you want to help us."

Mahoney said, "And remaining silent does not help us see you as a good man caught in a bad situation."

At last, Shariff nodded. "I am good man. We are good family. What do you want to know?"

Mahoney said, "Tell us about Sami Abdallah and his friends."

"I have nothing to do with these men," he said, taking the coffee. "The refugee agency placed us there. They were already renters when we come." Shariff said the men had all worked in various roles with the U.S. military, often as support staff. Abdallah, as we knew, had been a fixer for Special Forces. The two dead men in Abdallah's house had worked in a mess in the Green Zone in Baghdad. Kourie Mustapha and Umar Hassan, he said, had worked on the border with Syria. He could not remember what the two other dead men had done for the U.S. in Iraq, but it had gotten them preference for refugee status when America pulled out.

"What about you, Mr. Shariff?" I asked.

"I am an engineer," he said. "I worked on construction projects for the U.S. Air Force and the Army Corps of Engineers in the south of Iraq."

"And here?"

"I work for an engineering and construction company in Germantown. I just start there six months ago. Already they have promoted me twice."

Mahoney nodded. "Abdallah?"

Shariff blinked several times. "He is nice man sometimes. But he tried to get us to attend his mosque there. I told him we were not ready to decide such things."

"That make him mad?"

"It made him suspicious of us, I think," he said. "They all became polite, and we could talk about our families and our lives back home. But we were not friends."

I said, "Did you know they had the automatic weapons and the body armor?"

He shook his head, looking us in the eyes. "I had no idea. I was sleeping when the shooting started and I panicked, thought I was back in Fallujah. I never…" Shariff choked up.

"You never?" I said.

He cleared his throat, wiped at his eyes with his sleeves. "I never thought I would experience this kind of thing here, in America. I thought we had left that behind us."

"It's still a great country," Mahoney said.

Shariff's chin rose. "The best. Every day, we give thanks for being allowed to live here, to raise our daughters here."

I slid my phone across the table. "Have you ever seen this man visiting Mr. Abdallah or his friends?"

For several moments, the Iraqi refugee studied two pictures of the late Leslie Parks, one taken during his time in Iraq, the other more recent. He tilted his head, as if trying to get another perspective on the photos.

Finally, he said, "He's stiff on one side? Bad right arm?"

I glanced at Mahoney. Parks had been shot through the right arm when his convoy was attacked.

"Maybe," Mahoney said. "When was he here? How many times? For how long?"

Shariff said he'd first seen the man the same week they'd moved in. He'd arrived in a dark blue van with North Carolina plates. Abdallah had come out on the front deck of his house and greeted Parks like a long-lost friend.

"I am still moving things from our first place with the U-Haul," Shariff said. "So I am in and out all that day. He stayed maybe one hour and then he comes back the next afternoon. But this time, he backs van into driveway and goes to the barn. He is there maybe two hours, then he leaves."

Mahoney said, "You don't go over there? See what's going on?"

"I was putting up the swing and putting together the tricycles for my daughters."

"Then what?" I asked.

"He goes."

"And you remember him clearly?"

"Yes. He rubs his arm. It's bad."

I changed the photo on my screen to one of Marion "Captain" Davis. "What about this man? He ever come there?"

Shariff studied the picture. "No. Who is he?"

"Doesn't matter," I said, and I scrolled to the picture of Leslie

Parks and the bearded man on the Green Monster at Fenway. "What about him? Have you seen him?"

"This is the same man," he said. "The one with the bad arm."

"I'm talking about the second man, the one with the beard."

I blew up the man's face on the screen.

"It's possible," he said. "If he shaved his beard, it is possible he is someone I've seen."

"Where? When? How?"

Shariff raised his eyebrows. "Three, maybe four weeks ago? I am watching the girls play. Nina, my wife, she is sleeping. He comes in a pickup truck with a top. Abdallah is waiting for him. They go to barn. He leaves."

"What kind of pickup?" Mahoney asked.

He shrugged. "Silver. Maryland plates."

"You got a good look at him?"

He nodded. "When my daughter kicks the soccer ball, it rolls across the street. He came down Abdallah's drive to kick it back. So, close enough to see him."

"How long did he stay?"

"Longer than the man with the bad arm. Maybe two hours. He and Abdallah had coffee out on that front deck."

I said, "Did you ever see him use a funny-looking phone?"

He frowned. "No. But who knows what they did in that house."

"We're trying to figure that out," Mahoney said. "And we're going to have to keep you for the night. You'll get a place to sleep, and I'll make sure you are released early to go to the hospital to see your daughters and your wife, who we want to talk to as well."

"Thank you," he said. "I am not like those men. I swear to you on my father's grave I am not."

73

I SLID INTO BED beside Bree at ten past four. I didn't hear her when she got up at six a.m. My cell phone lit up at twelve minutes to seven.

Sampson was calling. My head felt like a freight train had hit it when I answered.

"There's been another Dead Hours killing," he said. "Baseball field on Tenth, not far from you."

"I know it. I'll meet you there," I said and hung up.

I stood in a cold shower for a full three minutes, didn't bother to shave, then quickly dressed and went downstairs, smelling coffee and bacon. I followed the aromas into the kitchen, where Ali was sitting at the counter talking to Nana Mama.

"What are you doing up already?" my grandmother said when she saw me. "Bree said you came in at four."

"And now I'm up at"—I glanced at the clock—"seven ten."

"You've got to get enough sleep, Alex. It's important for your health."

"Jannie says that all the time," Ali said. "And she should know."

I opened a cabinet, found a go-cup, and poured it full of black coffee. I sipped it, glad for the bitterness, which woke me up even more. "I agree with the both of you," I said, snapping the cover on. "I promise to catch up on my sleep when these cases are over."

Nana Mama sighed. "Which one has you up this morning?"

"A new Dead Hours victim," I said, moving past her.

"Bree took the car."

"It's seven blocks from here."

"What? Where?"

"Baseball fields near Tyler Elementary."

"Oh, dear God."

"I'll see you later," I said, and left the room and the house, becoming increasingly upset. I hurried down the road, sipping my coffee, nodding to people moving quickly in the chilly air. The closer I got to Tenth Street, the more I focused on the baseball field and the elementary school.

This would be the second time the Dead Hours killer had left a victim on a sports field near a school. Bart Masters, the fifth victim, had been found near a lacrosse field at Stoddert Middle School in Marlow Heights.

Uniformed police had Tenth Street shut off. I found Sampson standing on the pitcher's mound looking at victim number seven. He'd been propped up against the backstop behind home plate.

Like all the others, he was covered with a sheet. Bloody tears had seeped through the sheet and down the front.

"Who found him?" I said.

"Local guy out for an early run. He wore a headlamp, said there was steam coming off the body when he spotted it at five a.m."

Carly Rodgers, a deputy medical examiner, arrived on the scene.

"Hold up, Carly," I said as she started toward the body.

The ME halted, looked at me as I walked across the infield grass to her. "What's up, Dr. Cross?" she asked.

"That's soft soil there all around home plate. I'm thinking there have to be footprints." But when I checked the area, it looked freshly raked. The ground around the corpse had recently been scored as well.

"Are you kidding me?" Sampson said. "He kills the guy, puts the sheet on him, then hangs around to rake the area?"

"He's bold and doesn't want to be caught," I said, looking for the rake but not seeing it.

A criminalist arrived and began photographing the corpse in situ. We waited until he was done before going with Rodgers to the body. We told her about the steam coming off the body when he was discovered. "He'd probably been dead only twenty or thirty minutes at that point," Rodgers said, helping Sampson gingerly lift the sheet.

He was male, Caucasian, bearded, and bald. He wore a bloody blue tracksuit that said TYLER ATHLETICS.

"Oh, Jesus, he works for the school," Sampson said.

"Or he's a proud parent," I said, noticing a bulge in the right lower pocket of the jacket. With gloved hands I unzipped it and found a woven leather wallet. I eased it out of the pocket, opened it, and studied the DC driver's license and a district school employee ID. "Dalton McCoy. Thirty-nine. A physical education teacher here at Tyler."

Sampson squatted and gazed at the eyeless dead man. "Were you lured here, Dalton, or did you just blunder into him?"

74

AFTER EXAMINING MCCOY'S CORPSE, Carly Rodgers said he'd died around four thirty in the morning, which jibed with the jogger seeing steam coming off the sheet.

Sampson began organizing a door-to-door canvass of the houses around the baseball field and the school. I went up the street to the school's main entrance and found it open. I went inside. The principal, Helen Lawton, and her secretary had come in even though it was a weekend; Ms. Lawton was standing in the lobby talking to her secretary and wringing her hands.

I introduced myself. "I'm sorry to be here under the circumstances, Ms. Lawton. The body we found was one of your teachers, I'm afraid. Dalton McCoy."

One hand flew to her mouth and she gasped. The other hand sought the wall for support. "Oh my God. No."

Behind her, the secretary sat down hard on a chair outside the main offices.

"I'm going to need counselors," the principal said. "Mr. McCoy was one of the favorites here at Tyler." She began to cry. "This is going to shatter his wife and kids. Just shatter them."

When she composed herself, Lawton said that McCoy taught phys ed and was one of the most conscientious people she'd ever worked with, always enthusiastic, always learning, always motivating the kids and his fellow teachers. He lived in Laurel, Maryland, with his wife, Karen, and their young children.

"Any idea why he would have been on your campus at four thirty in the morning?"

"No," she said. "He often came in on the weekends to work on class plans. But not that early."

"Did he have a key to the school?"

"To the south entrance, the one bordering the playground and the baseball field."

Thinking that Laurel was at least a twenty-five-minute drive, even at that early hour, I said, "Do you know what kind of car he had?"

"Red Toyota Tacoma," she said. "He was very proud of that truck."

After a few more questions, I thanked her, offered my condolences, and asked that no one notify Dalton's wife. We wanted to break the news to her in person.

Walking back down Tenth Street, I scanned both sides of the road for a red Tacoma but didn't see it. I returned to the baseball field.

Sampson turned away from the medical examiner. I told him about my conversation with Helen Lawton and finished with the red Toyota Tacoma.

He dug in his pocket and came up with an evidence bag containing keys he said had been in McCoy's pants pocket. He pressed the panic button through the plastic.

A whooping noise came from over on I Street, just east of Tenth. He shut it off. We left the field and walked south on Tenth.

"I have to believe our guy made another big mistake here," Sampson said, gesturing to the well-maintained row houses that lined the west side of the street. People were looking out the windows at us. "Someone saw him, or one of those fancy doorbell cameras caught our guy."

"Good chance," I said. We turned left on I Street and immediately spotted the Tacoma halfway up the block on the opposite side.

We went to the little pickup. John opened the driver's door with the key fob. There was a Styrofoam cup of coffee in the holder and a zippered bag advertising a CrossFit gym in Laurel and a canvas briefcase in the passenger seat. Otherwise, the Tacoma was spotless.

The gym bag contained a change of clothes, jeans, a leather jacket, and a Washington Nationals ball cap. The briefcase held an iPhone, a fresh yellow legal pad, two new pens, an iPad, and a power cord.

I pressed the power button on the iPhone. The screen lit up and showed a picture of a beautiful brunette in her thirties crouched next to a little boy and girl playing on a beach.

"We need to go talk to his wife before she hears this from someone else," I said, seeing the phone was password-protected.

Sampson's face clouded, but he nodded. "She might know what he was doing here and what his passwords are."

I picked up the iPad. The screen was blank, the battery

dead. "Let's have the truck impounded in the meantime," I said, shutting the door.

"Here's your rake, by the way," John said, gesturing into the bed of the pickup.

There was indeed fresh sandy soil under the iron rake that lay in the back of the Tacoma along with several other gardening tools. After taking a picture of it all with our phones, we started back.

I happened to look through the ball-field fence all the way across to the playground.

"Son of a bitch."

"What?"

"There's someone here who should not be here."

Sampson followed my line of sight and said, "Oh, that's not cool."

"Yeah, I'll be right along after I nip this in the bud. Where did you park?"

"Tenth, north of Georgia," he said.

"I'll meet you there in ten," I said. I jogged east, crossed Eleventh, and headed north past the New Hope Free Will Baptist church.

When I was opposite the playground, I returned to the west side of the street and went to the chain-link fence, which put me about thirty yards from the small figure crouching by an internal fence and aiming a camera toward Rodgers and her assistant as they loaded the corpse of Dalton McCoy into the coroner's van.

"Ali Cross!" I yelled.

My youngest child sprang up, lost his balance, and almost fell into the big sandbox behind him. He managed to save himself but was shaken when he walked toward me.

"Dad, I—"

"You nothing," I said. "You are in an active crime scene."

"No, I—"

"No nothing, young man. I want you out of there and on a full march back home. I will deal with you later."

"Dad," he protested. "C'mon, I'm—"

"Marching straight home, or I will take that camera away and your laptop. And you are grounded until high-school graduation!"

75

BREE SAT IN HER office at the Bluestone Group headquarters in Arlington, studying faxed documents that Elena Martin had received the night before from the board member who'd alerted her to the FBI probe of Amalgam.

While Bree wasn't a wizard at this sort of thing, she had participated in enough investigations that involved financial chicanery to recognize some of the warning signs that might have attracted the Bureau's attention: Cash investments had come into Amalgam from offshore accounts in the Bahamas, the Caymans, and the New Hebrides, known money-laundering centers. The accounts were controlled by shell corporations registered in Lichtenstein and Panama, a method wealthy people and criminals used if they wanted to conceal their identities.

As she read further, Bree noticed that most of the sign-offs on the shady-looking investments carried the signatures of both Leigh Anne Asher and Craig Warren, Amalgam's chief financial officer. She found her boss's detailed notes from her conversation with the disgruntled board member.

Feels betrayed by Leigh Anne even if she is dead, Martin wrote. *Believes Leigh Anne and Warren walked a razor-thin line allowing some of the investments to occur. Believes the FBI saw it another way.*

Some of the shell companies may be connected to known organized-crime figures in Israel and Bulgaria? That's the sense he has.

Bree didn't understand that last bit and went to Elena Martin's office carrying the case file. She knocked on her boss's door. Martin, who was there even though it was a weekend, turned from her computer, looking like she hadn't slept in days.

"Pretty damning stuff, if I'm understanding it all," Bree said.

Martin raised both hands. "You think you know someone, especially after decades of friendship. How can I help?"

"There's something I don't get. In your notes about the possible offshore connection, there's a question mark. Then you wrote, 'That's the sense he has.' Who's *he*?"

"My source on the board."

"Okay. Was he interviewed by the FBI?"

"Briefly," she said. "It's there at the bottom of the page. He was approached about two weeks ago by an FBI agent. When my source saw the direction that the agent was taking with his questions, he said he'd feel more comfortable answering with an attorney present. They had a formal interview scheduled. It's there at the bottom."

Bree ran her eyes down the page and saw that her source had a meeting scheduled next week with FBI agent Charles Stimson. "Stimson," Bree said. "Do you know him?"

Martin shook her head. "I looked him up. Found very little other than he works out of offices in Reston. Residence in Groveton."

"I know a few people over at the Bureau," Bree said. "I'll make some calls and let you know what I find out."

She returned to her office and called Ned Mahoney, who answered on the third ring sounding groggy.

"I'm sorry, Ned, did I wake you?"

"Just getting up anyway," Mahoney said. "What's going on, Bree?"

"I told you that Leigh Anne Asher of Amalgam was on the downed jet, flying under a fake Irish passport."

"Seat two A. I remember."

"Seems that you guys had already been interested in Asher and Amalgam."

"That right?"

"Possible financial crimes. One of the agents involved in the investigation is a Charles Stimson. Works out of the Reston offices."

"Stimson?" Mahoney said. He paused. "I know *of* him. Strong on the white-collar-crime stuff. Does undercover work. Likes to stay out of the limelight."

"I'll give him a call," Bree said.

"If he doesn't answer, call his supervisor. Vicky Thomas. Here's her number. Tell her I sent you."

Bree put the number in her phone and said, "Thanks, Ned. I owe you one."

Yawning, Mahoney replied, "I'll cash it in someday soon, I'm sure."

They ended the call. Bree shut her door and dialed the FBI's Reston offices. She got an operator and asked to be transferred to Agent Charles Stimson.

The line rang five times before a baritone voice said, "You have reached the desk of FBI special agent Charles Stimson of the financial crimes unit. I'm away from my desk for a few days. Leave a message and I'll get back to you on my return."

As Ned had advised her, she called his supervisor, Vicky Thomas, and to Bree's surprise, even though it was a weekend, Thomas answered.

"Who is this? And how did you get this number?"

"Uh, this is Bree Stone. Ned Mahoney gave it to me."

"Bree Stone." Agent Thomas's tone softened. "You're Alex Cross's wife?"

"I am and I'm hoping you can help me." Bree explained about Leigh Anne Asher and Amalgam and the FBI investigating early investors in the company.

Thomas sounded quite a bit cooler when she replied, "You know I can neither confirm nor deny any investigations."

"Granted," Bree said. "Cards on the table? I'm not looking for anything that would be public. I'm trying to figure out what was happening on behalf of the Amalgam board members, who want to get to the bottom of this ASAP."

"I bet they do if there actually is an investigation under way. Who was the agent who contacted your board member?"

"Stimson. Charles Stimson."

There was a long pause before Thomas said, "Stimson. You're sure?"

"Positive. Why?"

After another silence, Thomas said, "Because Agent Stimson has been out of contact with this office for ten days and with his wife for more than twelve."

CHAPTER

76

THE WIDOW, KAREN MCCOY, stared at me and John Sampson, her chin quivering.

"No," she said in a low, airy, terrified voice. "That can't be right."

"I'm afraid it is," I said. "We found your husband's identification in his pocket. His Toyota Tacoma was there as well."

We were standing outside on her front porch. We could hear the television on inside the little Cape where this victim of the Dead Hours killer had lived.

McCoy's wife stared off into the distance, then plopped down on a wooden bench, put her face in her hands, and started sobbing. Grief and sorrow racked her for a good four or five minutes. You could tell she'd loved her husband deeply.

"We are so sorry for your loss, Mrs. McCoy," I said. "Is there someone we can call to come be with you?"

Before she answered, the front door opened. Mrs. McCoy

looked over at the little boy, no more than three or four, standing there in his pajamas.

"Mommy, why are you crying?" he asked, looking at her and at us uncertainly.

"It's okay, Frankie," his mother choked out. "Just go inside and finish your show."

"Will you come watch with us?"

"In a minute, baby."

He reluctantly shut the door.

Mrs. McCoy gazed up at us. "How do I explain this to him? He idolizes Dalton."

"It's going to be very hard, ma'am," Sampson said. "Which is why we can call somebody for you."

She nodded but looked miserable. "My sister, Judy."

Mrs. McCoy gave us the number. Sampson went down off the porch and called.

I sat beside her. "I know it's not enough, but we will catch whoever did this."

She shrugged. "He did it. That can't be taken back."

"No. It can't."

Mrs. McCoy broke down again, then put her hand across her mouth and shook her head violently. "I can't go to pieces. I just can't."

"That will come later," I said. "But I'd like to ask you some questions if you don't mind."

She swallowed hard. "Go ahead."

Over the course of the next few minutes, I learned that her husband had told her the night before that he was getting up for his five a.m. CrossFit class. She didn't hear him leave their bed. She had no idea why he would have been at Tyler Elementary at four thirty in the morning.

Sampson returned and said, "Your sister is on her way."

"Thank you," she said.

"Glad to help," Sampson said.

I asked if she knew the passwords for his phone, laptop, and iPad.

She gave us the phone and laptop passwords. "He doesn't own an iPad," she said.

"We found one in a briefcase in his truck," Sampson said.

Mrs. McCoy shook her head again. "We…he couldn't afford something like that. Money has been kind of tight."

We let it drop, though I suddenly wanted to know what exactly was on the iPad and indeed on all of McCoy's electronics.

"Is there anything else?" she said. "My sister will be right along. She doesn't live far, and the kids—"

"Just one more quick question," I said. "Did Dalton ever have problems with the law when he was younger? I mean, as a juvenile?"

She frowned, then nodded. "He was embarrassed about it. He stole a pair of cleats from a sporting-goods store in his hometown and got caught. They expunged it from his record when he was eighteen. Why?"

"Just something we noticed about several of the other victims," Sampson said.

"That they did something illegal as kids?"

"Correct," I said. "Whether it matters or not, we don't know yet."

A Jeep Wrangler came squealing into the driveway. An older woman in a sweatshirt, leggings, and running shoes burst out of it, calling, "Karen!"

Mrs. McCoy started crying again and ran to her. "Oh my God, Judy. What am I going to do?"

CHAPTER

77

BREE DIDN'T GET ALL the details, but based on what Agent Vicky Thomas was and was not saying, she figured that Agent Charles Stimson was gifted at undercover work and often went deep for three or four days at a time.

But twelve days without contacting his wife? Not a chance, according to Thomas.

"He's devoted to her," Thomas said. "She has early-stage ALS."

"That's a rugged road," Bree said. "Do you know what he was working on?"

"You know I can't—"

"Off the record? It won't even make my report."

"It better not."

"On my honor."

"He was interested in Amalgam. But he was more interested in the companies and people associated with Amalgam."

"Israelis and Bulgarians?"

"Among others."

"All foreign?"

"Not all. But there were Israelis and Bulgarians here that he was cultivating."

"Undercover?"

"At times."

"You think he was blown?"

"If he was, we haven't gotten confirmation. But he hasn't used any of the credit cards or identifications that are part of his cover. And he hasn't used any of his personal cards. And that's all you're getting out of me."

"You've been a big help."

"Nothing about any of this in your report."

"A promise is a promise. Not until you give me the okay. And thanks."

"We never spoke," Thomas said and ended the call.

Bree sat there at her desk a moment, pondering her next move. On a whim, she went to a law enforcement website and, using Alex's username and password, entered the Virginia DMV database and searched for Charles Stimson in Groveton.

She soon had the driver's license up on her screen. He had a big, blocky head, was a handsome guy with a nice smile. Six foot three. Two hundred pounds. Organ donor.

"Where are you, Charles? With the Bulgarians? Or the Israelis?" Bree muttered. She printed out a copy of Stimson's ID. She thought about calling up the missing FBI agent's wife or going over to talk with her. But under what pretext? And for what purpose?

Bree couldn't imagine Stimson talking about his undercover work with his wife, especially when she was not law enforcement. Sitting back in her chair, eyes closed, Bree wondered what else she did not know about Leigh Anne Asher and Amalgam and the Israelis and the Bulgarians and the undercover agent whose cover may or may not have been blown.

It seemed a given to Bree that Asher knew the FBI was looking at the investments. According to Elena Martin's source on the Amalgam board, Asher herself had decided not to notify the SEC about the inquiry.

But did Asher know the extent of it? The offshore accounts. The shell companies. Organized crime. The Israelis. The Bulgarians. And what the hell had she been doing in Florida using a fake Irish passport under her former name?

Bree remembered the photographs of the interior of the burned-out jet, how Asher's charred body hung there. Did any of the mysteries surrounding the Amalgam CEO matter anymore?

Then Bree realized that, with everything that had happened in the past few days, she'd forgotten the questions she'd asked herself: *Who was the guy hanging beside Leigh Anne Asher? Was he a stranger or her fiancé?*

To those questions she added another: *Or was the ring a fake, a way to ward off unwanted advances by strange men?*

Even though she did not want to, she called Ned Mahoney again.

"Bree," he said. "Was Thomas any help?"

"As helpful as she could be," Bree said. "I hate to ask, but one more favor?"

"If I can."

"Do we know who sat in seat two B on the American Airlines jet?"

"Everyone's been identified. We matched the manifests with the TSA records three days ago. Hold on a second."

Bree tapped a pen.

He came back. "All right, in that seat was Carson Daniels of Ada, Oklahoma."

"Ada, Oklahoma?" Bree said, wondering how Carson Daniels of Ada could have been engaged to Leigh Anne Asher. "Huh?"

"Want a look at his driver's license? I can send it."

"Sure," Bree said. "Why not? Do we know anything else about him?"

"Nope," he said. "We've been focused on catching who did it."

"Of course you are, and rightly so. I promise not to bug you anymore."

"You're family, so you're not bugging me," Mahoney said, and they said goodbye.

Ada, Oklahoma? Bree thought again. She turned to her computer and typed in *Carson Daniels* and the town. Up popped an address on Oklahoma State Route 3. Daniels appeared to have been thirty-five and unmarried. *Okay, but what does he do that gets him in first class on a flight from Florida?*

She dug deeper. Daniels was an independent crop-insurance agent. Was that enough? She supposed if he had lots of clients, it was. And Ada was certainly big-time farm and ranch country.

Her phone buzzed and her computer dinged, alerting her to e-mail from Mahoney. She called it up on her big screen and clicked on the image of Carson Daniels's driver's license.

Bree didn't get it at first. The glasses and the goatee threw her. But then she saw the resemblance. She whistled in disbelief.

And then she was so certain, she didn't even have to check the driver's license on her other browser to know that Carson Daniels of Ada, Oklahoma, and FBI special agent Charles Stimson of Groveton, Virginia, were one and the same.

CHAPTER

78

AFTER WE'D GIVEN MRS. MCCOY and her sister our cards and explained what was likely to happen next in the investigation, we headed back to Washington. Sampson drove. I sat there feeling exhausted and gloomy.

"Get some shut-eye," Sampson said. "I got more sleep than you did last night."

"Agreed, but I have to do a couple of things first," I said, yawning as I pulled out my phone.

I called Keith Karl Rawlins, a private consultant to the cyber-crimes unit at the FBI lab in Quantico, Virginia. Rawlins had dual PhDs from Stanford in physics and electrical engineering and a third doctorate from MIT in computer science. He was the smartest hacker I'd ever known.

"Alex Cross, as I live and breathe," Rawlins said.

"How are you, KK?"

"Not bad. Not bad at all."

"You still working in the basement?"

"I like to think of it as my subterranean lair, but yes."

"I need a favor."

"Of course."

"I'm going to courier over an iPhone, a laptop, and an iPad belonging to the latest Dead Hours victim. I have a password for the first two."

"That helps," Rawlins said. "What are we looking for?"

"A reason why a gym teacher would lie to his wife and drive from Laurel to Southeast to die at four thirty in the morning."

"Send them out here and I'll see what I can do."

"I'll messenger them as soon as I can," I said. I hung up and looked over at John. "Did we ever find out if that victim found in that park had a juvenile record?"

"I haven't had time to look at Henry Pelham," Sampson said. "But that reminds me—we have to see where we are on the DNA in the vomit we found at the scene. The way it looks is, the killer was the one who puked."

"Does Hanson with the state troopers know anything?" I said.

"Give her a shout. She might. And I'll messenger those things to KK. You go home and take a nap."

After John dropped me off at my house, I called the Maryland State Police homicide detective and got her voice mail. I left a message and was just shutting my eyes when she called back.

I picked up. "Hey there, Detective. Alex Cross here."

"I saw. You called?"

"I did. Have you been looking into Henry Pelham?"

"Quite a bit, though it's been tough. He has no living family and his coworkers said he was an introvert who never socialized. Neighbors barely knew him to say hi."

"Any chance he had a juvenile record?"

"Yeah, as a matter of fact, there was something when he was fifteen," she said. "But it was sealed and expunged at eighteen. Why?"

"Several other victims had juvie records that were expunged."

"Really?"

"Uh-huh. Nothing since for Mr. Pelham?"

"No. Quiet guy who led a quiet life."

"Any sense of where he broke the law as a juvenile?"

"Edgewater, Anne Arundel County, Maryland."

"Any idea who the prosecutor or judge was?"

"No, but the presiding judge at juvie in Anne Arundel has been around at least twenty years. You might give her a call."

Hanson gave me Judge Ernestine Ball's phone number and wished me luck.

I called the number and left a message, figuring that I wouldn't hear back soon because it was the weekend. Still, I identified myself and asked if I might have a few minutes of the judge's time on a sensitive case we were working.

Several moments later, a woman called back and said, "This is Judge Ball. How can I help, Dr. Cross?"

"It's a long shot, but I'm wondering if you remember a case eighteen years ago involving a fifteen-year-old from Edgewater named Henry Pelham?"

There was silence on the line before Judge Ball said, "You know I can't talk about juvenile cases."

"Especially ones that have been sealed and expunged," I said. "But these are special circumstances, Judge."

"How's that?"

"Pelham was shot to death by the Dead Hours killer."

"Well, I'm sorry to hear that, but that still doesn't change—"

"I'm sorry to interrupt, Judge, but at least five of the victims had juvenile records that were sealed and then expunged at age eighteen."

There was a pause. "Is that so?"

"Yes, ma'am. We're just trying to find a commonality beyond that if there is one."

A longer silence ensued before she said, "Was Mr. Pelham married?"

"No. He lived alone and had no living relatives. Neighbors barely knew him."

She took a long slow breath. "I was the judge on Henry Pelham's case. It carries my seal. It was expunged under my order."

"Yes, ma'am, but knowing what really happened might help us prevent another senseless killing."

Judge Ball cleared her throat. "Henry, who was fifteen, got into his parents' liquor cabinet, got loaded, and sexually assaulted a ten-year-old girl, a neighbor. He claimed to have no recollection of the experience and everyone who appeared in my court testified to the kid's character. He cried when he apologized in my court to the girl and to her family. There were no further incidents. End of story."

I hung up, went upstairs, and crawled into bed for a long nap.

79

BREE AND ELENA MARTIN entered the offices of Amalgam Corporation in Reston and asked to see Craig Warren.

The company's chief financial officer was in an emergency meeting following the death of the CEO—which was why the place was staffed on a weekend—so the two women asked for Leigh Anne Asher's personal assistant, Jill Jackson. The receptionist told them that Jackson was in Asher's office, cleaning things out before she moved on to a new job.

"That was quick," Bree said.

"We still want to talk with her," Martin said in her most intimidating voice.

The receptionist shrank a little and gave them directions to the corner office, where Bree and Elena found Jill Jackson on the floor with her back to the door, going through files and shredding them.

"Excuse me?" Martin said loud enough to be heard over the shredder. "What the hell do you think you're doing?"

Jackson jumped up and spun around, her hand on her heart. "You scared the bejesus out of me!"

"I would hope so," Bree said.

"What's going on here?" Jackson said.

"We asked first."

"I'm going through Leigh Anne's files, making sure they're in order."

Martin said, "Looks more like you're destroying things a federal agent would be interested in."

"I don't know what you're t-talking about," Jackson stammered. She was lying and not doing a great job of it.

Bree said, "I am two seconds from calling FBI agent Vicky Thomas and telling her what you're up to. She'll put you in handcuffs for obstruction of justice."

"So come clean," Martin said. "Tell us about Agent Charles Stimson."

Jackson looked from Martin to Bree and back. "Um, I believe Agent Stimson was looking at some of the early investors in the company. But that happened at Leigh Anne's request after she kind of figured out who they were."

"Oh, c'mon. Leigh Anne signed off on those investors along with Craig Warren."

Asher's personal assistant blanched, hurried past them, and shut the door. She turned, palms up. "That's because Warren told her that he'd done the due diligence on them. And things were happening so fast for Amalgam, she didn't have time to double-check his work. I swear that's true."

"A signature's a signature," Bree said.

"She knew she was in potential legal trouble, and she wanted a safe way out. That's why she called Agent Stimson. To lay it all out."

"Wait—she didn't call the FBI? She called Stimson specifically?"

Jackson licked her lips. "I don't know exactly how, but they knew each other. The FBI offices aren't far from here."

Bree and Martin continued to press Jackson and learned that Agent Stimson had looked at the evidence and immediately opened up an investigation focused on CFO Craig Warren and several Bulgarian and Israeli investors, who appeared to have ties to organized crime. Asher, Jackson said, cooperated fully.

"They spend a lot of time together?" Bree asked.

Jackson swallowed. "I guess. I didn't keep track of that. I'm sure, because of the investigation, they had to meet a lot."

Martin said, "Outside the office?"

"That's how you would do it. Right?"

Bree reached into the pocket of her jacket and came out with copies of the two driver's licenses. She showed the Virginia one to Jackson. "Recognize him?"

She shrugged and nodded. "Charles."

"How about this one?" she said, showing Jackson the copy of the Oklahoma license.

"Carson Daniels?" Asher's PA said, reading the name.

"Look closer," Martin said.

Jackson blinked and moved closer. "That looks like Charles Stimson too."

"Because it *is* Charles Stimson," Bree said. "Know how we found this driver's license?"

Jackson shook her head but looked as if she feared the answer.

Martin said, "Agent Stimson used it to get on the American

Airlines jet that went down. He was sitting next to Leigh Anne in seat two B."

Bree said, "They were coming back from Florida, where they'd been shacked up, all lovey-dovey. He even gave Leigh Anne an engagement ring. Did you know that?"

Jackson had held her own until then. But now she burst into tears and collapsed to the ground, moaning and blubbering. "No, no, no. It wasn't…it wasn't…"

Martin crouched by her. "It wasn't what?"

Jackson didn't reply until Bree handed her a box of tissues. Then she stammered, "It w-wasn't a fairy-tale story Leigh Anne told herself. It was real. They loved each other."

In fits and starts as she calmed down, the PA described how Stimson had come to Asher's apartment about fifteen months before. With Jackson's help, the Amalgam CEO had started showing the FBI agent documents surrounding the early investors.

"Like I said, they'd met before somehow, and he was trying to concentrate on the crime. But there were sparks flying between them." They tried to hide it, but Jackson was so involved in her boss's life, she knew an affair had begun within weeks of Stimson's arrival and subsequent investigation.

Bree said, "Did Leigh Anne know that Stimson was married and that his wife had ALS?"

Jackson's face fell, but she nodded. "She felt guilty, but Charles kept saying that he and his wife hadn't been together, really, in several years. He cared for her and all and would until she died. He told Leigh Anne that up-front and she admired him for it."

"Enough to have an affair with a married guy whose wife was dying?"

Jackson pulled her shoulders back. "Enough to fall in love with him. For real. And she believed Charles loved her too. And that ring? There's the proof of what Leigh Anne always used to say to me—'If it's real, love will find a way.'"

Elena Martin choked up and said, "Leigh Anne did say that. And then she'd watch one of those true-crime shows about husbands murdering wives and wives murdering husbands, and she'd say, 'Isn't it crazy what people will do for love and money?'"

80

I HEARD A FLOORBOARD creak and then soft footsteps; I felt a kiss on my forehead. Bree sat on the edge of the bed, smiling.

"How long have you been sleeping?"

"Not sure," I said groggily.

"It's six thirty. Dinner's almost ready. Why don't you take a shower while I tell you how my case of the missing executive turned out?"

Yawning, I nodded and shuffled to the shower in a way that made her laugh and say, "You really do need more sleep."

"Tell that to the killers and sociopaths," I said, turning on the shower.

I got in and let the hot water soak me while Bree told me about the FBI agent with a double life investigating the CEO with a double life. When she finished, I said, "Have you told Vicky Thomas?"

"She has an FBI team at Amalgam as we speak, seizing computers and paper records. I'll bet we see Craig Warren, the CFO, go down. I expect the IPO is off."

"What was the assistant shredding?"

"Leigh Anne's files pre-Amalgam. And probably personal stuff. I can't blame her for putting obstacles in our path. She was just trying to protect the reputation of someone she idolized."

I nodded, smiling, impressed once again at my wife's compassion for others, even people who got in her way. "Glad you closed the case."

"Me too. Ali says he's grounded?"

"Until after high-school graduation," I said, irritated again. "Even with kids as bright as Ali, you have to set boundaries. And showing up at an active major crime scene is breaking all boundaries in this house."

Her eyes widened. "He didn't tell me that. He said he was trying to help you."

"That kind of help will get me fired."

Bree agreed but said grounding Ali until graduation was a little extreme.

"I get it," I said, climbing out of the shower and toweling off. "I still love him, but he's got to be punished for this in a way that hurts."

"I'm sure you'll figure something out," she said. "And of course you still love him. Just because he's smart doesn't mean he doesn't need parenting."

"Exactly. And as long as it's done out of love, we're good."

Bree smiled. "Done out of love. I like…" She stared off into space as I dressed.

"Earth to Bree?" I said, buttoning my shirt. "What's up?"

She shook her head, then refocused. "Just something that

Leigh Anne Asher evidently used to say after watching one of those true-crime shows. 'Isn't it crazy what people will do for love and money?'"

"And power."

"The big three," she said just as Jannie knocked and told us dinner was ready.

More clearheaded now, I went down the stairs with Bree following, but she was off in the clouds again, no doubt contemplating Leigh Anne Asher's question of love and money.

Nana Mama brought a carved chicken to the table that she'd slow roasted in a mustard, saffron, and garlic sauce inside a ceramic pot. The meat was falling off the bone and smelled ridiculously good.

Jannie brought over bowls of roasted root vegetables and rice. Ali was already seated at the table—well, more like slouched at the table, head down, staring at his iPad.

"No electronics at the table," Nana Mama said sharply. "You know my rule."

Ali groaned, got up, put the tablet on the counter, then made a dramatic show of returning to the table and sitting down hard.

"What's up your butt?" asked Jannie, who'd come home to do laundry and have dinner.

"Nothing's up my butt," he shot back. "I just don't like injustice."

"Knock it off," I said, sitting down. "You're no victim here. You're lucky you weren't arrested for obstruction. So sit there, be quiet, eat your dinner, clean up, and go to your room."

"Dad," he said. "C'mon."

I stared at him until he shrugged and said, "Whatever."

The entire exchange put a damper on the mood at dinner,

though the meal itself was off-the-charts good. The chicken melted in your mouth, and the mustard, garlic, and saffron sauce on the jasmine rice had everyone fighting for seconds.

"You've outdone yourself, Nana," I said as the kids cleared the table.

"Wish I could take credit," she said. "I saw someone do it on one of my cooking shows. And a friend of mine from down the block brought me the saffron all the way from India."

"One hundred percent repeat, Nana," I said. "Right, Bree?"

My wife was staring off into space again. She startled and then said to my grandmother, "My God, if you don't repeat it, my life won't be complete."

Nana thought that was pretty funny. She cackled and said, "I had wonderful news today. The school district wants me to deliver more talks on YouTube because I guess my last one was a hit."

Ali frowned, put a stack of dirty plates on the counter, and went to his iPad. A moment later, he started laughing. "Nana, you've got like ten thousand views!"

"What?" we all cried. We crowded around his screen and saw it was true. And when we scrolled down to the comments, we saw remarks like *Need more teachers like this, challenging students in a kind way* and *A master class in Zoom teaching* and *Ninety-something great-grandmother has bored kids in the palm of her hand. Make more, Mrs. Cross.*

Nana Mama had tears in her eyes. "You see what happens when purpose comes back into your life?"

"Look," Ali said. "Like fifteen more people have watched it since we got on the page. You're not a star in the making, Nana. You're already a star!"

81

GRINNING FROM EAR TO ear, I left the kitchen and decided to watch a college football game to unwind. Jannie came in and sat at the other end of the couch.

Bree came over and sat next to me. "Good game?"

"Just started," I said.

Nana Mama came in holding several paperback books. "I've got some rereading to do before I go on camera and open my yap again," she announced to everyone's amusement. "I think I'll go up to my room for the night."

I got up and gave her a hug. "We're all proud of you, of what you stand for."

She got teary-eyed again. "It goes both ways. With all of you."

We all told her good night and we were returning to the game when Ali came in and started toward an empty seat. "Nana's got like another twenty views. I think she's going viral and—"

"Ali," I said. "Upstairs."

He stared at me incredulously. "C'mon, Dad."

"March."

He didn't storm out of the room and up the stairs. But it was close.

There was a spectacular, acrobatic catch by one of the wide receivers. It changed the mood considerably. During a commercial, Jannie said, "Bree, what's going on with Iliana's case?"

Bree startled again. "You know, Jannie," she said, getting up and grabbing her phone off the coffee table. "I was thinking the same thing just now."

She left the room, her thumbs working her screen, just as my cell rang. Caller ID said KK.

I answered. "Mr. Rawlins. Did you get the package?"

"About six hours ago," he said. "The laptop and the desktop opened with the passwords you gave us, but the iPad had not been set up for that yet. Meaning I got in and I found disturbing things and evidence of more coming. Can you get to a computer?"

Getting up off the couch, I said, "On my way."

"I'm not going to bore you with how I did it, but there's a video that was sent to McCoy using Tor."

"The encrypted messaging system, the onion-layer thing."

"Correct," Rawlins said. "But we have some cutting-edge technology here in the cybercrime lab that has broken through some of that encryption, enough that I was able to track the message back to a message board on the dark web and a member with the handle 'Fisher of Men.'"

"What kind of message board on the dark web?" I asked, climbing the stairs to my attic office.

Rawlins sighed. "One for pedophiles and the like."

My stomach turned. I entered my office, flipped on the light, and jiggled the trackpad to wake up the computer. "Is the video proof of it?"

"Yes. It should be in your queue."

"Then I don't have to see it."

"You need to see it because it was used as an advertisement of sorts, a taste of what the buyer could expect."

"Buyer?" I said, feeling more revolted. I went to my e-mail and found the attachment from Rawlins.

"Yes, buyer," Rawlins said impatiently. "And that's the thing. I think this is how your Dead Hours killer targets his victims. He lures them in with this video."

My cursor hovered over the attachment. I really did not want to watch it. "Look, KK, I'm going to take your word for it. I'm home, having a nice night with my family, watching the football game and—"

"You'll miss your chance, then, Cross," Rawlins shot back. "If I'm reading the decrypted fragments of messages to and from the killer right, he's got a new fish hooked. They're set to meet tomorrow morning."

I clicked on the video. The screen jumped to life, and I was immediately shocked at the depravity, the cruelty, the…thirty seconds in, I had to shut it off.

Feeling cold, feeling like the Dead Hours killer needed to be wiped off the face of the earth, I said, "Where and when is this meet supposed to go down, KK?"

82

BY TWO THIRTY IN the morning, John Sampson and I were set up across the street and down a hundred yards from the entry to a new residential development going in off the wooded Melford Road in Westphalia, an unincorporated area of Prince George's County.

Detective Marilyn Hanson was also watching from a different car with a different angle on the thirty acres of recently cleared land. Near the entrance, there were culverts and water pipes stacked by idle backhoes and bulldozers.

"Why here?" Sampson said, sipping at his coffee in the dark. "The others were in urban areas, except the guy in the national park, Henry Pelham. And then he goes back to the schoolyard. And now out here with whoever is supposed to be coming."

I shrugged. "Maybe he thinks the urban areas are too risky, so he's mixing it up."

"This just seems, I don't know, out of character," John grumbled.

"A curveball," I agreed. "Except for where Pelham was found. Any word back on the DNA of the vomit in that park?"

Sampson got a foul look on his face. "I asked yesterday, and they said there's a backlog, but they'd try tomorrow to at least get to the preliminaries."

Our radios crackled with Detective Hanson's voice. "Blue Dodge Ram, Maryland plates, coming your way. Driver is alone. Male. No firm visual."

"He see you?" Sampson asked.

"Negative."

Headlights slashed back near the entrance to the new development. The pickup truck made the corner and barely slowed passing the conduits and water pipes.

We were tucked in the parking lot of a landscape company. There was a sign out front set perpendicular to the road so it could be seen from either direction. When the truck headlights hit the sign, some of the light bounced back, giving me a quick but fairly decent look at the driver. He was older, Caucasian, glasses, hunched over the wheel and wearing a coat and dark ball cap.

He never looked our way and accelerated past us.

"You get a plate on him?" I said into the radio.

"Partial. You?"

"He went by kind of quick and the light on his license plate was dim."

"Convenient," Hanson said. "If he comes back."

But the pickup truck did not return. Indeed, for close to forty minutes, we did not see another vehicle on Melford Road.

Finally, at three twenty, a white Ford pickup truck came past us, heading toward the new development. I did not get as good a look at him as I'd gotten at the other driver, and I couldn't say much about this driver as the vehicle passed us.

The brake lights went on almost immediately. Then the headlights dimmed and the truck turned into the development under construction.

"You see him?" I said into the radio.

"I do," Hanson said. "How do we handle this?"

"We wait for whoever the second party is," I said.

"He tries to leave, I'm pulling him over."

"One hundred percent."

Sampson said, "That going to hold up? Just hate to see someone get cut free for lack of probable cause for a traffic stop."

I looked at him. "When we're dealing with people selling children, I think we're justified pulling this guy over every day of the week and twice on Sunday."

"I hear you," he said.

For fifteen minutes we waited. Hanson could still see the Ford, which had gone deep into the development and now sat there, lights off, engine idling.

At four a.m., Hanson said, "He's moving. Turning around."

"If you're going to stop him, do it before he gets out of that development," Sampson said. "We'll be right along for backup."

"Got that," the detective said.

We saw her headlights come on. She drove her squad car and stopped it so it was fully blocking the entrance to the construction site.

Sampson started our vehicle and drove up beside her, and we climbed out, hands on the butts of our service weapons. The Ford bounced along at a fair clip until the high beams caught us standing there. Hanson slapped a flashing blue bubble on the roof of her car and climbed out. The pickup kept coming.

Hanson and John both held up their badges. The truck slowed. A window rolled down, and a Hispanic male in his late forties looked at us with a puzzled expression.

"What's going on here, man?" he asked.

Hanson identified herself, walked to the pickup. "You are?"

"Enrique Morales," he said.

She asked him for his identification. He fumbled for it but eventually found a Maryland driver's license.

Hanson took it. "You live close by?"

"Close enough," Morales said. "Will you tell me what is going on?"

I said, "Why are you here in the middle of the night, Mr. Morales?"

"I couldn't sleep," he said. "I am under a lot of pressure, and I just came to the site to make sure I was on top of things."

Sampson said, "You're saying you work here?"

"I do," he said. With our permission, he reached over to the passenger seat and showed us a hard hat with the logo of the Lafford Construction company of Bowie, Maryland. He tapped a Lafford identification on a lanyard hanging from the rearview. "I'm the foreman on this job. Look in the back seat, you don't believe me."

Hanson shone her flashlight into the rear seat, revealing rolled blueprints and surveying equipment.

"I got a bad deadline, man," Morales said. "That's why I'm here instead of in bed with my wife. Why, who did you think I was?"

"We're not at liberty to say, sir," Sampson said.

"Well," he said, looking confused, "no one dangerous, I hope."

"Why would you say that?" I asked.

"I got fifteen men and more equipment coming at seven, that's why."

Hanson took a picture of Morales's driver's license, then handed the ID back to him. "Sorry to have concerned you, sir. We'll let you get on your way."

"Okay, then," Morales said and nodded. "Thank you."

The state police detective went to her vehicle, climbed in, started it, and backed up. Morales began to roll up his window.

I stopped him, said, "One more question?"

His brow furrowed. "If it gets me closer to my Denver omelet, yes."

"As a kid," I said, "before you were eighteen, ever get in trouble with the law?"

Morales looked at me with flat, dull eyes. "Me? Never. My mother would have beat me senseless, and my father would have done worse."

I smiled. "Just checking. Have a good day, Mr. Morales."

"I'm going to try, sir."

He rolled up his window and drove off.

Sampson said, "You believe him?"

I thought about the flatness and dullness of his eyes.

"No," I said. "I don't."

CHAPTER

83

SAMPSON DROPPED ME OFF at home around five thirty. I was beat, and other than my suspicions concerning Enrique Morales, we had nothing to show for the night's work.

K. K. Rawlins had to have misinterpreted the fragments of the Tor message he'd recovered from the iPad belonging to the Dead Hours killer's most recent victim. Maybe he had the date, time, or location wrong.

Who knew? I was so tired, I was almost past caring when I slipped a key in the lock and opened the front door.

The hallway and stairs were dark. I hung up my jacket, kicked off my shoes, and was about to start up the stairs when I heard a ding from the kitchen.

Five thirty was early even by Nana Mama's standards, so I padded down the hall and into the kitchen we'd added to the house a few years ago. I expected to find my grandmother hard at work, mixing blueberries into pancake batter or cutting bread for French toast. Instead, I found Ali sitting at the table eating soft-boiled eggs with toast and juice. He saw me and searched my face.

"Did you get him?" he asked.

"That is none of your business, young man," I said firmly. "Why are you up so early?"

Ali swallowed. "To talk to you about the Dead Hours investigation, about—"

I was at the end of my rope. I slammed my hand so hard on the counter, he recoiled and looked at me like I was a wild thing, which was the reaction I was after.

"Nothing," I said. "Nothing about the Dead Hours killer. At all. Do you understand, Ali?"

He stared at me, then shook his head ever so slightly.

"You don't understand that you could have compromised the investigation?"

"Not really, Dad," Ali said in a thin voice. "I just wanted to show you something. Please, I think it could help you."

"With what?"

"With the Dead Hours investigation," he said. "I found this—"

"Enough," I said and turned on my heel. "I'm going to sleep, and when I get up, you and I are going to—"

"Please, Dad!" Ali called out behind me.

I ignored him until I reached the bottom of the stairs and realized I could hear him crying as he said, "Please listen to me, Dad. Please. I think I found him, and you won't listen to me."

Hearing the pain in the voice of my youngest, I sighed and went back to the kitchen. He was still sobbing and wiping at tears.

"What did you find?"

Ali stared at me. "You really want to know?"

"I do. Whatever it is."

He watched me a moment more before saying, "Not *whatever*. *Whoever*." He reached for his iPad and began tapping on the screen. "I know you're going to want to kill me, but I've been at two of the three most recent Dead Hours crime scenes."

My head felt ready to explode. "What?"

"I'll explain later," he said. "And you won't be mad. Well, maybe a little mad, but you shouldn't be. Not after you see these."

He made a final tap on the screen and turned the iPad to show me two different pictures taken at the Bart Masters crime scene. They were crisp and clear and focused on an older, slightly hunched-over man with a full beard and shaggy silver hair. He held a cane and wore a tweed overcoat and matching snap-brim cap.

"Now, I wasn't at the Pelham scene, but the *Washington Post* was."

He clicked on a file and up came a picture of the scene beyond the yellow tape across the entrance to the national park. Perhaps twenty people were outside their cars looking at EMTs removing the bagged body of Henry Pelham.

Ali isolated a piece of the crowd and blew it up. There, four or five cars back, stood a man with red hair and a goatee wearing a dark blue windbreaker and cat's-eye sunglasses.

"Okay?" I said.

"Wait for it," Ali said, and he called up a picture of the crowd gathered across the street from Tyler Elementary and the Dalton McCoy crime scene. Again, he isolated someone in the crowd and blew up the image. This man's hair was dark and cut military tight. He wore mirror aviator sunglasses and a dark hoodie.

"I'm not seeing it," I said.

"I do," Ali said. "Do you know what a super-recognizer is?"

"I didn't know there was such a thing. You mean with artificial intelligence?"

He looked annoyed. "No, Dad. There are people who are born with super-recognizing abilities. They did a whole thing on them on one of Nana Mama's favorite shows, *Sixty Minutes*. We did the test and I got them all correct."

"Which makes you a super-recognizer?"

He nodded, tapped the screen. "They are all the same person, Dad. Shoulders hunched forward. The hair color and cut changes. So do the beard and mustache. The clothes and sunglasses try to fool you, but the cheekbones and jawline are absolutely the same."

I could see what he was talking about, but it wasn't enough to be definitive. At least not in my mind.

Until Ali tapped on the picture of the older man at the Masters crime scene. He blew up the right side of his head.

"Look at the ear," he said, magnifying it more. "He's got like half an earlobe sticking out from under the hair."

I squinted. It was true. I said, "But the photographs of the other men are from the wrong angle."

Ali nodded. Then he called up another photo he'd taken of the crowd at the McCoy crime scene. In it, the guy with the tight military haircut was almost broadside to the camera. I didn't need him to blow the picture up to see the man had half an earlobe.

I studied the pictures, seeing in my mind the silhouette of the driver of the blue Dodge Ram pickup that had gone past me and Sampson earlier in the morning. Was half his right earlobe missing?

"You believe me, don't you, Dad?" Ali said. "I'm right, aren't I?"

"I believe you've got something," I said. "But he seems awful old for a killer."

"And he limps," Ali said. "But he gets around fine. I have video of him beyond the baseball fence at the McCoy scene."

"Good video?"

He brightened. "Really good. You see him from every angle, Dad. He even takes off his hat. I'll bet you could use full-on facial-recognition software on him. Figure out who he is and why he keeps showing up."

I smiled and gave him a hug. "We just might try that once I've had some sleep."

84

BREE KISSED ALEX ON the cheek and headed to the bedroom door. "So, if Ali is right, is he still grounded until graduation?"

"Sophomore year," Alex grumbled. "Can you turn out the lights?"

Bree clicked them off and shut the door softly behind her, then checked her watch and swore softly. She ran down the stairs and into the kitchen, which was empty. She poured herself a go-cup of coffee, grabbed two of Nana Mama's muffins, and got her rain jacket out of the closet.

She'd no sooner gotten out on the porch and zipped her jacket against the dreary day than a dark sedan pulled up. The window rolled down, revealing Fairfax County police detective Marcia Creighton.

"Taxi's here," Detective Creighton called.

Bree went down the steps to the street and the car. She got in and laughed. "These new squad cars all smell the same, don't they?"

"Every one of them," Creighton said. "I think it's a mandatory spray."

"Did you check the Airbnb?"

"Last night," she said. "You were right."

"Thank God for bad housekeepers. Paxson?"

"Paxson," the detective investigating Iliana Meadows's murder said. "There were a few people I did not get to speak with the other day—the three coaches, actually."

"What about the roommate?"

"Kerrie Mountain. Nice kid. Very forthcoming, even after I went through their dorm room. Said she knew nothing about a sex tape or blackmail, but she did say Iliana had become irritable in the past two weeks. You said in your text that you had another theory?"

"I said I suspect something," Bree said, and explained.

When she was finished, Creighton nodded, said, "I hadn't thought of that."

"Neither did I, until last night."

Ninety minutes later, they exited the highway and got on Route 464, about four miles south of the Pennsylvania border, and soon after, they entered the quaint little town of Paxson, which was surrounded by wooded hills and farms.

Paxson bustled with midmorning activity despite the fact that it was a misty Sunday. A steady stream of students moved between the town and the Paxson State campus.

Creighton drove in the main entrance and found a spot in

visitors' parking. Bree and Creighton went to the administrative offices and had a talk with the bursar.

It had begun to drizzle when they found Iliana Meadows's roommate, Kerrie Mountain, studying in her dorm room. A short redhead with fair skin and freckles, Mountain was clearly devastated by Iliana's death and seemed to hold nothing back as they questioned her.

"I guess I knew she had money because she always had plenty to spend," Mountain said near the end of their conversation. "But I didn't know it was, like, that much."

Creighton said, "What do you mean?"

"I don't know," she said. "Kids on campus are saying Iliana had millions because of some accident that killed her father."

Bree moved around the dorm room, saw a keyboard, a mouse, and a dark screen. "She connected these to her laptop?"

Mountain nodded. "She said she liked to see things on bigger screens. Her laptop's missing, right?"

"It is," Bree said, moving the keyboard. "And so is her phone."

"You think the person who killed her took them?"

"Possible," Creighton said, watching her closely.

Bree turned the screen a little, noticed a small device in one of the USB ports. At first, she thought it was a thumb drive, but then she took a closer look. She turned the screen completely. "Do you know what this is?"

Iliana's roommate nodded. "It helps with Wi-Fi connections. Like an antenna. I've got one too."

"Where did you get them?"

Mountain told them. "We got a discount. Two for one. And the Wi-Fi seems better. Why?"

"I'll explain later," Bree said. "Don't touch them and don't talk to anyone about them until we return."

"No," she said. "I won't. I mean, I really don't know what's going on."

With a slight scowl, Detective Creighton crossed her arms and said, "Neither do I."

85

AS CREIGHTON AND BREE hustled through the light rain to the Paxson field house, Bree explained the devices and their ramifications.

"Jesus," Creighton said when Bree was done. "I never would have caught that."

"Alex showed me one once," she said. "Someone tried to use one on him."

"Okay, how do we handle it?" Creighton asked. "Strategically?"

"You're the one with jurisdiction."

"And you're a former big-city chief of detectives with way more experience."

"Make the questions sound routine at first, like follow-ups to some loose threads. Get them to answer before you tie them in knots."

The detective smiled. "I like that."

"Your call, but I'm willing to bluff on this one if we have to."

"Let's see how things go," Creighton said as they climbed the steps to the field house where the heads of the various athletic departments had offices.

"You've been here before," Bree said.

"Last week, but the coaches I wanted to talk with were all at another meet," Detective Creighton said, opening a door to the main office. "The staff are all here today, even though it's Sunday, because there's a big meet tomorrow."

Behind the front desk, an attractive young woman wearing a Paxson State Athletics hoodie was giggling at something said by a tall man wearing running shorts and a rain jacket.

Bree recognized him even before he'd twisted his head to see who'd come in. When he did, he sobered.

"Coach Leclerc," Creighton said. "One of the people we wanted to see."

"Didn't know you were coming by, Detective."

"A whim," Creighton replied. "We were in the area, and I had a few quick follow-up questions, if you don't mind."

Leclerc glanced at his watch, cleared his throat, said, "We're having a special speed practice right now, but sure, we can go to my office."

"And Coach Neely?" Bree said.

"Already outside with her team," he said, moving down a hallway.

"Let's go out there," Creighton said.

"It's raining."

"We won't melt," Bree said.

Leclerc shrugged and then took two sharp turns and pushed through a fire exit door. That put them in a tunnel that they followed to the small football stadium and track. Women's cross-country coach Marie Neely stood at the near side of the track looking at a stopwatch while Tina Dawson and several other girls came gasping across the finish line.

"Better," Neely said.

Breathing hard, Tina grimaced and said, "I don't know why I'm doing two-hundreds. I'm a distance runner, Marie."

"You qualified for regionals with that run at George Mason," Neely said crisply. "But if you want to compete at nationals, you will need a hard-sprint finish in you."

Tina finally noticed Detective Creighton, Bree, and Coach Leclerc. She wiped a strand of wet hair from her eyes. "Hello?"

Coach Neely turned and peered at them from under the hood of her rain jacket.

"They have some questions," Leclerc said.

"I'm running a practice," Neely said. "Big meet tomorrow."

"We'll ask between timings," Creighton said.

Neely looked at Leclerc, then sighed. "As you wish. Tina, you've got two more. Jog back. Stay warm."

"We'd kind of like Tina to stay," Bree said.

Tina appeared relieved. "I'd like to stay too."

Irritated, Neely said, "Put sweats on, Tina. Okay, ask away."

The Fairfax County detective said, "One of the things that Jannie Cross told us was that Iliana had confided in her that she wanted to talk with Bree because she was being blackmailed over a sex tape."

Coach Leclerc said firmly, "I still can't believe that Steve Hawley was—"

"He admitted to it," Creighton said, cutting him off. "He was being blackmailed as well. He's cooperating."

Leclerc stepped back. "I'm shocked."

"I am too," Coach Neely said. "But what does this have to do with us?"

86

DETECTIVE CREIGHTON LOOKED FROM the women's cross-country coach to the men's track coach to Tina Dawson.

"What was Iliana studying?" she asked. "Her major, I mean?"

Tina frowned. "I don't think she declared a major yet."

Coach Neely said, "Students have until the spring of their sophomore year to declare their major."

Bree said, "But you decided before classes even started, right, Tina?"

She nodded. "Computer science. I want a job eventually."

"Smart move," Bree said. "Closest thing to a sure bet these days. Growing field. Interesting work. A steady, reliable paycheck. Am I right?"

"Something wrong with that?"

"Nothing is wrong with that," Creighton said. "Especially for someone with your background."

Coach Leclerc said, "What the hell does that mean?"

Bree said, "Someone on scholarship. Academic and athletic."

"I'm proud of those scholarships," Tina said defensively.

"You should be. You needed them, and you got them."

"That's right, I did."

Creighton said, "Because you came from poverty in West Virginia and a broken home, and scholarships were your only way out."

"Yeah, we have nothing," Tina said in a soft snarl. "But my home isn't broken."

"Weakened, then. Your father died when you were ten. Mine accident, right?"

"Tunnel collapse."

"The mining company declared bankruptcy soon afterward, so you and your mother got very little."

"Enough for a year," she said. "Like I said, nothing. But we made do."

Bree said, "And you made do, and now you're here. But it must have stuck in your craw when you found out that Iliana Meadows's father also died in an industrial accident but she got millions."

Tina stared at her in bewilderment. "I did not know that."

"I think you did. No, I believe you did," Bree went on. "And it just ate you up inside. You barely scraping by, and Iliana able to rent a two-bedroom Airbnb because she didn't like the dump of a hotel the team was staying in."

Tina shook her head. "I don't know where you think you're going with this. But I have no idea how much money she had, nor do I care."

Creighton laughed a little. "Oh, you care. You care a lot, Tina."

Coach Neely said, "I think you need to stop whatever this is until Tina has talked with a lawyer."

"I agree," Coach Leclerc said.

Tina looked over at them in disgust. "I don't need a lawyer. All they do is take your money and run. I repeat: I had no idea she had money and I do not care."

Bree sighed. "The first week of school, you sold Kerrie Mountain and Iliana Meadows and I'm betting many more a device designed to improve their Wi-Fi."

For the first time, Bree saw Tina's eyes twitch with desperation. "They work," Tina said. "The Wi-Fi sucks in the dorms and they boost reception. I got them online from a wholesaler. I saw a need and I met it and made a little money. Again, what is wrong with that?"

Bree smiled at her. "What's wrong is that those devices are more than boosters—if they are even boosters at all. At the very least, they are keystroke loggers."

Tina's nostrils flared. Creighton said, "They record everything someone using the computer types in and calls up. You knew all about Iliana's money. And you knew about something else."

Bree said, "You found e-mails and texts from Iliana to her former coach. He told her he'd made a sex tape of the two of them. A perfect wedge for someone wanting to pry some of that money out of Iliana's hands, money that would be at least a little payback, some balance when it came to her father's and family's worth."

Creighton said, "And it worked. Using an encrypted messaging system, you told them you had the tape and demanded fifty thousand dollars from each of them payable in cryptocurrency. Iliana paid. Her old coach mortgaged his house to pay."

Tina just stood there looking evenly at them all, steely. "No. Never."

Bree said, "But then Iliana balked when you asked for another hundred thousand dollars. And then there you were at her Airbnb, her supposed friend, listening to her problems, telling her before she went out on her run that she should pay, that the tape coming out would destroy her reputation."

Tina shook her head in disgust. "You don't know what you're talking about. And remember, I got to the Airbnb after you and Jannie did."

"Because you'd already been there and gone," Creighton said. "We found blood evidence in the shower drain in the second bedroom."

Bree said, "Probably came off your skin and clothes when you climbed in there. The blood spatter made by the sharp rock you hit her with got all over you and landed in a trap in the drain. Along with your DNA."

Tina's jaw trembled. Suddenly, she spun around and bolted.

Creighton and Bree took off after her, chasing her up the track. Tina might not have been a sprinter, but she quickly opened up a gap.

Bree was ahead of Creighton but still fifty yards from Tina when she veered off the track and vaulted over the low chain-link fence that surrounded the field.

"There's a road below there!" Creighton gasped.

Bree sped up, reached the fence, looked down a steep embankment, and saw Tina was slipping and sliding near the bottom. She heard the grinding roar of a semitruck as it rounded a close corner. "Tina!" Bree yelled. "Don't!"

But Tina had already seen the Mack truck, and in the second that followed, Tina Dawson, gifted athlete, envious blackmailer, and cold-blooded murderer, stepped off the embankment and into the road and was hit before the driver could even touch the brakes.

87

BREE CAME HOME LATE that evening, traumatized and depressed after seeing Tina Dawson commit suicide by semitruck rather than face arrest and prison for Iliana Meadows's murder. Jannie was equally shaken when Bree called to tell her the person and reasons behind her friend's death.

"That's so sad," Jannie said after hearing of Tina's end.

"It's crazy what people will do for love and money."

When she hung up, Bree sat across the kitchen table from me, looked at her beer, and said, "I already feel punch-drunk."

"I felt the same way when I woke up today."

"Get anything done since?"

"A little. I sent Ali's photos and the video to Keith Karl Rawlins. He's going to run biometrics on the old guy with the weird earlobe."

"So wait and see."

"Story of a detective's life sometimes." Indeed, I'd found that during big investigations, the days were long and grinding, and the results seemed to seep in. But every once in a while, especially when we were getting close, a sudden torrent of information would flood in and change the entire course of the case.

Which is what happened the next morning when K. K. Rawlins called me as Sampson was driving us to work in his Jeep Grand Cherokee.

"Got him," Rawlins said.

"You're kidding me," I said, putting the phone on speaker.

"I don't kid. Well, rarely. It's definitely him. Got hits out of Interpol, Scotland Yard, and IAFIS."

"Interpol?" Sampson said.

"The earlobe thing gave him away. He's a British national. Former Special Air Service commando and armorist. Interpol and FBI files on him say he appears to have become a contract hit man after leaving the armed forces, but he's never been nailed for it."

"No sheet on him?" I asked.

"No, there's a sheet. He just did five years in federal prison in Colorado. He was suspected in the killing of a top bank executive in Denver with ties to the old Alejandro cartel. But they were able to convict him only on illegal weapons charges.

"He was evidently caught building and in possession of automatic ghost guns. The judge gave him ten years, but some legal nonprofit I've never heard of got him released for medical reasons last February."

I was scribbling in my notebook as fast as I could. "Name?"

"The old guy or the legal group?"

"Both," Sampson said.

"Padraig 'Paddy' Filson. And the legal group is the Exoneration Project."

"Never heard of either of them," I said. "But his release puts Filson on the streets a month before the Dead Hours murders began."

Sampson said, "Any idea where Filson is now?"

"No," Rawlins said. "But he's got a federal parole officer."

"Got a number?"

"And a name," he said, and gave them to me.

John said, "Great work, KK. Any word on the DNA from the Henry Pelham site? The vomit with the blood clots? I know there's a backlog."

"Huge logjams upstairs, but now that we have a name to check, I'll go up and get it to the front of the line ASAP. Promise."

As soon as we ended the call, I punched in the number for Filson's federal parole officer. Jeannie Michaels answered on the second ring.

I identified myself and inquired about Padraig Filson.

"Paddy?" Michaels said. "What's he on the edge of now?"

"Edge of?"

"On the edge of something bad but not over the line, so he can't be convicted of anything. It's the story of his criminal career."

"Repeat offender?"

"Did time in Scotland and France before his daughter moved here to Denver and he followed. Didn't take long before a shady banker was executed, and ATF caught Paddy building untraceable machine guns. So, again, what's he on the edge of now?"

I told her about the Dead Hours murders.

"Could be him," she said after a pause. "I mean, the whole

327

thing with the sheet and shooting out the eyes seems wildly out of character, but it's possible."

"You know where he is?"

"Two weeks ago, he was in Ohio," the parole officer said. "But at the moment, no, I don't know. He's been moving around. Working at various Amazon warehouses."

Sampson said, "He got released for medical reasons?"

"Paddy's terminal," Michaels said. "Slow-moving cancer with no cure. Maybe a year to live now."

"Can you do us a favor and ping him?" I said. "Get on the phone with him long enough to track his location?"

"Well, we weren't scheduled for a check-in until the day after tomorrow, but I'll give him a try. No promises. He uses one of those damn phones with the prepaid cards and keeps it off most of the time."

We'd no sooner gotten to Metro PD headquarters than the federal parole officer called us back.

"You're lucky I've got U.S. marshals across the hall," she said. "They do this kind of phone tracking of fugitives all the time. Anyway, they set it up before I called Paddy, and they traced his location. He told me he's in Omaha, but they have him in Springfield, Virginia. Outside an Amazon warehouse."

88

BY THE TIME WE reached the Amazon fulfillment center in Springfield, Virginia, about five miles southeast of downtown Washington, DC, Paddy Filson had finished his overnight shift and left.

The warehouse supervisor said he had no permanent address for Mr. Filson. He believed that Filson, like a lot of people who worked at the fulfillment center, lived in some kind of mobile home or trailer.

"Try the Burke Lake campground or Pohick Bay," he said. "They're the closest."

We got back in the car, pulled up a Google map of the area, and saw Burke Lake to our west less than three miles and Pohick Bay farther to our southeast.

"Burke first?" I said.

Sampson shook his head. "My gut says he's at Pohick. Look

how close that campground is to Accokeek and that national park where they found Henry Pelham."

"Other side of the river," I said. "He has to drive all the way north to the bridge and then come back down."

"It's still close," Sampson said. "But we'll check Burke Lake first."

Fifteen minutes later, we were waved through the gate. The manager said he had only ten campers this time of year, what with the weather getting colder. None of the campers matched the photograph we showed him of Filson.

"He's at Pohick," Sampson said when we left. "I'm feeling it."

It took us more than half an hour to get there. In the light, steady rain, autumn leaves were falling on the narrow route east off the interstate.

When we reached Pohick Bay Regional Park and the entrance to the campground, we found the guard shack empty but the gate open. A sign there said WINTER FEES COLLECTED ONCE A WEEK.

An older woman walking a dachshund appeared. We drove up to her. She acted suspicious until Sampson showed her his badge, and I showed her a picture of Filson.

"Gray, blue, and white Forest River Arctic Wolf fifth wheel," she replied. "Dark blue Dodge Ram pickup. He's been here long as I have. Works at Amazon and talks to no one. What's he done?"

"We just want to ask him a few questions about Amazon."

She laughed. "I can tell you all about Amazon."

"We'll find you afterward," I said.

"One thing you should know before you go down there— he's got guns. Weird ones."

"What do you mean, weird?"

"Like I think he builds them. In the trailer."

"Thank you," I said. "You've been a big help."

As we pulled away from her, both Sampson and I were thinking about the recent firefight we'd survived outside Sami Abdallah's home.

John said, "Backup?"

"Let's drive by," I said. "See what we see and then decide."

The campsite was heavily wooded and spotless but for the leaves falling on the pavement. We rolled slowly down the slick access lane.

There was some kind of rig—motor home or travel trailer— parked in almost every site, including the one on the far right, closest to the bay itself, a new fifth-wheel insulated trailer beside a midnight-blue three-quarter-ton Dodge that faced the lane.

"Same truck that went past us the other night," I said, then saw that the pickup's rear cap window was up and the tailgate down. I caught movement. "He's in the back of the truck. I'm going."

As Sampson started to take the curve in the lane back to the entrance of the campground, I eased open the door of his Jeep Grand Cherokee. He tapped the brakes. I stepped out and walked with the Jeep long enough to close the door softly.

Sampson rolled on around the loop and out of sight. The wet leaves and the rain dripping from the trees covered the sound of my footfalls as I drew my weapon and went around the back of the trailer, sticking to the taller dead grass to keep silent.

Gun up, I stepped out sideways from behind the back of the trailer and saw Filson facing away from me on his hands and knees in the back of his truck, rearranging plastic bins and crates. He was wearing a different coat than he'd been wearing

331

in Ali's pictures, a shorter one that revealed a pistol in a holster on his right hip.

For a second, I questioned my decision not to wait for backup. But two steps later, I was right behind him and to his left, just off the edge of the tailgate.

Holding the gun double-fisted, I aimed at the back of his now shaven head, the point where it met his spine. An instantaneous death shot.

Calmly, softly, I said, "Police, Mr. Filson. If you go for that gun, I will blow your head off. I cannot miss from this distance."

The older man tensed at the first words out of my mouth, and I thought from the way his right shoulder twitched that he wanted desperately to go for his gun. But then his back just kind of sagged.

"That's it, then," he said in a heavy brogue. "What would you have me do?"

"Lie down in the truck, facedown, fingers laced behind your head."

Filson complied just as Sampson ran up, his service weapon drawn.

"He's armed," I said. "Right hip. We'll pull him out by his feet."

With each of us aiming a gun at him with one hand, we dragged him back far enough to strip the pistol from its holster.

"Any other weapons?" I asked.

"Not on me," Filson said, still facedown with his hands behind his shaved head.

"Roll over and get out," Sampson said.

He rolled over awkwardly, then scooched out, looking much older than his sixty years. When he slid off the tailgate, John holstered his weapon, spun Filson around, and put zip cuffs on him.

"You're under arrest for the Dead Hours killings," Sampson said.

Before he could read the man his rights, Filson smiled oddly and said, "Well, then, you've come to the right place, haven't you?"

89

IT BEGAN TO RAIN hard. We put Filson in the back of Sampson's car and alerted the FBI to bring criminalists to the campground.

After two local Fairfax County Sheriff's deputies arrived to seal off the scene, the rain let up a bit. John and I entered the trailer, put on gloves, and began to search.

It didn't take much time to find the long coat he'd been wearing in Ali's first pictures and then the windbreaker from the *Post* pictures. He had a drawer full of cheap sunglasses and a stack of white sheets on one of the bunks. Beneath the sink we discovered gunsmithing equipment, including a miniature lathe and drill press.

There were boxes of handload bullets of several calibers in the cabinets above the fridge. Wrapped in a white pillow-case under some blankets in the storage space beneath the master bed, there was a handcrafted weapon that looked like a miniature double-barreled side-by-side shotgun, except with a custom pistol grip.

I cracked the breech and found two .25-caliber bullets in the chambers. When I lifted the gun and aimed at my reflection in a mirror, there was no question that at short range, Filson's double gun would blow out both my eyes.

"We got him," Sampson said. "It's over."

"Fat lady's singing," I said. "But I still want some answers."

"If he'll talk."

"He'll talk. I can see it. He wants to tell us all about it."

Because the murders occurred across multiple state and district lines, we decided to take the confessed Dead Hours killer to the federal detention facility in Alexandria until a judge could determine which jurisdiction to try him in. Filson said little during the drive, even when we passed groups of television reporters outside the campground and near the detention facility. We used the underground entrance and had Filson booked and then taken to an interrogation room, where we let him stew until two in the afternoon.

When Sampson, Detective Marilyn Hanson, and I entered, Filson had changed into an orange jumpsuit and was shackled to his chair by his ankles. His wrists were in handcuffs, and he was forced-smiling, as if he were trying to enjoy himself or cover some pain.

"Padraig Filson," I said.

"Call me Paddy," he said in a brogue, sitting back in his chair with a grim expression on his face. "Everyone does."

Sampson said, "You turned down legal representation?"

"Public," he said. "I'll go private if need be. How did you get me?"

"Your earlobe," I said.

"Damn thing," he said, wincing. "Al-Qaeda sniper shot it half off in Afghanistan twenty years ago."

Detective Hanson said, "Are you in pain, Paddy?"

He forced the smile again. "Twenty-four/seven from various causes."

Sampson said, "You're sick."

"Terminal," he said. "Matter of months now, and there'll be a big slide before a crash, and then I'll be free again, beyond your reach."

I said, "You believe in life after death?"

"I do. We are spirits having a physical experience."

Sampson said, "Do you expect to be judged for what you've done?"

Filson shrugged. "Don't know. But if I am, I believe I'll be found justified."

Hanson sat back in her chair with an angry look on her face. "Justified? You feel you were justified in killing seven men in cold blood?"

Filson nodded, smiled at her. "One hundred percent. And beyond that, I'm not saying another word without a glass of Jameson in front of me."

I said, "Booze? We can't do that."

"Look, Cross, I am dying. Oxy doesn't do a damn thing for the agony I get in. The only thing that kills the pain is Jameson. The good stuff. Bring me a bottle of that, and I'll talk all day and into the night."

CHAPTER

90

IT TOOK A LITTLE while, but soon enough we had a bottle of the "good stuff," Jameson Black Barrel Irish whiskey, and set it on the table in front of Filson.

He looked at us snobbishly. "Well, it's not Rare Midleton, is it?"

Detective Hanson looked disgusted. "You think we're going to spring for a three-hundred-dollar bottle for a confessed assassin?"

"Aye, once you've heard the evidence against him," he said. "But Black Barrel will do in the meantime. Can you pour me more than a wee bit, Dr. Cross?"

I opened the bottle, poured two fingers into a paper cup. Filson picked it up with his handcuffed hands and poured it slowly into his mouth. As he did, his shoulders dropped and his core relaxed in a way that made me realize how tight he'd been holding himself. There was no doubt the man was suffering.

When the whiskey was gone, he put the cup back on the table and nodded. I poured him a second round and he left it there.

"Look," Filson said. "I have seen the hard evidence against the men I killed. Each and every one of them needed to be eliminated before they scarred someone else for life and many lives beyond them. Trauma gets passed along, you know, generation to generation. Like a virus."

Over the next hour, which we recorded with multiple cameras, Paddy Filson sipped Irish whiskey and told us he'd seen juvenile records that were supposed to have been expunged and linked to every one of the Dead Hours victims.

When Daniel Kling, the first to die, was sixteen, Filson said, he raped an eight-year-old boy after he himself was earlier abused by a family friend. Victim number two, Theo Leaver, had been high on meth when he attacked and raped an elderly woman. Another victim, Lavon Kyle, molested two six-year-olds when he was twelve.

It went on. Trey O'Dell, the newlywed who'd told his wife he'd stolen a pair of cleats from a sporting goods store when he was fourteen, had actually sodomized a ten-year-old girl. Bart Masters, found off the lacrosse field, had been abused repeatedly as a child by an aunt's boyfriend, and he in turn had started abusing a neighbor's children when he was ten.

"When Henry Pelham was fifteen, he got drunk and assaulted a ten-year-old neighbor girl," Filson said. "And Dalton McCoy? When he was fifteen, he forced a twelve-year-old boy to rape his twelve-year-old girlfriend at gunpoint. And yet, even his records were sealed and supposedly expunged so he could start his life over at eighteen. Clean slate. No record. Free to destroy people's lives again."

I said, "We've seen no record of anything as adults. They were never charged again. They never made the sex-offender registries."

"Because they were smart. They kept their lusts hidden on the dark web. The virtual world was where they connected."

Sampson said, "And where they bought?"

"Correct. All the men I shot led secret lives where they paid to act out their twisted fantasies, most of the time on children being held as sex slaves."

"And you know this how?" Detective Hanson asked skeptically.

He cleared his throat, looked nauseated. "There are videos."

"For all of them?" I said.

"Some multiple. Seems it's not enough for them to act out their perversions. They want the memory of it on video to be enjoyed over and over again. Or at least until they've raised the money to act out some new dark fantasy."

"Jesus," Hanson said, trying to come to grips with what Filson was describing. "And how did you get hold of these videos and tie them directly to your victims?"

"They were sent to me over Tor," Filson said. "They also had to be watched within an hour of reception or they got nuked. No trace after sixty minutes. It's how we communicate, how we've communicated almost since the beginning."

I said, "Who is *we*? You and who else?"

The dying assassin laughed and sipped his whiskey. "You know what, Dr. Cross? I've tried to figure that out. I really have. But I honestly don't know who calls the shots and pays the bills in this particular business."

Sampson said, "So you were paid."

"Aye. Paid well."

Hanson said, "Where's the money? How much?"

Filson laughed again and drained the whiskey. "Can't tell you that. Otherwise what's the point of it beyond a little cleanup of the nastiness under the rug?"

I held up both hands. "We're going in circles, Paddy. Why don't you start at the beginning and tell us how it all started."

CHAPTER

91

PADDY FILSON TOLD US he started feeling sick early in the second year of his incarceration at the Rifle Correctional Center outside Glenwood Springs, Colorado. His visits to the prison infirmary had proved useless until a bone in his arm snapped for no good reason and he complained loud enough to get his blood tested.

"Turns out, I was already a dead man walking," Filson said. "Rare form of blood cancer. Slow creeper. Incurable. Makes my bones brittle. They told me I had a year, fifteen months, max."

Filson said he posted the news on prison social media and set about preparing himself to die in captivity. Shortly afterward, he was contacted by a legal group called the Exoneration Project that offered to take up his cause.

He messaged back and forth with a woman named Elizabeth Brenner who said she would be the lead lawyer for his case.

"I told her they had me cold on the weapons charges," Filson said. "I *was* building ghost machine guns. But in my defense, it was only to see if I could do it. I had no interest in selling those kinds of weapons to people who had no clue how to use them."

"And?" Sampson asked.

"She said that it didn't matter. They would ask for my release based on the terminal diagnosis. A mercy thing. And it would save the corrections department a lot of money. An economic thing. I didn't think she had a chance, but two days later, there I am, walking out the front door of the Rifle, a free man."

Filson claimed he was picked up by a young woman named Phoebe who said she worked for an affiliate of the Exoneration Project and that Elizabeth Brenner was sad not to be there herself. Phoebe drove him to the outskirts of Denver and stopped beside a steel building in an industrial area. Phoebe told him to go in a certain door, where someone associated with the Exoneration Project was waiting to discuss his health care and a possible well-paying job. Essentially broke coming out of prison, he got out of the car and went through the door.

Filson entered an empty, cavernous space, dead center of which there was an overstuffed chair and a table with a glass and a bottle of Jameson whiskey on it.

"I wasn't going to turn that down after years in the hole," Filson said. "So I sit there and pour myself one, drink it, and then the lights go off. I'm sitting there in the dark and there's this guy talking through some kind of distortion machine to mask his voice."

"C'mon," Hanson said.

"On my mother's grave," Filson shot back. "Anyway, he tells me he represents people trying to clean up society, trying to take out the rapists and molesters before they can scar another generation. Then he tells me he'll pay me fifty K for each life-long sexual predator I take out. He'll show me the evidence and let me make up my own mind.

"He also said I'd be doing the world a favor in my final months, using my skills for a greater good. I thought about it for two seconds and took the contract."

Filson said he was given enough cash to buy the truck and the trailer and was told to go to Washington, DC, and wait. He saw the evidence against Kling a week later and shot the man four days after that.

I said, "You look proud of it."

"Aye. He deserved it. I made the world a better place."

"And got paid for it," Hanson said.

"Aye. But don't worry. The money will do some good for a little boy I met once, a good little boy who deserves a better life. I've made sure of that. And don't bother with the Exoneration Project. It was a fake project with a website. It was taken down not long after I took the job."

I rubbed my temple. "You have no idea where the money came from?"

"Payment was in crypto, so I don't think I could figure out the source if I tried a decade, and I don't have a decade," Filson said.

Sampson said, "Give us access to your crypto accounts."

"No."

I said, "I know cyber experts at the FBI lab at Quantico who will be able to trace these people."

"Highly doubt it. He seemed mighty sure he couldn't be touched."

Hanson said, "The guy speaking through the distortion box?"

"That's right," Filson said and drained another double shot of whiskey. "The Maestro himself."

Hanson did not react, but Sampson and I both sat forward fast.

"What did you just call him?" I said.

"The Maestro," he said, his head retreating. "It's what Phoebe called him afterward, when she drove me to a hotel."

CHAPTER

92

COLD RAIN FELL ON Captain Davis when he walked out of George Washington University Medical Center around three in the afternoon, feeling raw inside, scrubbed clean, a new man, clear-eyed and ready to face the music.

He pulled the hood of his jacket up over his head and began to walk toward Foggy Bottom and the river. Rain or no rain, he needed time to think and prioritize, and he'd always done that best while walking.

I'm not listing these in any order, he thought. *That comes later. Rehab is definitely a priority.*

Davis knew he had a ways to go, knew he needed a good dose of long-term rehab before he could say he'd kicked his drinking habit. And he would go to rehab. He would.

It was a priority, he decided, but not number one. Not yet. *Fiona Plum.*

In his gut, he could feel that was the number one priority—to go see Fiona. Make amends. Apologize and seek her forgiveness. Once he had that, Fiona's forgiveness, Davis would do whatever it took to resolve his issues with alcohol for good. At that point, his sobriety would become the priority for the rest of his life.

But right now, it's Fiona and how much I let her down.

Captain pulled out his phone, and for the first time in four days, he turned it on.

Almost immediately, it started dinging with text messages and e-mails marked urgent. Davis ignored them, feeling shivery as he called up the Uber app.

He typed in Fiona Plum's address in Alexandria and hit Enter. Two minutes later, a black Nissan Sentra pulled up.

"You Marion Davis?" the young man driving said.

"That's me," Davis said and he climbed in the back.

"Traffic's going to be bad with the rain. And they're saying maybe snow tonight."

"I believe it. Hey, can you turn up the heat? I've got a little chill."

"You got it."

By the time they reached the Fourteenth Street Bridge, Captain felt like he was drying out in more ways than one. He started going through his messages and frowned. There were at least ten from Fiona. The first ones were asking where he was and saying she was worried about him. But the last three or four were begging him to surrender to the FBI.

What the hell was going on? He'd been released from federal custody the day before he checked himself anonymously into the detox unit at GW Medical Center.

Several texts were from his attorney, also advising him to turn himself in.

Davis now felt as upside down as when he'd been entering detox.

Someone's framing me. I'm positive. Or is it just paranoia? Yeah, well, it's not paranoia if someone's really out to get you, is it?

Soon after passing Reagan National Airport and exiting the GW Parkway, the Uber driver went by a liquor store. Davis suddenly wanted a drink. No, he desperately needed one.

Within seconds, the need became an obsession. He could almost taste the beer and chaser sliding down his throat, giving him relief, fortifying him, giving him the courage to face every one of his shortcomings and drown them in alcohol.

He almost told the driver to go back to that liquor store, but a voice inside him said that would be the end of whatever future there might be with Fiona Plum. He simply could not face her with booze on his breath.

Not a chance. She would smell it. No doubt.

Davis felt his heart race and noticed his hands were trembling. Not as much as they had been when he was going through full-blown withdrawal but bad enough to make him wonder if he had the emotional and physical strength to face Fiona in person.

And then it was simply too late. The driver turned onto her road. A moment later, her little Craftsman bungalow with the attached garage came into view.

A dark gray Sprinter van with the signage for a painting service was backed up to the mouth of the garage, which was lit up inside. Davis thanked the driver, got out, and noticed the WET PAINT sign on Fiona's front door.

Steeling himself, he walked toward the house, listening to the drumming of the rain on the roof and the van as he walked up the side of it. The rear double doors were open, almost flush to the frame of the garage door.

He had to turn himself sideways to get past the frame and the van door. As he did, he saw a big, swarthy guy, shaved head, come out the door to the house. He was dressed in a paint-spattered coverall and carrying a paint can and a crescent wrench in hands covered in blue disposable gloves.

The painter smiled when he saw Davis as if he were half expecting him, or expecting someone, anyway. There was something oddly familiar about the guy, but Captain couldn't place him. "Hey there," Davis said.

"Hey there yourself," the painter said in a Middle Eastern accent. He put down the paint can and came toward Davis, whose back was to the open van. "You're Marion Davis, aren't you?"

"I am."

"It's funny. That's my name too."

"Really?"

"True," he said, smiling. "Coincidence, huh? Miss Plum could not believe it."

"I bet not. Where is she? Fiona?"

The other Marion Davis grinned again. "She's right behind you, Captain."

The football coach turned, peered inside the rear of the van, and saw Fiona Plum blindfolded, gagged, and bound with duct tape. A split second later, the crescent wrench smashed into the back of his head, knocking him out cold.

CHAPTER

93

JOHN SAMPSON AND I jumped out of his Jeep Grand Cherokee down the street from a split-level ranch house in suburban Rose Hill, Virginia, a ten-minute drive from the federal holding facility in Alexandria.

We'd left Paddy Filson in a hurry despite the fact that he'd just implicated the vigilante group Maestro and, by extension, our archnemesis M in the Dead Hours killings. They'd orchestrated them, in fact, if the assassin was to be believed.

But Ned Mahoney had called us in a panic. A nearly naked woman had collapsed and gone into cardiac arrest in her garage in Rose Hill after telling her neighbor she'd been drugged by the terrorist who'd shot down AA 839 with a machine gun.

"I'm on my way, but you can get there faster than I can," Mahoney said, and we'd bolted, leaving Detective Hanson to continue the interrogation of the Dead Hours killer.

The rain had turned less torrential by the time we reached the yellow tape a sheriff's deputy had put across the driveway. After showing him our identification, we walked up to the garage, where we saw a buxom woman in lavender lingerie sprawled on the concrete floor, brunette hair covering her face.

"Who found her?" Sampson asked.

"Lady across the street, there on her porch," the deputy said. "She said the deceased is Rosella Santiago, who inherited this place from her uncle two years ago."

I squatted down and used a pen to push back her hair.

Sampson whistled. "I know her."

"I do too," I said. "Our friend from the sports bar. The siren who was with Captain Davis when he disappeared before the shootdown."

We both hustled across the street to talk with fifty-two-year-old Agnes Mellon, who'd been out walking her miniature poodle, Muffin, in the rain when Rosella Santiago staggered into her open garage and called weakly for help.

"She looked bombed, out of it on something," Mrs. Mellon said. "And then she fell, and I ran up there with Muffin. She looked at me dazed and said in this slurred voice, 'He did this to me. Machine-gun guy. Shot down the plane.' That is what she said. Exactly."

"Thank you for calling it in," I said. "Have you seen him? This machine-gun guy?"

She shook her head. "I'm not the nosy neighborhood-gossip type. I have a busy enough life of my own. I just happened to see her go down in the garage."

"What about the other neighbors?"

"You can try."

Ned Mahoney came running toward us through the rain. Sampson's phone buzzed with an alert.

He looked at it and said, "Marion Davis! He's surfaced. I've got him using an Uber half an hour ago. He went to Fiona Plum's. He's got to be there right now!"

"I'm on my way there," Mahoney cried; he spun around and ran back to his car. "Search that house! Talk to the other neighbors!"

CHAPTER

94

IN FIONA PLUM'S GARAGE, the man who'd renamed himself Marion Davis stared at the inert form of his namesake lying in the back of the van with the English teacher. He hyperventilated at his good fortune. He'd believed that sooner or later, Captain Davis would return to Plum's house, that it was just a matter of time.

He had been waiting for barely two hours, and here was the former football star already! Marion Davis looked at his watch and saw it was a little before five p.m.

He'd figured the next strike for the following night at the earliest. But he could change the schedule. He could go tonight, couldn't he?

Marion Davis felt his heart racing. He could go tonight. He could go now.

He pushed Captain Davis deeper inside the van, bound his wrists and ankles with duct tape, and put tape across his mouth.

Satisfied, he got out, shut the rear doors to the vehicle, and removed the painter's coverall.

Marion Davis went back into the house and turned off the lights. The garage light went off last. Five minutes later, he was driving away from Plum's neighborhood.

He pulled into a strip-mall parking lot, drove around the back of the stores into an alley with dumpsters, stripped the magnetic painting company signs off the side of the van, and put them in an empty dumpster. Then he drove west at a sedate pace due to the relentless rain. Another good omen, as far as he was concerned.

The storm and the coming night would shield him from prying eyes as he moved into position for the shot. All he needed now was continued low cloud cover and a little ground fog to make the hunting conditions absolutely ideal.

CHAPTER

95

SAMPSON AND I LEFT Agnes Mellon, returned to Rosella Santiago's house, and started going through it while a Fairfax County medical examiner and two criminalists photographed and documented the scene in the garage.

John went upstairs; I moved through the kitchen and living area, which were immaculate and smelled slightly of bleach. Sampson returned and said the upstairs was the same. He'd found a vacuum cleaner in the master bedroom closet. Its bag was gone.

We looked in the trash cans in the garage, but they were empty as well. Around the back of the house, I spotted a bulkhead, which meant there was a basement. We found the door to it off the laundry room and walked down a flight of stairs into a well-equipped woodworking shop: A bandsaw. A table saw. Two lathes. A drill press and multiple hand tools above a long bench.

Sampson opened a door and found another workroom, this one for metals and electronics.

"It's him, Alex," he called out a few moments later. "It's definitely him."

I followed John inside and saw him photographing two diagrams he'd found pinned to the wall. At the top of each it said RAYTHEON CORP., FIM-92 STINGER. The diagram on the left showed the inner workings of the surface-to-air missile. The right detailed the Stinger's infrared homing system.

"He's been working on the missiles," Sampson said. "Right here."

"And he's got them with him," I said. "Keep looking. I'm talking to the neighbors."

I knocked on the doors of several houses to either side of Santiago's but found no one home. I was crossing the street to try Agnes Mellon's neighbors when Ned Mahoney called.

"No Fiona Plum. No Captain Davis. But there was a brutal letter to him from her. Said she never wanted to see him again if he didn't get help."

"Her car there?"

"Yes."

"Is the place spotless?"

"You could eat off the floor. Some tarps in a hall and unused paint cans in the garage."

"He was here. We found diagrams for the Stinger missiles."

"Son of a bitch."

"Put out a heightened alert on Davis."

"On it," he said and hung up.

I knocked on the front door of Mellon's neighbor to her left and got no answer. But the door of the house to the right of hers opened before I could knock.

A male in his late teens who told us his name was Rex said, "What's going on? Is Rosella dead?"

I nodded.

"Wow, that's sad. What happened?"

"Someone drugged her, and she told your neighbor before she died that it was the guy who shot down the American Airlines plane."

"No shit," Rex said. "Damn it, I knew that dude was wrong."

"What dude?"

"Davis. Marion Davis. The dude she lived with."

I swallowed hard. "As in Marion Davis, the NFL player?"

"Football? He was big but he didn't look big enough for the pros."

I pulled out my phone and called up a picture of Captain Davis. "This him?"

The teen glanced at the photo. "Nah, nothing like him."

I asked Rex to describe Rosella Santiago's live-in.

"Around five ten, maybe a hundred and ninety pounds? Real thick guy. Looked and sounded Arab to me. Brown eyes. Short black hair."

"Beard?"

"Nope."

I called up another picture, this one of Leslie Parks and his mysterious friend Ibrahim in Fenway Park. "What about this guy?" I asked, showing him the photo.

Rex took the phone and studied it a few seconds before nodding. "He's shaved the beard and cut his hair. But that's definitely Marion Davis."

"Does he have a vehicle? Davis?"

"Yeah, one of those high-ceilinged vans. A Mercedes."

"A Sprinter?"

"That's right. Dark gray. Signs for his painting service on the side."

"Virginia plates?"

"Pennsylvania," he said. "And I think it's a rental."

"How do you know that?"

"There was a QR code on the driver's side, lower left corner of the windshield. I used to clean cars at Avis at night. They all have them."

96

THE RAIN CONTINUED AS night came on. Marion Davis drove steadily north on I-95, past Laurel, Maryland.

His mind kept looping in and out of the plan, looking for any weaknesses and finding none. Davis had done his homework meticulously over the past several months. He glanced at the digital clock on the console: 5:45 p.m.

It was a good night to die, he decided. If all went well, dying would not be necessary, but Davis was mentally prepared if need be.

He got off the interstate at the Savage exit and took a right. A minute later, he pulled into the drive of a Colonial that was empty and for sale. He opened the garage door with the remote he'd stolen at an open house for the place the week before, pulled in, shut the garage door, and got out of the van with his tools.

Davis lifted the hood and found the wiring and chip for the Mercedes tracking and security system. He clipped the control leads and crushed the chip, then retrieved a set of Florida license plates from beneath the passenger seat. He exchanged the Pennsylvania plates for the Sunshine State plates, tossed the others in a trash can, returned to the driver's seat, and sent a text over his burner phone to a memorized number: Are you still selling that Chevy?

Without waiting for a reply, Davis put on heavier clothes—a Canada Goose parka, wool pants, and knee-high Muck boots—and got back on the interstate heading toward the Beltway and the District of Columbia. A half hour later, he was south of DC, exiting at the Lorton, Virginia, exit, when his phone buzzed with a text: Chevy sold, sorry.

Davis's heart began to pound. *We're on.*

He heard noise coming from the rear of the van, looked over his shoulder, and saw Captain Davis sitting upright and glaring at him.

"Good," Marion Davis said. "I was hoping I hadn't clipped you too hard. It's actually easier if you're awake."

Captain Davis struggled against the tape around his wrists and ankles. But Marion Davis had done the job right. The captain could struggle all he wanted; it would do him no good.

"You don't remember me, do you?" Marion Davis asked, not caring that his captive couldn't answer. "Ibrahim Obaid. We met once. At Leslie Parks's place in North Carolina when you were posted at Fort Bragg. We didn't talk long. I was leaving. You were just coming in." Marion Davis laughed bitterly. "I knew who you were, of course. Leslie had told me all about you. How you were the man in the cockpit who bombed my village in Iraq, how you were responsible for the deaths of so many in my family."

He fell silent for a moment, letting that sink in. "You were the perfect man to take the fall for me, Captain. Guilt-ridden for what you did there, which turned into a drinking problem that got you fired from the American Airlines pilot program, and then your ex-girlfriend finds out the drinking was all about the atrocities you committed. Poor unstable woman— she killed herself and her daughter over it. All I had to do was change my name from Ibrahim Obaid to Marion Davis and the game was on."

Obaid—he thought of himself as Obaid again, now that he was looking at the original Marion Davis—laughed as he took a right onto Ox Road heading north. "The game is still on, Captain, and once again you are going to take the fall. Along with poor Fiona Plum."

He heard her whimper almost directly behind him. "Ah, she's awake too. So much the better. She loves you, you know, Captain. And what have you done for her in return? Nothing. Absolutely nothing. Another reason to get rid of you for good."

Traffic built as the rain began to turn into sleet. It came down in curtains, and they were crawling along with cars honking all around them.

Bam! Bam! Bam! Bam! Bam!

Obaid, startled, looked over his shoulder and saw Captain Davis pounding the back of his head against the wall of the van. Obaid pulled a sound-suppressed pistol from the center console and aimed it at the ex-coach. "One more and I'll put a bullet through her brain," he said. "I promise you that."

Captain Davis's face went red and he tried to scream through the duct tape.

"You'll kill me?" Obaid said and laughed. "No, I don't think so."

Traffic lightened as they passed into a wooded and less dense residential area. He turned the radio to an all-weather station and was happy to hear that the temperatures would drop and the storm would gain strength; there'd be snow and wind gusts approaching thirty miles an hour.

Obaid did the calculations in his mind, contemplating the direction of the shot and the angle of the wind. If he had it all straight, he couldn't miss, not with the Stinger's infrared homing system. And every test he'd conducted in the past three days said that Leslie Parks had been right. Despite the system's age, despite all the U.S. efforts around the globe to eradicate the shoulder-to-air missiles, the FIM-92 Stinger in the crate behind him would not only work but show the world the fragility and fraught future of air travel.

Obaid smiled, looked over his shoulder at Captain Davis, and said, "When you're done tonight, Captain, the airline business will be in turmoil, and the precarious economy of this country will lurch, stagger, and fall."

He returned his attention to the road. "And when I'm done, Captain, it will never rise again."

97

NED MAHONEY ALERTED MEMBERS of his AA 839 team, still operating out of the big tents opposite National Airport, about the new developments. The FBI was talking to the security chiefs of the major auto and truck agencies, looking for a dark gray Mercedes Sprinter van with Pennsylvania plates rented to a Marion Davis.

While they did, Sampson and I searched the internet for anyone who had recently changed his name to Marion Davis. We got a hit in West Virginia.

Sampson and I were in Sampson's car in front of Rosella Santiago's house when Ned called to say that no Marion Davis had rented a Sprinter van in a five-state area. I said, "Try Ibrahim Obaid. He changed his name to Marion Davis late last year. The application says he is a naturalized American citizen, living in Charleston, West Virginia. Emigrated to the U.S. under U.S. Army sponsorship a few years ago. Guess who he listed as one of his references."

"Leslie Parks?"

"Bingo."

"I'll call after running Ibrahim Obaid," Ned said, and he hung up.

The temperatures were plunging. The all-news radio station was warning of a serious storm, with the sleet turning to snow.

"Home?" Sampson said, starting the car.

"Until we hear something different," I said.

Sampson turned on the wipers; they slapped at the frozen rain and pine needles blown on the windshield. He put the car in gear, and we drove away from Rosella Santiago's house feeling helpless.

Ibrahim Obaid, a terrorist playing a long game as Marion Davis, was clearly ahead of us.

"What's his target?" Sampson asked. "And why does he have Captain Davis and Fiona Plum with him?"

That surprised me. "You think he does?"

Sampson nodded. "We know Captain Davis took an Uber to her house. We know she's missing. We know Obaid ran a painting business. We know a painter was there."

"True on all counts. I think he's going to continue the frame-up of Captain Davis. And maybe make Fiona Plum part of it."

"Exactly my thinking," Sampson said. "So what's his target?"

"And when?"

Before we could discuss possible answers, my phone rang. Mahoney said, "Ibrahim Obaid leased a dark gray Mercedes

Sprinter van from a West Virginia company. We've got the West Virginia plate numbers."

"Not Pennsylvania?" I asked.

"No, but it doesn't matter. We've got the codes for Mercedes's version of an OnStar system. It's dead or in a dead spot, but we had him last about fifteen minutes ago on a residential street outside Savage, Maryland."

"Savage?" Sampson said. "That's not far from the Baltimore/Washington International Airport."

"Jesus," Mahoney said. "Good call, John. We've got agents and police on the way. I'm on the way too."

He hung up as we were getting on I-395 east of Annandale, Virginia.

"Head north?" Sampson said. "Or home?"

"Both the same way," I said. "Give me a minute to think about it."

I did, trying to look at everything that had happened in the past day, not only the capture of the Dead Hours killer and his claim to be linked to M and Maestro, but the leaps and bounds we'd taken in the investigation of the downing of AA 839. I thought about Ibrahim Obaid and every twist and turn of his journey—working for the U.S. military with Leslie Parks, then killing Parks; changing his name; stealing the Browning machine gun and the Stinger missile system; shooting down the jet; killing Rosella Santiago; and, if John was right, kidnapping Captain Davis and Fiona Plum as part of an elaborate frame job.

I called Mahoney back. "That tracking system still off in the Sprinter?"

"Affirmative, but we've got an address for where they last had it. I'll give it to you. Follow me north."

"I don't think so, Ned. Something tells me he's doubling back. John and I are going to head west, cover the bases. Can you give us someone at Mercedes who can tell us all the places he's been recently?"

"I can. Here's the number. Her name is Carolyn Mayfield."

CHAPTER

98

SHORTLY AFTER DARK, AS the temperatures dropped into the twenties, and the sleet turned to snow, Ibrahim Obaid took a right off the highway onto Tanner Lane, the entrance to Chantilly Crushed Stone, Vulcan Materials, and Virginia Paving, which owned pieces of a giant gravel pit there.

Obaid stopped the Sprinter at the gate next to a booth with a security guard, a guy in his late thirties, dark features, and also wearing a Canada Goose jacket with the hood up. Obaid looked at the booth's camera as the guard opened the window. The tiny red bulb that should have lit up to indicate the device was recording remained dark.

All was going according to plan.

"I'm placing an order," Obaid said.

The guard said, "Good luck finding anyone. Once they heard all the snow was coming, they freaked and left."

"Eight to fourteen inches overnight, I heard."

"Same."

"Too bad about the Chevy."

"Early bird gets the worm," the security guard said, and he hit a button that raised the gate. "Godspeed, brother."

"And to you, brother," Obaid said.

He drove forward onto an inch of fresh, wet snow over pavement that quickly gave way to pressed gravel, which was slick and rutty. He was happy that the van was all-wheel drive.

The guard had been right—there were no personal vehicles at Chantilly Crushed Stone, Vulcan Materials, or Virginia Paving. And all the dump trucks and dozers in the pit were idle and empty.

Obaid drove down into the pit and went past the vehicles, beneath the conveyor belts that fed the gravel sifters, and by a steel maintenance shed. All dark. The terrorist felt a thrill go through him. He could not have asked for better conditions and felt truly blessed this night.

On the northwest side of the pit, where vehicles either turned around or continued down into the deeper excavations, Obaid drove forward and stopped. He turned off the headlights and put on his yellow fog lights, which shone down rather than out. He retrieved a pair of heavy bolt cutters and a headlamp with a soft red filter from the floor on the passenger side. He put on the headlamp, pulled up the hood on his jacket, got out, and was hit with driving, wet snow.

He walked forward through the snow about twenty-five yards to a chain-link fence and proceeded to cut out a section about twelve feet wide and drag it aside. Back in the Sprinter, he brushed the snow off his clothes, put on his seat belt, and looked over his shoulder into the dark rear of the van.

"Hold on tight, now," Obaid said to Captain Davis and Fiona Plum. "Things could get a little bumpy here."

Obaid turned on the parking lights to add to the glow from the fog lamps, put the van in gear, and stomped on the gas. The Mercedes fishtailed and then caught enough traction to accelerate forward through the gap he'd cut in the fence. Obaid hit the opening a little to the right, scraping the side of the van as it gained speed. He saw the edge of the ditch ahead, tugged the wheel left, and braced for impact.

The van shot through the air, cleared the ditch, and slammed down on the shoulder of a snow-covered road paralleling the rear of the gravel pit. The Sprinter slid and for a moment Obaid thought for sure he'd gone too fast, that he was about to sail off the other side of Perimeter Road and smack into the trees.

But Obaid managed to get the van under control. He stopped, did a three-point turn, and sped east into the gloom and the storm, once again firmly convinced that God was on his side.

Using an app on his burner phone, he quickly found Striker Avenue and took a left on it, glad to see he was the only vehicle that had passed this way since the snow began. The woods were thick on both sides and continued all the way to where Striker hit a T at Structures Road. He pulled the van into a turnout on the other side of the intersection and shut the vehicle off. Snow tapped against the windshield.

Obaid took the suppressed pistol from the console, put his hood back up, turned the red headlamp back on, and got out. Over the storm's sound and fury, he heard the roar of a big jet not far off and he could not control his excitement. He had not anticipated the storm, but everything else was going exactly as he'd envisioned! He turned his back to the wind, eager to complete his plan.

Then he went around the back of the Sprinter, opened the rear double doors, lifted his gun, and shot twice.

CHAPTER

99

U.S. ROUTE 50 IN Virginia was a mess an hour after dark that evening. It was snowing as hard as it had been raining earlier in the day. The roads were freezing up, and more than an inch of snow had fallen when Sampson took the turn onto Tanner Lane.

We'd gotten through to Carolyn Mayfield at Mercedes, and at our request, she'd run the data from the Sprinter van for the past two weeks, looking for repeat visits to any addresses or areas. What immediately caught our attention was a number of visits to a gravel pit south of Dulles International Airport.

We pulled up to the security gate, and the guard looked surprised when he opened the window. "Pit is closed," he said in a Middle Eastern accent.

Sampson showed his badge. "You see a gray Mercedes Sprinter van come in here recently?"

I watched the guard closely. He glanced down and to the left before returning his gaze to John. "No. Everyone is gone two hours ago."

I looked forward past the gate and saw snowed-over tracks. The snow had started only an hour before.

"We want to take a look for ourselves," I said.

The guard looked nervous now. "Is impossible. Must have permission or you have warrant. Come back tomorrow."

I leaned over in my seat, showed him my FBI credentials, and said, "This is a federal investigation. Now lift the gate or we will have you arrested for obstruction."

The guard stared at us for a second before the gate rose. Sampson put the Grand Cherokee in gear, and we drove through.

"Follow those tracks," I said.

I looked over my shoulder and back through the rear window with the wiper blade clearing the snow. The gate lowered. The guard came out of the shack and looked after us as we rounded a curve in the road.

"I can barely see the tracks. Snow's piling up," Sampson said.

"Then go faster," I said.

Sampson put the SUV in four-wheel drive and sped up. With the wind and the new snow, it was difficult to stay on the tire tracks as they curved around the gravel pit. We lost them at one point and had to backtrack; we found them going down into the pit itself toward a line of dump trucks and bulldozers.

There was less wind down in the bottom and we were able to stay with the tracks beyond the northwest corner of the pit, where we found a gaping hole in the perimeter fence of Dulles International Airport and tire tracks going through it.

"Call Ned," Sampson said, driving slowly through the hole in the fence. "Get flights shut down. He's in there!"

I dug out my phone. "No bars!"

John slammed on the brakes. "And no way across."

I looked forward and saw a ditch; on the other side of it was a road with tracks heading west. "He got across!"

"Had to have jumped it," he said, slamming the Jeep in reverse. "Try my radio!"

We went skidding back toward the fence. I got Sampson's walkie-talkie.

John said, "Hold on," and hit the gas hard. We shot ahead.

We did not have enough speed to clear the ditch fully. The front wheels hit the far side of the ditch, smashing the bumper and headlights and jerking us hard against our seat belts, but the forward momentum carried us up and onto the snow-covered road.

Sampson clawed at the wheel and managed to straighten us out before we went off the other side.

"My Jeep!" He groaned. "And we can't see squat without lights!"

I unbuckled my shoulder harness, dug out my Maglite, rolled down the window, and clicked on the light. I hung out the window and played the beam across the road.

"There's your tracks," I said. "Stay on him. Wait! He turned around!"

Sampson skidded to a stop, turned the SUV around, grabbed his radio, and said into it, "Metro Dispatch. This is John Sampson, over."

Only a hiss came back.

"Must be some kind of frequency jammer on airport grounds," he said, and he looked at his phone. "No bars."

"He's taking a left!" I said, my hand freezing from holding the flashlight out the window.

Sampson took the left and accelerated up Striker Avenue. The tracks were more distinct now. We were closing the distance.

Two minutes later, we hit a T with Structures Road and saw the tire tracks turn into a pullout on the opposite side. There sat the gray Mercedes Sprinter.

The rear doors were open. I shone the light in and saw a green wooden crate, the lid off, and under the lid a pair of legs in jeans and running shoes.

I raced to the back of the van, Sampson right beside me. He yanked away the wooden crate cover, revealing Fiona Plum.

With all the blood, I thought for certain she was dead. But John jumped inside and felt her neck for a pulse.

"She's alive, but barely," he said. "She needs an ambulance pronto."

I thought about the Google map of the area that I'd studied as we drove to the gravel pit. "We put her into your car. You drive back to Perimeter Road. Take a left, then the first left onto Willard Road, then the first right onto Live Fire Road. Follow it to the end. I'm pretty sure the airport fire station is there. Tell them to shut the airport down."

"Where are you going?"

A jet roared, taking off to our northeast. I gestured with the flashlight at snowed-over footprints headed into the woods and toward the airport.

CHAPTER

100

STILL IN SHOCK OVER the shooting of Fiona Plum, Captain Davis, holding the loaded shoulder-mounted missile launcher Obaid had forced him to carry, slipped and stumbled amid the falling snow. Davis's mouth, wrists, and ankles were no longer duct-taped, but he was unsteady, and he almost went down there in the forest, a quarter mile from Dulles International's south runway.

But the terrorist grabbed him by the back of his jacket and kept him upright. "Not yet, Captain," Obaid said calmly. "We've got important work to do here in memory of dear Fiona."

Davis's pulse soared along with his anger. He suddenly and overwhelmingly wanted to get extremely violent with this man. Brutal, in fact. He wanted to kill Obaid for what he'd done to Fiona Plum and the passengers of AA 839.

The terrorist seemed to sense the rage building in Davis because he pressed the muzzle of the suppressed pistol to the back of the former pro football player's neck. "It would be a damn shame to end it here, Captain, but I will if I have to. We're not far now, and with the snow, I could drag your carcass into position. So move."

Davis told himself he'd cooperate for now, wait for his chance. By the dim light of Obaid's headlamp, he began creeping forward again on the snowy game trail they'd been following the last hundred yards. He squinted into the driving snow, shifting the missile launcher to guide it around trees and branches. He could just make out the lights of the terminal and the flashing light of the control tower ahead.

Then the first strong beam of light from the tower hit Davis's eyes, and it triggered a terrible memory of the flash of his rockets hitting a village he had been told was a stronghold of the Islamic State. He remembered the moment after he'd fired the rockets, remembered watching their contrails rip down through the sky as children ran from their homes and into the streets.

Then he remembered the muzzle flashes when Obaid shot Fiona.

This was worse, Davis decided. This was personal. This was someone he...loved.

He had, hadn't he? He'd loved Fiona's quirkiness and her smile and the way she adored him and laughed at his jokes no matter how corny. And he'd been so grateful to her for standing up to him, for forcing him to take a cold hard look in the mirror.

But now she's dead. And so are those children.

"I'm sorry for killing them," Davis said. "Your family."

"Shut up, Captain," Obaid replied. "They're gone no matter how sorry you are. And you'll get no forgiveness from me. Not tonight. Not ever."

"Then why not just shoot me and get it over with? Why kill innocent people?"

"Because that's what you did. It's the only argument men understand."

"What?"

"An eye for an eye, Captain," Obaid said. "It's there in the Bible. It's there in the Koran. An eye for an eye."

Davis could see the colored lights that ran east to west along the southern runway, which was being plowed. He noticed for the first time that his sneakers were soaked and his feet were freezing. So were his hands.

A jet took off from the runway west of the terminal. It passed directly over them in the woods.

"Keep going," Obaid said. "Get right up there to the edge of the trees."

The snow was falling at a rate of two inches an hour now. White sheets of it billowed across the airport grounds and looked like smoke in the wake of the plow, which was far down the south runway when Davis got to the last line of trees.

"Put the launcher down and sit by that tree," Obaid said. "I'm giving you the best seat in the house, Captain."

Davis felt like puking when he set down the Stinger missile launcher and collapsed in the snow against the trunk of a leafless oak not two hundred yards from the runway.

"Hands," Obaid said after taking off a knapsack and setting it down.

Davis held his hands out and watched the terrorist zip-tie his wrists together. "They'll know it wasn't me," he said when Obaid stuffed his pistol in the pocket of his parka and picked up the Stinger launcher. "They'll know I was held against my will."

"It doesn't matter in the long run," the terrorist said, shrugging.

In the distance, from the far end of the northwest runway, a jet revved its engines and came roaring at them.

CHAPTER

101

FLASHLIGHT IN MY LEFT hand, pistol in my right, I followed the tracks of the two of them moving single file along a deer trail through the snowy woods. My mind kept racing.

Who was I hunting here, just Obaid or both Obaid and Captain Davis? I believed it was just Obaid. But for the moment, I had to assume both men were part of the conspiracy.

With the flashlight on, I could move fast and close the gap between us. But unless I spotted them first, the light could attract their attention. If they were armed, one or both could shoot me before I could defend myself.

I cupped the business end of the Maglite with my left hand, aimed it directly at the ground, and moved slower. Then I heard a jet take off and cross above the woods ahead of me.

They've got a Stinger inside Dulles. The hell with your safety, Alex. Catch up!

Throwing caution to the storm winds, I turned the Maglite on high and ran as fast as I could along the men's tracks. As the jet gained altitude and headed east, I heard another engine, closer and almost directly north of me, moving west.

I broke from the woods onto Willard Road, which ran diagonally toward the south runway at Dulles. The snow was three inches deep by then and untouched save for the tracks of Obaid and Davis, which crossed the road and disappeared into the next block of trees.

I saw lights slash to my north, in the direction of that second engine, and I instinctively abandoned the tracks and sprinted toward the runway.

CHAPTER

102

CAPTAIN DAVIS SAW THE lights of the jet accelerating down the west runway, coming directly at them through the driving snow. Ibrahim Obaid pulled the key on the Stinger that blocked the trigger from firing.

"Even if you shoot them down, kill them all, it won't bring your family back," Davis said. "And it won't shut down the airlines or the economy. Not for long."

Obaid did not look at him. He illuminated and aimed through the sighting system mounted along the barrel of the shoulder-to-air missile launcher. "Nothing will bring my family back," Obaid said. "That's the point. I have nothing to go back to, Captain. And the airlines? If this doesn't do it, I'll shoot down another and then another." He laughed and glanced over at Davis. "What? You don't think I have other sources of weapons? Leslie Parks had many stashes and he told me about all of them before he died."

The terrorist laughed again and settled behind the Stinger's sights.

The jet was coming fast now.

Davis could see the nose rising off the runway five hundred yards away.

Obaid's shoulders tensed.

Davis rolled over onto his knees, struggled to his feet, lowered his head, and charged at the terrorist.

He smashed into him, knocking Obaid down, then he went down himself. The terrorist screamed in pain and rage and hammered Davis in the forehead, slashing him with the back of the Stinger launcher.

Davis saw stars and lost consciousness for a second. When he came to, Obaid was on his feet and had the launcher shouldered again.

"You can't stop fate," the terrorist said, swinging with the United Airlines jet as it passed overhead. "The heat-seeking system loves the rear engine."

He pulled the trigger.

But rather than a whoosh of fire, a feeble puff of flame exited the back of the launcher barrel. The missile shot up and out, got three hundred feet into the air, and lost thrust; it dived down into the woods and hit a tree.

An explosion rocked the snowy forest, lit it up for a second like a flare. The United jet disappeared into the clouds.

"It's over!" Davis yelled as blood poured into his eyes from the gash. "You lose!"

"Never," Obaid said, setting down the launcher. He grabbed his knapsack and got the second rocket-propelled grenade out. He loaded it into the launcher as another jet began to accelerate at them from the north end of the west runway.

103

THE HUGE DUMP TRUCK with the snowplow was turning around when I burst from the trees and ran across the VORTAC road onto the runway, waving the flashlight and my pistol wildly at the dump-truck driver and hearing a jet begin its takeoff from the north.

The driver threw his brights on and accelerated. I realized a gun wasn't the best thing to be waving at him, so I dropped it in the snow, pulled out my credentials, and waved them instead.

For a second, I thought for sure he was going to run me down, but then the plow skidded to a stop. I snatched up my pistol, sprinted to the passenger side, got up on the step, and opened the door. I saw a grizzled Black man in his fifties behind the wheel.

"I'm Alex Cross," I said, gasping as I climbed in. "I work for the FBI. There's a terrorist on the grounds. He's got a missile."

"You're shitting me."

"No, sir," I said, seeing the jet lift off east of us and cross over the top of the runway we were on. "Call the tower. Tell them to stop all—"

Just then, through the snow, I saw a flash to our two o'clock, no more than a quarter of a mile away. Something arced into the sky, then fell and exploded with a brighter flash. The United Airlines jet gained altitude and vanished into the clouds.

"Son of a bitch!" the driver said. He threw the dump truck in gear, punched the gas, and raised the plow so it covered the lower windshield. "Grab that radio there. Call ground control. Tell them you're with Sweet Al Dupris on the south runway."

I snatched up the radio mic as he kept shifting gears and we accelerated east toward the explosion site. "Ground control, this is Alex Cross, a consultant with the FBI," I said. "I am with Sweet Al Dupris in his plow on the south runway. There is a terrorist on the grounds with a Stinger missile. Call the tower. Stop all takeoffs. Repeat, stop all takeoffs."

"Who the hell is this?" a woman came back. "Put Dupris on."

I held out the mic and pressed the transmit button. Dupris said, "He's not shitting you, Alfie. Call the tower. Shut all flights down."

A tense voice came over the radio. "This is Lieutenant Paula Renfrew with the airport's fire and rescue department. We have a DC homicide detective here with a severely wounded woman. He's saying the same thing. There's a terrorist with a missile on the grounds!"

To our ten o'clock, and to my dismay, I saw another jet beginning its takeoff down the runway toward us. I swung my attention back to two o'clock and peered through the storm in the direction of those flashes we'd seen.

For a moment, I saw nothing but big white flakes slashing the windshield.

But then a figure appeared at the limit of the dump truck's headlights, running out of the woods through the snow. In the next second, I made out the missile launcher up on his shoulders.

"There he is!" Sweet Al shouted.

I lowered the window so I could lean out and shoot at Ibrahim Obaid if we got close enough. The jet was still coming fast at us from our left, about six hundred yards away.

The terrorist shouldered the launcher. Over the radio, we heard someone in the air traffic control tower yell, "Delta one-one-seven, abort takeoff! Repeat, abort takeoff!"

Captain Davis burst out of the woods and ran right at Obaid, who saw him coming. He clubbed the former NFL player with the launcher, knocking him down. To our left, the jet's engines cut off, and the plane began to skid and slide.

Obaid saw what was happening and ran up the rise onto our runway; the Delta jet fishtailed, then went completely sideways. The left wing almost touched the ground before the plane finally stopped, just short of the end of the runway.

The terrorist, no more than eighty yards from us, shouldered the launcher again. I leaned out the window, trying to aim through the snow.

Before I could shoot, Sweet Al laid on the horn and slammed the dump truck's accelerator. Obaid glanced our way, squinted at the headlights, looked back at the crippled jet two hundred yards away, and realized it was too late.

He swung toward us, went to his knees, and fired from less than fifty yards.

The fifty-year-old RPG blew a gout of flame out the back of

the launcher. The missile erupted from the barrel, ripped low right at us, and exploded against the massive plow blade.

The brilliance was blinding. The noise was deafening.

The dump truck shuddered, and its tail end lurched left and slid.

We went off the runway and down the bank and came to a stop almost at the trees. My vision returned and I saw we had not run Obaid over.

The terrorist had dropped the RPG and was running down the bank toward the woods about forty yards from us. Despite the blood running from his head wounds, Captain Davis was on his feet again, racing after him. His hands were zip-tied.

Obaid must have heard Davis coming because he stopped, pulled out a pistol, and pivoted to shoot the former pilot. Davis tried to duck out of his line of fire but slipped and sprawled on his belly in the snow, right in front of the terrorist.

Obaid aimed his pistol.

I fired my gun several times out the open window of the dump truck and hit Obaid square in the chest with the first and second shots and in the face with the third.

The son of a bitch died where he fell.

104

One week later
Georgetown University Medical Center

THE ELEVATOR DOOR OPENED. Captain Davis, sporting a large bandage on his forehead, pushed a wheelchair containing a wan but very much alive Fiona Plum out of the elevator, across the lobby, and out the front door into the brisk fresh air.

Bree, Sampson, and I started clapping. "You made it!" Bree cried.

"I did," Fiona said, giving us all a weak smile.

"And so did I, thanks to all of you," Davis said. "Especially you, Dr. Cross, and you, Detective Sampson."

"Our great pleasure, Captain," Sampson said.

"You had a hand in saving a lot of people," Mahoney said. "We thank *you*."

I nodded. "If it weren't for your relentless attacks on Obaid, who knows what might have happened?"

Mahoney added, "And again, I deeply apologize for ever suspecting you of involvement in such a heinous scheme."

Sampson said, "We're all sorry for not believing you were being framed."

Davis put his hand on Fiona Plum's shoulder. "It's all water under the bridge now, but going through all that forced me to see what was missing in my life. Right, my dear?"

The English teacher grinned and held up her left hand, revealing a large diamond engagement ring. "Right, Captain."

We cheered and hugged them. Both Davis and Plum started crying.

"I honestly feel like the luckiest woman alive," she said.

"And I'm the luckiest man alive," Davis said, wiping the tears from his eyes. "Do you know what this fine woman did the second she had enough strength?"

"Oh, Captain," Fiona said.

He said, "She called Hampstead, the headmaster at the Charles School, and told him she was quitting and we were suing him and the school unless he reinstated me as coach."

"And?" I said.

"I'm back on the field this afternoon," Davis said, grinning.

"Exactly where he should be," Fiona Plum said. "But now I just want to go home and recover and plan our wedding. Thank you all again."

Two EMTs helped Davis lift her wheelchair into the back of a private ambulance he'd hired. With promises to be in touch soon, they drove away through the last of the slush from the big storm.

Sampson said, "I'm off to pack. Willow and I are going to Disney tomorrow."

Bree said, "She must be out of her mind."

John laughed. "It's all she's been talking about since I booked it a few days ago."

I said, "I could use a few days off myself."

Bree said, "I second that. How about Jamaica for a long weekend before Christmas?"

"Oooh, I like that idea."

Mahoney's phone dinged with a text. He read it and looked up at us. "Paddy Filson died twenty minutes ago of a heart attack in his cell in Alexandria."

"Jesus," I said. "I wanted to talk to him about Maestro again."

"I did too," Bree said. "See if there was any connection to Malcomb."

For the past few months, Bree had become convinced that our old nemesis M, the leader of the vigilante group known as Maestro, was Ryan Malcomb, a brilliant, reclusive billionaire who ran a cutting-edge data-mining company called Paladin in Massachusetts.

I said, "How about we postpone the vacation until after Christmas?"

"Take a flight to Boston?" Bree asked.

"I think it's time we put an end to M and Maestro," Mahoney said, nodding.

"I do too," I said. "Once and for all."

Have you read them all?

ALONG CAME A SPIDER

Alex Cross is working on the high-profile disappearance of two rich kids. But is he facing someone much more dangerous than a callous kidnapper?

KISS THE GIRLS

Cross comes home to discover his niece Naomi is missing. And she's not the only one. Finding the kidnapper won't be easy, especially if he's not working alone . . .

JACK AND JILL

A pair of ice-cold killers are picking off Washington's rich and famous. And they have the ultimate target in their sights.

CAT AND MOUSE

An old enemy is back and wants revenge. Will Alex Cross escape unharmed, or will this be the final showdown?

POP GOES THE WEASEL

Alex Cross faces his most fearsome opponent yet. He calls himself Death. And there are three other 'Horsemen' who compete in his twisted game.

ROSES ARE RED

After a series of fatal bank robberies, Cross must take the ultimate risk when faced with a criminal known as the Mastermind.

VIOLETS ARE BLUE

As Alex Cross edges ever closer to the awful truth about the Mastermind, he comes dangerously close to defeat.

FOUR BLIND MICE

Preparing to resign from the Washington police force,
Alex Cross is looking forward to a peaceful life. But he can't
stay away for long . . .

THE BIG BAD WOLF

There is a mysterious new mobster in organised crime.
The FBI are stumped. Luckily for them, they now have
Alex Cross on their team.

LONDON BRIDGES

The stakes have never been higher as Cross pursues two
old enemies in an explosive worldwide chase.

MARY, MARY

Hollywood's A-list are being violently killed, one-by-one.
Only Alex Cross can put together the clues of this
twisted case.

CROSS

Haunted by the murder of his wife thirteen years ago,
Cross will stop at nothing to finally avenge her death.

DOUBLE CROSS

Alex Cross is starting to settle down – until he encounters a
maniac killer who likes an audience.

CROSS COUNTRY

When an old friend becomes the latest victim of the Tiger,
Cross journeys to Africa to stop a terrifying and
dangerous warlord.

ALEX CROSS'S TRIAL
(with Richard DiLallo)

In a family story recounted here by Alex Cross,
his great-uncle Abraham faces persecution, murder
and conspiracy in the era of the Ku Klux Klan.

I, ALEX CROSS

Investigating the violent murder of his niece Caroline,
Alex Cross discovers an unimaginable secret that could
rock the entire world.

CROSS FIRE

Alex Cross is planning his wedding to Bree,
but his nemesis returns to exact revenge.

KILL ALEX CROSS

The President's children have been kidnapped,
and DC is hit by a terrorist attack. Cross must
make a desperate decision that goes against
everything he believes in.

MERRY CHRISTMAS, ALEX CROSS

Robbery, hostages, terrorism – will Alex Cross make it
home in time for Christmas . . . alive?

ALEX CROSS, RUN

With his personal life in turmoil, Alex Cross
can't afford to let his guard down.
Especially with three blood-thirsty
killers on the rampage.

CROSS MY HEART

When a dangerous enemy targets Cross and his family,
Alex finds himself playing a whole new game of
life and death.

HOPE TO DIE

Cross's family are missing, presumed dead. But Alex Cross
will not give up hope. In a race against time, he must find his
wife, children and grandmother – no matter what it takes.

CROSS JUSTICE

Returning to his North Carolina hometown for the first time in over three decades, Cross unearths a family secret that forces him to question everything he's ever known.

CROSS THE LINE

Cross steps in to investigate a wave of murders erupting across Washington, DC. The victims have one thing in common — they are all criminals.

THE PEOPLE VS. ALEX CROSS

Charged with gunning down followers of his nemesis Gary Soneji in cold blood, Cross must fight for his freedom in the trial of the century.

TARGET: ALEX CROSS

Cross is called on to lead the FBI investigation to find America's most wanted criminal. But what follows will plunge the country into chaos, and draw Cross into the most important case of his life.

CRISS CROSS

When notes signed by 'M' start appearing at homicide scenes across the state, Cross fears he is chasing a ghost.

DEADLY CROSS

A shocking double homicide dominates tabloid headlines. Among the victims is Kay, a glamorous socialite and Cross's former patient — and maybe more. But who would want her dead, and why?

FEAR NO EVIL

Alex Cross ventures into the rugged Montana wilderness where he's attacked by two rival teams of assassins, controlled by the same mastermind who has stalked Alex and his family for years.

TRIPLE CROSS

Hunting an elusive killer who targets families around Washington, DC, Cross must work harder than ever to discover the truth.

She's landed the case of her life.
But now her life is on the line.

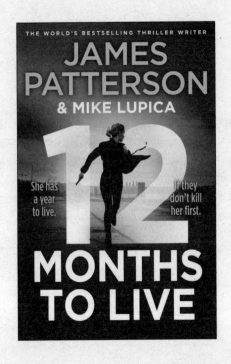

Read on for an exclusive extract . . .

ONE

"FOR *THE* LAST TIME," my client says to me. "I. Did. Not. Kill. Those. People."

He adds, "You have to believe me. I didn't do it."

The opposing counsel will refer to him as "the defendant." It's a way of putting him in a box, since opposing counsel absolutely believe he *did* kill all those people. The victims. The Gates family. Father. Mother. And teenage daughter. All shot in the head. Sometime in the middle of the last night of their lives. Whoever did it, and the state says my client did, had to have used a suppressor.

"Rob," I say, "I might have mentioned this before: I. Don't. Give. A. Shit."

Rob is Rob Jacobson, heir to a legendary publishing house and also owner of the biggest real estate company in the Hamptons. Life was good for Rob until he ended up in jail, but that's true for pretty much everybody, rich or poor. Guilty or innocent. I've defended both.

Me? I'm Jane. Jane Smith. It's not an assumed name, even though I might be wishing it were by the end of this trial.

There was a time when I would have been trying to keep somebody like Rob Jacobson away from the needle, back when New

York was still a death penalty state. Now it's my job to help him beat a life sentence. Starting tomorrow. Suffolk County Court, Riverhead, New York. Maybe forty-five minutes from where Rob Jacobson stands accused of shooting the Gates family dead.

That's forty-five minutes with no traffic. Good luck with that.

"I've told you this before," he says. "It's important to me that you believe me."

No surprise there. He's been conditioned his entire life to people telling him what he wants to hear. It's another perk that's come with being a Jacobson.

Until now, that is.

We are in one of the attorney rooms down the hall from the courtroom. My client and me. Long window at the other end of the room where the guard can keep an eye on us. Not for my safety, I tell myself. Rob Jacobson's. Maybe the guard can tell from my body language that I occasionally feel the urge to strangle him.

He's wearing his orange jumpsuit. I'm in the same dark-gray skirt and jacket I'll be wearing tomorrow. What I think of as my sincerity suit.

"Important to *you*," I say, "not to me. I need twelve people to believe you. And I'm not one of the twelve."

"You have to know that I'm not capable of doing something like this."

"Sure. Let's go with that."

"You sound sarcastic," he says.

"No. I *am* sarcastic."

This is our last pretrial meeting, one he's asked for and that is a complete waste of time. Mine, not his. He looks for any excuse to get out of his cell at the Riverhead Correctional Facility for even an hour and has insisted on going over once more what he calls "our game plan."

Our—I run into a lot of that.

I've tried to explain to him that any lawyer who allows his or her client to run the show ought to save everybody a lot of time and effort—and a boatload of the state's money—and drive the client straight to Attica or Green Haven Correctional. But Rob Jacobson never listens. Lifelong affliction, as far as I can tell.

"Rob, you don't just want me to believe you. You want me to like you."

"Is there something so wrong with that?" he asks.

"This is a murder trial," I tell him. "Not a dating app."

Looks-wise he reminds me of George Clooney. But all good-looking guys with salt-and-pepper hair remind me of George. If I had met him several years ago and could have gotten him to stay still long enough, I might have married him.

But only if I had been between marriages at the time.

"Stop me if you've heard me say this before, but I was set up."

I sigh. It's louder than I intended. "Okay. Stop."

"I *was*," he says. "Set up. Nothing else makes sense."

"Now, you stop me if you've heard this one from me before. Set up by whom? And with your DNA and fingerprints sprinkled around that house like pixie dust?"

"That's for you to find out," he says. "One of the reasons I hired you is because I was told you're as good a detective as you are a lawyer. You and your guy."

Jimmy Cunniff. Ex-NYPD, the way I'm ex-NYPD, even if I only lasted a grand total of eight months as a street cop, before lasting barely longer than that as a licensed private investigator. It was why I'd served as my own investigator for the first few years after I'd gotten my law degree. Then I'd hired Jimmy, and finally started delegating, almost as a last resort.

"Not to put too fine a point on things," I say to him, "we're not just good. We happen to be the best. Which *is* why you hired both of us."

"And why I'm counting on you to find the real killers eventually. So people will know I'm innocent."

I lean forward and smile at him.

"Rob? Do me a favor and never talk about the real killers ever again."

"I'm not O.J.," he says.

"Well, yeah, he only killed two people."

I see his face change now. See something in his eyes that I don't much like. But then I don't much like him. Something else I run into a lot.

He slowly regains his composure. And the rich-guy certainty that this is all some kind of big mistake. "Sometimes I wonder whose side you're on."

"Yours."

"So despite how much you like giving me a hard time, you do believe I'm telling you the truth."

"Who said anything about the truth?" I ask.

TWO

GREGG McCALL, NASSAU COUNTY district attorney, is waiting for me outside the courthouse.

Rob Jacobson has been taken back to the jail and I'm finally on my way back to my little saltbox house in Amagansett, east of East Hampton, maybe twenty miles from Montauk and land's end.

A tourist one night wandered into the tavern Jimmy Cunniff owns down at the end of Main Street in Sag Harbor, where Jimmy says it's been, in one form or another, practically since the town was a whaling port. The visitor asked what came after Montauk. He was talking to the bartender, but I happened to be on the stool next to his.

"Portugal," I said.

But now the trip home is going to have to wait because of McCall, six foot eight, former Columbia basketball player, divorced, handsome, extremely eligible by all accounts. And an honest-to-God public servant. I've always had kind of a thing for him, even when he was still married, and even though my sport at Boston College was ice hockey. Even with his decided size advantage, I figure we could make a mixed relationship like that work, with counseling.

McCall has made the drive out here from his home in Garden City, which even on a weekday can feel like a trip to Kansas if you're heading east on the Long Island Expressway.

"Are you here to give me free legal advice?" I ask. "Because I'll take whatever you got at this point, McCall."

He smiles. It only makes him better looking.

Down, girl.

"I want to hire you," he says.

"Oh, no." I smile back at him. "Did *you* shoot somebody?"

He sits down on the courthouse steps and motions for me to join him. Just the two of us out here. Tomorrow will be different. That's when the circus comes to town.

"I want to hire you and Jimmy, even though I can't officially say that I'm hiring you," he says. "And even though I'm aware that you're kind of busy right now."

"I'd only be too busy if I had a life," I say.

"You don't have one? You're great at what you do. And if I can make another observation without getting MeToo'ed, you happen to be great looking."

Down, girl.

"I keep trying to have one. A life. But somehow it never seems to take." I don't even pause before asking, "Are you going to now tell me what you want to hire me for even though you can't technically hire me, or should we order Uber Eats?"

"You get right to it, don't you?" McCall asks.

"Unless this is a billable hour. In which case, take as much time as you need."

He crosses amazingly long legs out in front of him. I notice he's wearing scuffed old loafers. Somehow they make me like him even more. I've never gotten the sense that he's trying too hard, even when I've watched him killing it a few times on Court TV.

"Remember the three people who got shot in Garden City?" he asks. "Six months before Jacobson is accused of wiping out the Gates family."

"I do. Brutal."

Three senseless deaths that time, too. The Carson family. Father, mother, daughter, a sophomore cheerleader at Garden City High. I don't know why I remember the cheerleader piece. But it's stayed with me. A robbery gone wrong. Gone bad and gone tragically wrong.

"Well, you probably also know that the father's mother never let it go until she finally passed," he says, "even though there was never an arrest or even a suspect worth a shit."

"I remember Grandma," I say. "There was a time when she was on TV so much I kept waiting for her to start selling steak knives."

McCall grins. "Well, it turns out Grandma was right."

"She kept saying it wasn't random, that her son's family had been targeted, even though she wouldn't come out and say why. She finally told me why but said that if I went public with it, she'd sue me all the way back to the Ivy League."

"But you're going to tell me."

"Her son gambled. Frequently and badly, as it turns out."

"And not with DraftKings, I take it."

"With Bobby Salvatore, who is still running the biggest book in this part of the world."

"Jimmy's mentioned him a few times in the past. Bad man, right?"

"Very."

"And you guys missed this?"

"Why do you think I'm here?"

"But upstanding district attorneys like yourself aren't allowed to hire people like Jimmy and me to run side investigations."